Fake ~~Flesh~~

Josje Weusten

Copyright

For Veerle and Stine,
keep singing each to each.

Contents

PART I

Present Day
Maastricht, the Netherlands

A truth in art is that whose contradictory is also true.
(The Truth of Masks—Oscar Wilde)

CHAPTER 1

MARTIN

'Did you hear the rumours?!'

'I luvvv rrrumourrs!' Martin shouts back at Elon over the loud music in the bar, something jazzy. He's working a thick German accent, gargling the r in the back of his throat, an attempt to mimic actor Christoph Waltz. 'Tzel me more!'

In one gulp, Martin knocks back the rest of his Alfa pilsner and reaches for the next one on the blackened counter. He is careful not to waste his drink. He's thirsty. His woollen sweater is killing him, but he's perfectly in tune with the dress code for tonight—the ugly Christmas jumper. He chose to wear a blue one with Jesus and the text *Birthday Boy*.

The sweaters were Zac's idea. A stupid idea. Christmas sweaters are something from vulgar comedies and who genuinely likes those? His own suggestion—black suits with bolo-ties, much like John Travolta in *Pulp Fiction*—didn't make the popular vote. It would've been the stylish choice though. Besides, it's the third of January. Christmas is over.

Despite the ridiculous dress code, Martin has been looking forward to this evening in the pub with his fraternity mates. Especially after that run-in with Eveline. He spent the whole afternoon with his girlfriend. He even cooked his famous risotto, seasoned with lemon and pepper. Lots of pepper, that's the secret.

Afterwards, they watched a documentary on the gold-coloured two-seater in his room. It was a loud programme about women who liked to dress up as mermaids. Being in the third year of her psychology Bachelor, Eveline loves these kinds of things. She was glued to the screen. Some women in the show claimed they only felt like themselves when dressed up. That deep down they *were* actual mermaids.

It couldn't have interested him less. Annoyed, he looked sideways at Eveline. She was wearing his old hooded sweater, a faded black one with frayed hems. He had given it to her when she had complained about being cold earlier that evening. Even in the worn jersey, his girlfriend looked stunning. She is an absolute knockout—long blonde hair, dark blue eyes with golden streaks around the pupils, and a body that blew every man away. He wouldn't want to risk losing her.

Martin was thus careful not to voice his frustration with the programme. Eveline had called him narrow-minded for less. Instead, he checked the messages on his phone, most of them responses to a post from Zac. It was a clip of a half-naked woman in an office space. She was desperately trying to cover her breasts with her arms, when a bloke in a suit walked by and put up his hand in front of her—*The guy who invented the high five.* Martin hadn't been able to stop himself from laughing.

Eveline looked up, disrupted. She was right in the middle of a scene in which a woman showed off her new mermaid outfit. Without any irony, the voice-over commented dispassionately that there were three different tail-types. His girlfriend glanced down at his cell. As soon as she saw the post, she shame-stared at him—'Well go off then. Go! To your new dick network.'

Martin is thus relieved to be here in their regular bar. With the boys, he doesn't have to watch his words. They all share the same love for old films. Fincher, Tarantino, and the like. It's the main reason why he decided to join them. The entire frat would be here this evening, up for a night of fun before the second semester hits them.

Except for Jens that is. He had gone home to his family in Germany for the Christmas break. His train back to the Netherlands had been cancelled because of a bomb threat. The umpteenth in the past month, all of them fake. Much ado about nothing, if you'd ask Martin. He doesn't care Jens cannot make it. He's a bit dull, too serious, like most Germans. And as long as Zac is there...but as usual his best friend is late.

Elon has turned on his e-cigarette and is gearing up

for his big reveal: the rumours. It's not allowed to smoke anything in the bar, but the owner generally turns a blind eye.

'Allegedly...' Elon starts, circling the sleek metal stick between his fingers. The green light at the tip is flickering, eager for his drag.

Martin listens with half an ear and scans the dimly lit space. Nothing ever changes in the bar. That's probably why he likes it so much. From the out-of-use perforated dartboard in the back to the dusty black-and-white pictures of previous owners and once-famous movie stars above the counter: they have all remained untouched. The red-cedar floorboards are sticky from days-old spilt beer and the billiard table is as pruney as the nearly deaf barkeeper behind the tap. Still, no sign of Zac.

Martin takes another sip of his pilsner.

'Martin, my man! Hot in here, innit?' Zac suddenly rings in his ear. The slap from his best friend on his back is hard and unexpected, and Martin almost chokes on his drink. The beer runs out of his nose.

His friend snickers, while Martin dries his wet chin. He clears his watering eyes with the sleeve of his jumper. Zac is wearing a T-shirt instead of a sweater, on it a picture of Santa in a bathing suit. Martin could have known. Zac always has to stand out, be the centre of attention, never one to shy away from a prank or two.

The shirt is so tight Martin can see almost every line of his friend's pecs. Zac has tied his shoulder-long blond hair in a bun. Together with his stubbly beard, it gives him a rugged but approachable look. Manly and sensitive. A chick magnet.

Martin used to be annoyed by the fact that his friend can hook up so easily with every girl he likes. Not anymore. Not since he has Eveline. He knows Zac likes her too. Zac can't keep his eyes off her when she's along. But she's with him, not Zac, but *him*.

Martin takes a big swig of his drink to wash down the acid taste of the coughed-up beer and offers his friend a pint.

Zac is quick to take it off his hands, bawling, 'To a good start of the semester!'

'Hear, hear! And you joined right in time,' Martin yells. 'Elon has another juicy story up his sleeve!'

Zac signs to the bartender to lower the music's volume. Eyeing up Elon, he smiles, amused. 'Now which girl have you entrapped this time?'

Elon isn't as handsome as Zac, but he turns quite a few heads, and he knows it.

'It's nothing like that, Zac.' Elon grins. 'It's about Prior.'

They all know Jude Prior. Who doesn't? He is famous, or at least his films are—*The Detainees. The Exiles. The Insurgents.* All big cult hits. And the main reason why Martin and Zac are here today, to study in the film art programme in which he teaches. In Maastricht of all places.

'Now it's getting interesting. Come on, don't hold back,' Zac replies.

'I heard about it from Anaïs, you know, the one with

the big tits.' Elon cups his hands in front of his chest and pouts to express his appreciation. 'Haven't you seen her? Man, how can you have missed her? Trust me. You'd love to pull her. She's on my list. Anyway, Anaïs showed me the whole thing, and she—'

'What thing?' Martin is fearing the worst.

Elon waves them to come closer. He knows how to build in drama. 'It won't take long before it goes viral. A video in which he...'

Anxious, Martin stares at the two blinking red lights on Elon's sweater: Rudolf the Reindeer's balls, which Santa is kicking. He wipes the cold sweat out of his neck, but the drops run down his back and into his butt crack.

§

The lecturer, a middle-aged woman in a severely cut suit, is about to start when Zac rushes into the lecture theatre. He nearly slips. The wooden floor has been waxed during the Christmas break. The wax still spreads its piney perfume.

Martin waves at Zac and points to the empty seat he saved for him. Zac hasn't responded to any of his calls or messages since Martin hurriedly left the pub last evening. Martin needs to talk with him. They have to fix this. Zac must know this too. So why does he take a seat at the back? Didn't he see him sitting on the corner of the front row?

Zac is flirting with the red-haired girl next to him, telling her one of his slapstick-ridden anecdotes for sure.

She laughs. His friend is wearing a deeply cut V-necked shirt and he leans in shamelessly to give her a glimpse of his chest.

Annoyed, Martin tosses back his hair, which is damp. He hasn't stopped sweating since Elon dropped his news on the video of Prior. Martin takes off his black leather jacket and carefully hangs it over the back of his seat, then pulls up the foldable table attached to his chair. It's half a desk actually, barely covering a quarter of his lap.

Crap! There's a syrupy substance all over his hands. Someone must have spilt it on the desk. Orange juice maybe or it might have been Coke once. He doesn't want to risk getting any of it on his jacket, which, although tattered, was his dad's once.

Martin hastily wipes his fingers on his trousers, then realises his mistake. He'll smell sickeningly sweet all day. Zac most definitely will make fun of him. Martin quickly tries to come up with a film quote to counter his friend's jokes later. *Well damn if I ain't so sweet, I make sugar taste just like salt.* A twisted Kurt Russell. Old perhaps, but classic. No, of course, why didn't he think of that immediately? He can always count on Prior for the right words: *I don't need to eat no popsicles. I'm sweeter than a toy with googly eyes.*

He chuckles and feels relieved somehow. There's no reason to. Not yet. But Zac will know what to do. His friend won't let him down. *They hadn't come here to fear. They hadn't come to die. They had come to win.* Together they will find a solution. Hell yeah, the two of them, Martin Hermans and Zac Bleecker, they are special.

He and Zac have been hanging out almost daily since the introduction week of the Faculty of Film Studies, which most students and staff members endearingly call FFiS. Martin, however, refuses to use the crippled acronym invented by the university.

Sure, it isn't the Amsterdam Film Academy. They wouldn't have him. Martin had to apply for one of the programmes in Maastricht instead. It's all about history, genre and cultural impact, the analysis of viewpoint and *mis-en-scène*. He doesn't learn how to shoot. He merely gets to take movies apart. Yet none other than Jude Prior teaches some classes. It's a highly competitive master, not everyone gets in, but he and Zac did. And it still is one step closer to his dream of becoming a filmmaker.

'*Id est*, always make sure to ground your claims in facts. And back statements with references to peer-reviewed research. Questions?' the professor finishes up her lecture, clearly not expecting any.

It's late afternoon, the last class of the day, and everyone is eager to leave. The professor starts to gather her things, like the students around him. All of them girls. He and Zac are the only men *and* the only Dutch in this year's cohort. Some are already heading to the door when Martin raises his voice, 'Sure, facts are important, but what about truth?'

He posed his question without hesitation, loud enough for everyone to hear it. 'What's that?' the professor inquires nonetheless. 'And introduce yourself please.'

'Martin Hermans. What about truth instead of facts?'

'Explain,' she commands and walks to the end of the wooden dais. Her earrings—crystal threaders, almost reaching her shoulders—dance in hypnotising horizontal circles. 'Go on. We don't have all day.'

Martin uneasily moves back and forth in his swing-back-seat until the student to his right gives him a poke with her elbow. 'Uh, well...there are facts, and they serve their purpose, but literature, films...don't they touch upon greater truths?...about life, death, loss...love, which are to be felt, and lived?' While he is talking, the professor stares out over his head at the wall. Is she even listening? Offended, he ends his speech with a question, 'And isn't it through art, through fiction, that we can experience such truths?'

The girls who are still in the room, surely twenty, have stopped packing their bags to watch them—him and this middle-aged woman—waiting for what is to come next.

Martin doubts she has heard a word of what he has been saying. He's thus surprised when she looks down on him to answer slowly in a tone which allows no dispute, 'That's irrelevant. Facts and data alone make up scientific knowledge. Of course, we should account for interpretation, perspective and context, but everything else is opinion, entertainment at best. To think differently about this can be dangerous. Hubris isn't solely something for Greek tragedies.'

She turns to the lectern to pick up her leather auburn bag, a clear indication that she's done with this. But before she can reach for it, Martin replies, a lot softer now, 'No...I think you're wrong...there are different truths, based on facts, but also on emotions, and if you wish, opinions. Art, fiction, mere fiction...as Oscar Wilde says, *is there anything as real as mere* fiction? It gives us access to other identities. Fiction makes it possible to live through experiences which aren't our own.'

The professor ignores his words and glances at her watch. 'That's it for today. Out you go.'

Insulted, Martin remains seated as the professor rushes off with her bag clenched under her arm. She probably didn't hear him. Yes, that must be it. Still, why does he feel so humiliated then? His fellow students are leaving too.

Trying to ignore the dull thuds of their seats as they flip back into place, he stares at the ridge of the high gabled roof. Silver-coloured figures dangle from the beams and rafters, strung up on steel strings. Some modern artwork he never noticed before. He tilts his head. What is it precisely? Some strange trapeze act or is he witnessing a hanging?

Only then he realises he has completely forgotten about Zac. Martin turns round to look for his friend, but he's already gone. He could kick himself. Why did he get carried away in that pointless discussion? He should focus on one task at a time. He needs to find Zac and get that video offline. Hurriedly, Martin shoves his stuff in his scuffed backpack and puts on his jacket. Maybe he can still catch him.

He runs through the faculty building. Martin is about to shout Zac's name when he's pulled into an empty side-corridor. Zac holds him firmly in place against the wainscoted wall, gripping him forcefully with both hands.

'Jesus, Martin, chill,' his friend hisses in his ear.

'Zac, what did we do? We...'

Zac's already angular features harden and his grasp tightens. Martin wriggles to loosen his hold. He merely succeeds in getting him to let go with one hand. The other remains clamped in place.

Zac is so close Martin can smell him—Axe and Gauloises. He suspects that Zac merely likes to light the French sticks for the way they make him look. Martin has never seen him inhale.

'Can you take it down?' Martin pleads, his usually deep voice reduced to little squeaks.

'If that gives you peace of mind.' Zac's words bounce off the grey terrazzo floor. 'It won't make much of a difference. The internet doesn't forget. What are you so worried about anyway? It was an anonymous account. If we keep our heads down, we're safe.'

'Yes, I know, but what about Prior? This'll harm—'

Zac is quick to cut him off, his tone appeasing, 'Naah, it'll blow over. Still, we can't tell anyone. Can I trust you?'

'Of course you can trust me.'

'Then forget about it, Martin.' Zac's blue eyes look

friendly again. He winks. 'Go home and bang Eveline.'

§

The warmth of his dorm room is welcoming and reassuring. Martin isn't entirely convinced everything will sort itself out. But who knows? Maybe Zac is right. Maybe they're lucky.

The echoes of his irregular breathing still stick in his throat. He decides to open a bottle of wine from the collection he inherited from his father. Besides his jacket, one of the few things he left him. It'll calm him down. Help him to see things in perspective.

Martin dithers near the steel wine rack at the foot of his bed. The Malbec's high alcohol content tips the balance. He searches around for a glass that is more or less clean, sits down on the couch, and fills it to the brim. Strong, dark, violet, fruit flavours...The wine needs to breathe for half an hour to release its full vibrancy. He takes a big gulp anyway.

He might as well take Zac's advice. Slouched, Martin prises his phone out of his jeans pocket. He owns a heavy thick model. It's outdated and slow, but tangible, unlike today's devices. He checks the screen. It's seven p.m. First some music. Michael Kiwanuka, *Cold little heart*. The acoustic version from the soundtrack of Prior's film *The Exiles*, of course. Gentle, soft, soothing. *Did you ever notice? I've been ashamed.* Then he messages Eveline—*Your body is 65% water and I'm thirsty. Come over?*

Is it his fourth or fifth drink? Who cares? Martin

empties the bottle into his glass. It's getting late, and his girlfriend has still not replied. He takes a handful of the Bolognese-flavoured potato chips he found at the back of a cabinet in the rundown communal kitchen. One of his roommates strategically hid the green bag behind the mouldy cereal box no one dares to touch. He'll replace it tomorrow.

With seasoned fingers, Martin browses through Eveline's online posts on his phone. There's a pic from four minutes ago. He zooms in. His girlfriend appears to be having a good time without him. Eveline is raising a glass with Aperol-Spritz, her favourite, while being held on her feet by some bloke behind her. She will surely have sex with him tonight.

The idea of her sleeping with another man doesn't appeal to Martin. Eveline was the one who'd suggested they have an open relationship, merely one month into their dating. She thought the romantic ideal of monogamy to be 'another patriarchal construction to control women'. Martin felt no need to hook up with other people. He still doesn't, she's all he needs. What's wrong with being exclusive, with choosing each other? That's not what he said however. Dazzled by the fact she wanted to be with him and too afraid to lose her, he would've agreed to any condition she'd set to make it last. He only managed to put in that their friends were off-limits. Luckily, she agreed to that.

He unzips his pants. In his imagination, she's at least his, and his alone. And it will take his mind off the video, if just for a couple of minutes. Yet when he closes his eyes before he comes, Martin doesn't see Eveline, but Prior. Bend over, his pants around his ankles, his professor teasingly watches over his shoulder, right at him. Martin desperately tries to stop his cum, but it's too late.

§

It's nearly morning when the dorm's doorbell rings. Martin glances through the sole window in his room. Eveline's blonde hair sticks to her cheeks in sand-coloured strands. It's raining. He presses the button on the wall next to the window to let her in. The opener is timeworn and doesn't always work. This time, after a loud buzz, the door opens without a hitch.

'Hey, there you are.' He is genuinely relieved to see her. Eveline is soaked. The water drips on the dirty lilac carpet in his room. That someone once considered carpet in a student house was a good idea is beyond him.

His girlfriend deposits her canvas tote bag on his desk and scans his room disapprovingly. Martin wishes he'd tidied up. Eveline hates clutter. Clothes and dirty dishes lay around, and dozens of books cover the floor. Mostly novels, old classics in Dutch, English, German, and French: *Das Parfum, La Bête Humaine, The Great Gatsby, Disgrace,* and *Tirza.* Not his film books of course. Those are on display on the bookshelves against the wall. Eveline decorated the ledges with multi-coloured Christmas lights before the holidays. The one above his bed holds his favourites: *The Principles of Screen Writing* which used to be his father's, and all the works on and by Prior he could lay hands on.

Eveline reaches for the striped green tea towel on his clothing rack. 'I see you haven't taken down the Christmas lights yet.'

'Yes, I know, Christmas is over. I'll do it later today. How was your night?'

She shakes her head, signals she's not in the mood to talk about it, and abrasively dries her rained-out hair with the towel. Martin leans forward and pushes some damp locks to the side. He can smell the scent of yesterday's guy on the skin of her neck—something smoky—but decides not to press on.

Instead, he nods to the screen of his laptop next to her bag on his desk. 'I have an idea for a script.'

He opened the file a minute ago when she knocked on his door. It's a diversion. He had been meaning to tell her what happened, with Prior, the video, all of it. When the moment drew closer, he backed out. She wouldn't understand, not get it was a joke.

'Another one?' Eveline sounds surprised. She sits down on his bed.

'Yes, well, you know how it is. Art is my way of coping.' Martin tries to sound light-hearted. Does she notice anything different about him? Does she believe him? He should be more concrete. 'It's about the COVID-pandemic.'

'That's not very original, perhaps—'

'I have something different in mind for how to tell

it,' Martin interrupts her. 'Visually, I mean. To depict multiple connected stories and blend them at the end.'

Eveline grins. 'That sounds as complex as you.'

Her careless teasing comforts him and he smiles. 'Yes, maybe, but in some regards I'm simple.'

He gets up, slowly unbuckles his belt and takes off his pants. 'Is that ok?' Martin whispers as he pulls her closer to him.

As soon as she nods, his hand slides under her dress.

§

A repetition of uncanny pinging sounds wakes him up. Martin sits on the side of his single bed and rubs his head. He's about to reach for his phone when Eveline pulls him back into the warmth of where his body lay.

She'd put on one of his shirts for pyjamas, the chequered green-blue one. Her own clothes are lying on the heating. Her panties hang inside out on the thermostat valve. Dried fluids glisten on the black cotton.

'Hmmmm.' Martin clamps her fingers around his half-swollen cock.

Eveline yawns and withdraws her hand. 'Again?'

'Gladly. Give me a minute. I'll take a leak first.'

She laughs. 'You sure know how to seduce a girl. No, thank you. I've had enough. A coffee, however...'

Martin already heads out to the bathroom, before Eveline gets to finish her sentence. He doesn't bother to put on his boxer shorts first.

'With milk,' she calls after him.

Martin briefly checks his hair in the bathroom mirror and rearranges it. He needn't have. His hair always looks good. Pleased with himself, he stands over the toilet. The urine spatters against the sides of the bowl. With his free hand, he opens the messages on his phone.

What the hell? Ninety-six messages?!

They're all from his frat mates. It wasn't uncommon for their group conversations to spin out of control but like this? Startled, he almost drops his cell. Martin manages to grab the phone before it falls into the water. Oh, blast! He has peed down the inside of his leg. It's on his foot as well. He'll have to shower before returning to the bedroom, to Eveline. Like this, he'll have no chance of more sex. But first, he has to know what everyone is so worked up about.

Martin opens the original message in the conversation. It's from Elon, a link to a news item—*Production Company Washes Hands of Jude Prior. Streaming Services Take Prior Films Down.*

No, no, no, this can't be happening. The guff is all over the news, and everyone confirms it. The lies, they make them true. They are 'surprised', but also 'always thought so', 'in the back of their minds, they suspected it'.

There's no way he can put this right anymore. All hell has broken loose. Oxygen, he needs air, to breathe. Without flushing, Martin rushes out into the hallway and slams through the door into his room, nearly throwing himself into the book piles on the floor.

»«

CHAPTER 2

EVELINE

Eveline cannot help but stare at her boyfriend. She's lying on her stomach with her feet on the large lumpy pillow, her head at the foot of the bed. Her elbows are half-sunken in the soft mattress, and her chin is resting in her hands. She had been dozing off again when Martin barged back into the bedroom with an unsettling suddenness. The heavy fire-resistant door banged loudly into the wall.

Martin was completely beside himself. He didn't reply when she asked what was going on. Instead, he started to pace like a caged animal. He hasn't stopped since. Her eyes follow his restless movements. His genitals dangle along with their rhythm. Up and down, left to right. Their fleshy furiousness captivates her gaze.

He smells strange. She didn't notice it immediately. Yet when he passes near to her there's no escaping. Piss. Unmistakable. Eveline gets up to open the window, and wavers in front of the full-length, steel-framed mirror close to it. She's wearing one of Martin's plaid shirts, the sleeves rolled up, the front unbuttoned. He has the shirt in every thinkable colour scheme. Eveline likes this one on him as the ocean-green brings out his eyes.

She watches her otherwise naked body in the mirror and bends forward. She'd like to have more perky breasts. Eveline realises it's not feminist to think that. She should be happy with her body. But however how hard she tries to embrace her breasts, they keep bothering her the same, like they have been since her early teens.

She first became aware of their "flawed" nature—although again, she shouldn't think in those terms—during a sleepover at Kiara's. It was Kiara who suggested they'd do the pencil test together. Some beauty vlogger whom her best friend followed had been posting about it. The test turned out to be simple. To find out if their breasts were firm enough, they were to place a pencil in the fold under them. If the stick fell within seconds, their chests passed the test.

How old had they been? Sixteen, Seventeen maybe? Either way, Eveline remembers the sound of Kiara's pencil as it fell on the wooden floor. Pleased, her friend shook back her curls, which she had recently dyed in a bright red, the first of many colours to follow. While Kiara beamed with pride, it remained dead silent on her own side. Eveline feels ashamed thinking back at the joke that Kiara made next—'My goodness, Eveline, I think you need a pencil case instead.'

Quivering, she pulls the shirt panels back over her chest and studies the many film posters Martin has used as wallpaper. Mostly pictures of his beloved Prior films. There's also an old one of a wet blonde girl in a white bikini, emerging from a wild sea with a black knife in her hand. Then, there's his self-made collection with directors' quotes in calligraphic letters:

Read, Read...If You Don't Read,
You Will Never Be a Filmmaker

All You Need for a Movie is a Gun and a Girl

What a pretentious nonsense.

The thudding of Martin's pacing has stopped, and she turns around to find him standing in the middle of the room, frozen for a moment. Her boyfriend gapes at her as if only now noticing she's there as well and understanding that he needs to explain his behaviour.

Barely understandable the words shoot out, 'Prior... my teacher...his films...'

She could use the coffee she asked him for earlier. She's getting hungry too. It's well after noon and she hasn't had something decent to eat since the croissant on the way here this morning. There's a coffee bar across the street. It's part of a chain, but they make decent cappuccino and sell sandwiches. Looks like they won't be heading there soon.

Martin's cheeks are flushed and there's sweat on his upper lip. He rattles, '...the media, they're after him. There's a video...Well here. Watch.'

It's a short clip, a little less than two minutes. The resolution on his old phone is poor but Eveline can see and hear enough for it to make her skin crawl. 'Oh my God. How awful!'

'Isn't it?' Martin exclaims fiercely. 'Look, here, interviews with actors he shot with. They're so quick to wash their hands of him. The poor man. I should do something to help. I should—'

'Really Martin? *That's* what you are so worked up about?' Eveline interjects.

'No, no. You don't understand. It's not real—'

'You don't get what it's like for us women, do you?'

'Please list—'

The book hits him right in the balls. Martin folds double, moans, cries and smiles at the same time—a painful grimace. Eveline didn't aim for his crotch. In fact, she didn't aim at all. She was so angry, she grabbed whatever was closest to her. Her boyfriend falls onto the floor, his hands in front of his testicles, groaning.

'I'm so sorry. I didn't mean to...do you have an ice pack?' Eveline's voice is tight.

She opens the door of the small freezer under Martin's desk. There are some containers with leftovers, probably frozen take-away, and a Smirnoff bottle in it.

'...Give...' Martin wheezes, still wincing, pointing at the bottle, '...that'll do...'

He unscrews the red top with his teeth, takes a large slug, and places the cold bottle against his crotch.

The book she floored him with lies between his feet. On the cover, there's an image of a young man sitting near a shoreline. He's leaning forward to gaze at his reflection in admiration. The painted muscles in his neck stand out and his thick blond hair falls over his forehead. *The Picture of Dorian Gray—the uncensored edition.*

Eveline squats down next to the novel and observes Martin with concern. 'Are you ok?'

His breathing slowly returns to normal. He doesn't look at her. He doesn't even turn his head in her direction. 'Damn it, Eveline. Why do you always have to get so hysterical?'

That's all it takes to trigger her rage again. Hysterical? Always? He *really* doesn't get it. She takes off the chequered shirt, *his* shirt, and briskly puts on her panties and T-shirt bra, a wired one for support. Pulling her dress over her head, she storms out of his room.

§

The bar's copper doorknob is shaped like a cocktail shaker. It feels cold and sleek when Eveline folds her hand around it. The fight with Martin has been weighing her down all day. She's in dire need of a drink and some entertainment tonight.

She had asked Kiara to come as well, but her friend couldn't make it. It isn't the first time Kiara has "better" things to do. Eveline hasn't seen her much lately. Without classes together it turns out to be difficult to stay connected in the same way as in secondary school. In their final high school year, Eveline had tried to convince her best friend to enrol in psychology as well. Yet Kiara was set on taking law.

Company or not, she can use a drink. Eveline turns the doorknob, but the wooden door doesn't give way and she has to put her shoulder against it to open it. It's still early in the evening. There are only a few other people in the bar. Despite being half-empty, the space feels intimate. With its art deco-inspired low tables and velvet armchairs, the decor exudes a 1920s speakeasy vibe. Everything bathes in a yellow and pink diffuse glare of bare lightbulbs and hidden tubes.

From the outside, you'd never guess at all that splendour hiding behind the building's facade. There are no windows, no neon signs, just a wooden green door. The only clues are the doorknob and the small plaque next to the doorbell with an engraved command—*Press for Drinks*. You have to be part of the city's in-crowd to notice, to know, which makes Eveline feel like she belongs.

Sitting down on a rotating barstool, she orders a gin mule. The bartender skilfully scoops the ice cubes in a crystal highball, measures the doses of gin and ginger beer, and stirs the drink with a twisted spoon. She doesn't fancy his full blond beard and round spectacles, nor the suit he wears, but the routine with which he makes the drink is comforting. Eveline casts him a brooding smile. She knows it's unethical to pick him up. Sure, she's allowed to, she and Martin have an agreement. Still, they just had a fight.

'I never drink alone,' she whispers nonetheless.

'We're not allowed to drink with customers.' The bartender has a slight accent, most likely German. Eveline can't make out for sure and she doesn't care enough to ask. He looks at her and takes another glass. 'But one won't hurt. I'm Roy by the way.'

'Eveline.' She smiles seductively.

Roy reaches for the Beefeater bottle and pours it into the glass until it's one-quarter full, then fills it with tonic.

They clink.

Eveline signs at the bottles in the floor-to-ceiling oak rack behind him. 'Which drink is the most difficult to make?'

'The Commonwealth, without a doubt. It has seventy-one ingredients.'

'Seventy-one? Oh my gawd. Is it any good?'

'It's an experience.'

Eveline tilts her head pleadingly. 'Will you make me one?'

'Later maybe. You'll have to excuse me now.' He points his bearded chin in the direction of the door—new customers are walking in—then winks at her. 'I have the early shift. I'm done in two hours.'

When his shift ends, it almost goes without saying that she goes back with him to his place. It's right in the centre, but smaller than she anticipated. A tiny studio room of fifteen square metres if not less. The room is furnished with care with what appear to be second-hand pieces. Against the wall, there are two dark-blue plastic chairs and a glass coffee table, serving as a stand for a large fern. There's a study book next to the plant: *Project Europe: A History.* The cover is frayed at the edges.

So he's a student, European Studies probably. The bartending must be a side job. Eveline picks up the book to glance at the blurb on the back:

Today it often appears as though the European Union has entered an existential crisis after decades of success... Kiran Klaus Patel's bracing look back at the myths and realities of integration challenges conventional wisdoms of Europhiles and Eurosceptics alike.

Boring, not something for her at least. Eveline puts it back on the table. Looking up again, she notices the picture above the single bed. A framed photograph of a picnic with two women and a man by a pool. The women are dressed in swimsuits and engaged in a serious conversation with each other. The man is slightly out of focus, his pixels a bit blurry. He's fully nude, lying on his side, serving no other purpose than to pleasure the women whenever they so wish. Now *that* intrigues her. She studies it closer.

Roy comes up behind her and kisses her neck.

'Do you like it? I took it. It's inspired by *Le déjeuner sur l'herbe,*' he whispers the French words in her ear.

Eveline mischievously starts to unbutton her dress. 'You want to talk breakfast already?'

§

She is usually at her best in the morning, in the seemingly infinite space between the end of one day and the beginning of the next. A space she's able to stretch to fit her like a glove. But today the morning doesn't feel right.

Eveline is careful not to disturb Roy, who's still sleeping. Or was it Ray? She doesn't recall. Did she have that much to drink? Rrrayoooy. Raoy. Whatever his name, she doesn't want to wake him up.

She scans his room to plot her way out. It's dusky. The curtains are half-closed. She can merely make out some contours of the furniture and the outline of her dress, within hand's reach on the floor near the bed.

However lost in the moment she was last evening, currently the dawn and a mild hangover carry a different awareness. She wants to be gone before Raoy wakes up. His synthetic bedding doesn't breathe and is clinging to her thighs like duct tape. She has to struggle to get out.

Raoy turns on his other side and the bedsprings squeak. Eveline holds her breath. Luckily, he continues to sleep. A flicker of remorse—or is it guilt?—runs down her spine. She shouldn't have slept with him. The sex hadn't even been that good. He turned out to have just reasonably skilled fingers.

She believes hands give away a lot about how a man performs in bed. If he's selfless or selfish. She's usually good at reading them. This time she made a lapse in judgement.

Eveline tries to shake off the shame of the fresh memory. Martin has good hands. She spotted that the first time they met. Light, thin fingers and palms smaller than hers. Their effect is generally unparalleled. However, lately, he doesn't use them in the same way anymore. Or at least not as often as he did.

She has tried to return to that split-second of forgetting, looking for it between the sheets in different beds and in the hands of other men. Hands with various smells, skin, and age, leathery, soft, with or without cigarette stains, scars, moles, freckles, cracks, sharp nails, bitten ones. She makes them stain her and the bedding, but they all feel the same: different.

She wonders what it means. As she studies psychology, she knows all too well that sex is about exposure, about vulnerability. However brief, messy, shaming or faltered, you always learn something about yourself and the other person. Whether that's a pleasant truth is another matter.

Eveline sighs and grabs her dress from the floor to slip into it hastily. By touch she makes her way through the room, to the door. The sun isn't up high enough to shine its red morning light through the curtains' opening. Where's the door handle? She curses under her breath.

'Are you leaving already?' Raoy switches on the bed light.

Shoot. The handle is two centimetres below her left hand. She turns around to apologise. 'You were sleeping so deeply. I didn't want to wake you.'

'Et le petit déjeuner, Eveline?'

His accent lies thickly on his voice. It's certainly German. He turns the 'j' into that typical 'ch' sound.

'I have to run. Some other time maybe.'

'Can I have your numb—?'

'I know where you work.'

She'll have to strike her favourite bar from her list. Raoy is nice and witty, and under normal circumstances, she wouldn't have minded meeting up again. Now, it would remind her of her mistake. She hurriedly leaves his room.

In the entrance hall of the block of student flats, she digs her phone out of her bag. It's a depth filled with hair elastics, two Durex Wild Berry packets—one empty and one half-full—and five different lipsticks in nearly the same vintage pink shade. She has never been good at making choices.

Her phone is brand new. Eveline has had it for a week and still needs to get used to it. She has a subscription to a digital news service, two even. Kiara thinks it's a ridiculous waste of money. She struggles for a couple of seconds to open her favourite news app. A feast of bad messages emerges:

Live: Mob-Killing in Berlin—False Pics to Blame

Exclusive: Antitrust Probes against OMG-Media

*Breaking: 152 Climate Refugees Drown
in the Mediterranean Sea*

There's a message from Martin as well. Fight or no fight, it's their first anniversary today. He wants her to meet him at *Lumière* cinema at eleven a.m. It's sweet of him to think of it, to make an effort. Perhaps they simply needed a short break from each other.

It doesn't surprise Eveline that he has chosen the cinema for their celebration. It was where he took her for their first date as well. Eveline can't remember which film it was. She doesn't care too much for films, but for him, they're a religion. Martin even has a weekend job checking tickets in *Lumière*.

She decides to stop at one of the many takeaway coffee bars on her way to the cinema to buy a peace offering. The barista hardly notices her when she enters the almost empty place. A middle-aged couple and a lonely bearded man somewhere in his seventies are sitting at the Formica tables in the back. The barista is leaning on the counter with her elbows, watching the big TV screen in the front.

Eveline peeks over her shoulder to see what's on: two crying children and a woman in the middle of a busy street across from a metro station—*Berlin Bomb: mum tells how she and her kids fled.* Old news. That terrorist attack happened two days ago and it was foiled in time.

'Lucky they shot and killed him before he could hurt anyone,' the barista mutters to no one in particular.

'Can I order?' Eveline is getting impatient.

'Just a minute.' The woman turns up the volume to hear the interview with the mother.

A picture of the bomber emerges on the screen; a white extremist, with short-cropped blond hair.

'Hello?' Eveline snaps. It's nearly eleven.

The barista sighs annoyed. 'Ok. What will it be?'

'A double espresso and a flat white with an extra shot of oat milk.'

Unlike Martin, Eveline likes her coffee like her men—white and cloudy. Her sexual preference for troubled Caucasians makes her somewhat uncomfortable. It feels racist somehow. She doesn't know why and if it is, but she will never acknowledge her predilection in public.

While she waits for her order, Eveline decides not to tell Martin about her fling with Raoy. Normally, she tells him everything, perhaps not right away, but she finds it important to be honest. Although her boyfriend says she doesn't have to, she wants him to know the truth. But this one might hurt him too much. It might make things between them more awkward.

She realises she probably smells of Raoy. If she doesn't want Martin to find out, she'll have to do something about that. There's no time to go home for a quick rinse down. Eveline fishes her deodorant from her bag and sprays herself generously. Her clothes, her hair, her armpits. She ignores the disgruntled looks from the barista. Vanilla and cherry blossom. That should do the trick.

§

Martin is already waiting outside of the cinema when she arrives. He's wearing that worn leather jacket again. It's at least two sizes too big for him. She doesn't like how it makes him look, which isn't only a lot younger but also helpless in an almost childlike way.

Eveline takes a sip of her hot coffee and offers Martin the cup she bought him. Taking it off her hands, her boyfriend leans in to kiss her. Eveline remembers she might taste like Roy as well. She went down on him big time. Even though the coffee will have washed most of him away, it's better not to take any chances. At the last second, she angles her face to one side and Martin's lips land on her cheek.

'What's the plan?' she tries to sound upbeat.

'You'll see.' Martin plays along equally cheerfully, raking his fingers through his dark brown hair.

Apparently, they're going to pretend as if nothing happened. Martin doesn't say a word about yesterday and she would be the last one to bring it up. He had it coming. Eveline feels sorry nonetheless. Would his balls still hurt?

Martin opens the glass sliding doors to the closed cinema with his staff key card. They're the only ones in the building this morning. There's something uneasy about its complete emptiness. As they walk through the large hall, the lights turn on automatically, alarmed by their movements.

Martin wavers in front of the wide open doors to one of the cinema rooms. He plays with the zipper of his jacket and blows his hair out of his eyes. 'Eveline? I...I've done something stupid...'

Is he going to bring up their fight after all? She eyes

him, annoyed. Martin coughs and mumbles something. Then he stares out at the white projection screen in the front. Although the silence stretches uncomfortably long, Eveline doesn't feel like asking him what is going on.

When Martin finally talks, he sounds steady again. With a flair for the dramatic, he waves at the rows of grey fake leather chairs. 'We have the whole place to ourselves. I handpicked the film *and* I brought a bottle of pinot noir!'

Eveline laughs, relieved. Martin likes red wine, not simply as a drink, but as a conversation topic as well. Her boyfriend leads her over to chair number eight on the last row. It's the best seat according to him. She would have preferred the love chair further down in the middle, a double seat without armrests to separate them from each other. But not wanting to be a spoilsport, she sits down. After tossing his jacket on the chair next to her, Martin disappears into the back to start the film.

An eerie sequence of droning noises is roaring through the surround speakers as he returns. The opening score sounds like something coming out of the old synthesiser gathering dust at her mum's house. When Eveline grew up, her mother played in a moderately successful band, *Pixie's Flix*, and she was hardly ever at home. There had been numerous babysitters and au pairs to care for Eveline, while her mum 'toured the world'.

In reality, the band never made it outside Germany, Belgium, and the Netherlands, but her mother made a lot of money nonetheless. Eveline has just a faint idea of who her dad is. One of the many men her mother hooked up with after a gig. She's seen an unclear picture of him.

How long has it been since she spoke with her mum? Nine months, ten? A while in any case. She should visit her mother soon. Maybe she'll merely give her a call. Her mother doesn't miss her anyway. As far as she's concerned, mothering comes down to picking up the bills. Unlike her boyfriend or her fellow students, Eveline doesn't have to work to pay for her studies. With her mum's allowance, she can lead a life of relative luxury.

Martin shifts restlessly in the chair next to her. The film he picked turns out to be a love story between a man and a computer program called *Her*. He probably thought it romantic. Eveline can, however, not settle into it. Martin keeps interrupting to explain something about the camera angle, and the lighting, and to tell her his favourite line from the movie—*The past is just a story we tell ourselves.*

Annoyingly, her boyfriend insists they watch the entire credit role as well. When it's finally done, he reaches inside the left pocket of his leather jacket and takes out a little package. It's gift-wrapped in shiny pink-striped paper. Martin puts on a big smile as he hands it to her.

Eveline takes another sip of the wine bottle—Martin didn't bring glasses—before she unwraps it slowly. A flesh-coloured vibrator shaped like a bunny emerges. The skinned rabbit fits precisely in the palm of her hand.

Her boyfriend picks it up and dangles it in front of her eyes from the key chain it's attached to. 'It made me think of you. You can take it everywhere in your bag. Look, it has nineteen different vibration modes.'

Eveline feels offended. She hates sex toys. Her jaw tightens at the sight of it and her hands curl into fists. This has nothing to do with what she considers real sex, real intimacy, and what they share, their relationship.

Martin is all excited about it, however. He presses the many buttons, turning it on. 'Here, feel, this is the fastest setting.'

The vibrator's high-pitched buzz cuts through the air between them, sounding like a bumblebee on the attack. Martin leans forward intending to give her the throbbing plastic thing. It might as well be a hand grenade with the pin out. No way is she going to touch it again. Instead of reaching out, she clenches her knuckles more firmly. Her fingernails dig deep into the flesh of her palms.

Unaware of her rejection, Martin has already let go of it. In a strange almost slow-motion-like pace the pink toy tumbles down. It hits the velvet floor with a small thump. Thrilled at its unexpected liberation, the bunny starts to spin around wildly.

»«

CHAPTER 3

DITTE

Stress has settled between Ditte's shoulders. She circles them backwards and forwards, stretches her arms upwards, and repeats the movements three times. Her spine cracks, but her shoulders still hurt.

Ditte leans back in the stick-back chair at their kitchen table. Her husband Jeppe found the white wooden chair, one of six, in the local thrift shop. That's how he has put together most of their interior. Their home is a carefully curated combination of second-hand steals, heirlooms, and his art.

Jeppe has taken the kids out, so she can get some work done, but the afternoon has got away from her. As always on Fridays, Ditte is preparing the classes for the next week. Still, even the thought of teaching cannot lift her spirit today. Ever since that lecture at the beginning of the week, she has been feeling strangely puzzled. It dealt with one of her favourite topics: the differences between primary and secondary sources and, most importantly, how to evaluate their trustworthiness.

Ditte hadn't been able to start her class on time. As usual, she had to wait before all the students had taken a seat. One of them even slipped when running into the room. She couldn't blame him for being late. The lecture hall is located in the back of the faculty building, at the end of a maze of hallways, corridors and wooden staircases in a variety of styles. The result of centuries of architectural add-ons. As such, it marks the difference between staff and students. They get lost easily, while she and her colleagues find their way with ease. Ditte doesn't like how the building humbles the students.

She had to work hard for their attention that afternoon. As creative types, her students are more interested in fiction than facts. Yet, there's an unspoken agreement that she has the final word. She hadn't been prepared for how that young man challenged her authority. Martin it was. Martin Hermans. She won't forget the name.

He kept flipping his dark-brown hair back while he talked. An annoying habit. Ditte had averted her gaze to be able to listen without prejudice. Instead of him, she stared at one of the framed poems on the walls. There were many world-famous ones—*The Hill We Climb, We Wear the Mask, Immigrant, One Art*...This one, however, was only locally renowned. It was in Dutch, which she could read fine by now. Dutch isn't so different from Danish. *Spreek als je kunt...Dat was de kunst*. However, the deeper meaning of the poem was—like nearly all poetry, whether in Dutch, Danish or whatever language—an enigma to her.

Although she wasn't looking at Martin, his confident tone had bothered her. He spoke with the bravura which comes with the luxury of going through life unmarked—white, male, and probably cis-gender and heterosexual as well. Ditte doesn't like to make assumptions about something as changeable as gender identity and sexual preference, but she couldn't help doing so when he spoke.

She could easily have put him in his place by pointing out how he had misquoted Oscar Wilde. There had been something fragile in his voice, making her decide not to. It was probably the right decision. Still, she can't rid herself of the feeling she has missed something crucial there, at exactly that moment. It reminds her of the days when the housekeeper has been to their home—some furniture has been moved and she can't quite figure out which pieces.

Ditte sighs and gets up from behind the kitchen table to open the dishwasher. She puts in the dirty breakfast plates, smudging her fingers with strawberry marmalade and chocolate spread.

Then of course, there's Jude. She hasn't heard from him in days, whereas normally they always have lunch together. Now, he doesn't respond to her messages or calls. Has she done or said something wrong? Ditte wouldn't know what. Besides, if she had, he isn't the type to hold a grudge. Jude is a true Brit—at least, what she thinks Brits are like, which is probably a stereotype—thoughtful with a sense of self-mockery. Most academics lack the latter quality. She too takes herself far too seriously.

Ditte met Jude first during the faculty barbeque at the opening of the academic year, when she started working here a couple of years ago. Their kids were about the same age. They quickly set up play-dates, and numerous dinner parties irrigated with wine followed. Countless evenings they've sat in this kitchen—she, Jeppe, Jude, and his life partner Alexander—talking for hours, laughing, and confiding their deepest thoughts to each other.

Ditte selects the eco-programme and turns on the dishwasher. At the same time, her youngest daughter Louna runs into the kitchen, her caramel curls dancing up and down. Jeppe is on her tail. Their almost one-year-old son Razi is asleep in the yarn sling-wrapped around his chest. They have returned from their walk. The light patter on the staircase to the second floor of their oldest, Alma, gradually reaches the kitchen. She's on her way to her room, probably to play with one of her beloved Playmobil sets.

Louna gives Ditte one of her inexorable hugs, squeezing most of the air out of her lungs. Ditte laughs, a signal for her daughter to grab her more tightly.

'Careful, Louna,' she warns her semi-sternly. 'You'll be covered in chocolate. My hands are dirty from the dishes.'

Jeppe leans across from them against one of the magnolia-coloured kitchen cabinets, a mild smile on his lips. He observes the goodhearted wrestling between her and Louna while combing through his full beard with his fingers, which, unlike the blond hair on his head, is light reddish.

Ditte fell for him when they first met during an exposition organised by the local art club of which her dad was the treasurer. Jeppe had finished his series *Danish Cows in Green from Above,* which was on display there as well. He had told her about the cows, their names, where they lived, and how intelligent they were, and she had been smitten.

'Did you hear from Jude?' Jeppe asks. He must be concerned too, as he likes Jude a lot as well.

'No, nothing yet. I'll try to call him again later,' Ditte replies, fixing her eyes on Louna, who has started to skip around the kitchen.

Her daughter is humming a Danish tune, which Ditte often sings to her—*Alt hvad hun ville var at danse.* All she wanted was to dance.

§

In shock, Ditte gazes at the red-painted mouth of the university's spokesperson. She's called Nina and is barely in her thirties. Her face is marked by a faked kindness, reminding Ditte of the preschool teacher of her youngest of three children. Nina pronounces every syllable with care, but to Ditte the sentences sound muffled, like underwater noises. Only some words seep through—'Jude', 'intolerable', 'sexist'.

Ditte and her colleagues were summoned to the lecture hall first thing this morning. Even the receptionist and the janitor got sent inside. Nina made sure the high wooden double doors were closed before she dropped the bomb: the faculty was going to distance itself from Jude Prior in a press conference.

Voices of confusion and protest swelled like a sea. Jude isn't only a professor, but a famous film director too. He's the showpiece of the Faculty of Film Studies. Then Nina showed them the video of Jude, and everyone went dead silent.

Nothing good has ever come out of a woman unless she gave birth to a brilliant film director like me... actresses, without me, they would amount to nothing. They cannot even remember their lines.

Every word Jude spoke is etched in Ditte's mind. She feels betrayed, insulted, and enraged. At the same time, she has a hard time believing it. Ditte doesn't know a more emancipated man than Jude, apart from her husband Jeppe. Would her best friend think so little of women?

Although the evidence is irrefutable, the video somehow makes her feel *like a terribly real thing in a terribly false world.* As if she's trapped in an unimaginative version of Lewis Carroll's wonderland. It was her close friend for sure on the screen. Yet something is off.

She tries to focus on Nina again, who's urging them to sit quietly through the conference, which is about to start in an hour in the very same lecture room.

Nina speaks slowly, emphasising nearly every word, 'The front rows are reserved for the press. You will be sitting in the back. Do not talk with them. Do not answer their questions. Leave that to me or the Dean. Trust me, you don't want to be associated with this. I'm here to look out for you. Keep comments to yourself. Everyone has to pull in the same direction to take the faculty through this media storm. If you can't do this, then you should leave.'

Someone behind Ditte remarks below his breath that this isn't fitting for a university, which is supposed to be a stronghold of free speech. Probably René. Or is it Elisabeth? Still, everyone remains seated.

'Good,' Nina goes on, relieved. 'My assistant will collect your phones and other devices. Naturally, we don't want any unauthorised recordings circulating afterwards.'

There are some grumbles, but in the end, all her colleagues toss their cells in the wicker basket the assistant holds out to them. No one wants to miss what is about to happen. The basket looks like the one Ditte uses once a year to collect Easter eggs with her kids. Except for the dotted ribbon Ditte tied to the handle. Reluctantly, she too throws her cell into it.

§

Every available seat has been taken by increasingly boisterous members of the press. Ditte and her colleagues are standing packed together in the back of the lecture hall. Nina has positioned herself as a shield between them and the assembled gaggle, not realising it's the Dean she should have been worried about.

Eric has groomed himself carefully for the occasion. His blond-grey hair is cut short at the sides and he's clean-shaven. If he received instructions from Nina to keep it to the point, he has forgotten them. More likely, he's having his moment.

Ditte is astounded by the fuss the Dean is making out of the press conference. Eric is elated. His Adam's apple moves rapidly above the collar of his perfectly fitted white shirt. The glimmering darkness of his equally tailor-made jacket bolsters his blatant tone.

'Playwrights are generally less emphatic than normal people. My ground-breaking research has shown this indisputably. You can find my seminal publication—an absolute must-read—on my research page. Wait, I'll show it. Here it is.' Eric clicks the remote in his right hand. With the link to his webpage, a bright-coloured headshot of him in traditional academic dress emerges on the wall-fitting screen behind him. 'Now, we may assume that what goes for playwrights goes for screenwriters as well. Perhaps Prior also lacks empathy, this would explain...'

Eric has always hated having to ride on Jude's coattails. Ditte suspects him of finally seeing an opportunity to get rid of the man who has cast a shadow over him. He consistently refers to Jude by his last name only. There's a disdain in how he stresses the first r and the i, cutting the o short.

Ditte has never liked Eric. The Dean had been the

most important reason she was reluctant to move her family to Maastricht, a few years ago. Her first meeting with him was online. She had applied for a position as an associate professor in European history.

The Faculty of Film Studies wasn't her first choice. They didn't even have a history department, she'd be a member of the film analysis group. She'd be the only historian working there. Sure, one of her future colleagues, Gus, was a renowned film art historian, but that didn't count. It was, however, a permanent position. Those were hard to come by in academia. Besides, she saw and sees the merit of teaching future filmmakers how things actually went down.

Ditte had dressed herself with care for the job interview. She's aware she turns heads and that it matters, unfortunately. When you're a woman in academia, looking pretty, let alone sexy, is often not advantageous. She's bound to be taken less seriously. Hence, she had decided to go for a plain professional look. A black woollen dress with long sleeves and a high turtleneck. Simple, conservative almost. Apart from her earrings, crystal threaders, which were a gift from her father. She never goes anywhere without them.

It hadn't been the first time people were taken by surprise when meeting her. Her father had insisted on giving her a common Danish name, as well as her mother's last name. Not because he was a feminist, which he was, but because he thought it would improve his daughter's chances in a society in which prejudice tends to prevail despite good intentions.

Besides, her dad didn't truly have a last name. No one in Somalia did at the end of the 1980s. He had to fabricate one when seeking asylum in Denmark. That, and the fact he came by boat at the age of nineteen is about all Ditte knows about her father's life before he came to Denmark. To this day, her father has remained silent about the ordeals he must have gone through.

He has overwritten the terrible preceding events with a romantic tale of how he met her mother. Whenever anyone wants to know about his past, he tells the same anecdote. That he saw her mum in a grocery store and asked her how to pronounce the Danish names of some vegetables, and that she asked him the Somalian names in return.

Eric had so obviously expected to see someone else on his screen for the job interview. Somebody more Danish-looking—blonde with pale skin. He wasn't able to hide his astonishment. Webcams capture everything, they magnify every facial expression, including bewilderment.

He tried to talk over his faux pas but made it worse. Like now, Eric went on about all the important and famous people he knew and his own, obsolete, semi-psychological publications about the personality traits of artists.

The whole situation, the man himself, was all so uncomfortable. Ditte had almost killed her camera. Her finger was already on the button. She was, however, pregnant at the time. And she was, and is, the one providing for their family. Jeppe takes care of the household and the children. True, he's an independent artist too. He sells about one or two of his abstract landscapes from a bird eye's view for a decent amount. Yet, it isn't enough to make a living. It's merely a nice little extra. And so, despite all the red flags, she swallowed her pride.

At present in the lecture hall, Eric has started to criticise Jude's artistic work in front of the increasingly confused journalists, 'We can see how his sexism feeds into his films, *The Exiles* for instance...'

Ditte has seen *The Exiles* on a screening night, organised by the faculty itself for goodness sake. Sure, the female protagonist was naked in one scene and it was suggested the male antagonist performed oral sex on her. Still, it happened at her request, and even then, he explicitly asked for consent.

It had struck her. Men in films usually took women. In this one, the woman was confidently the taker. She made sure it was about *her* pleasure. The shooting of the scene felt atypical as well. It was mostly from her perspective. As a viewer, you were thus looking with her at and down on the man. Ditte found that interesting, but sexist? No.

However loathsome Jude's remarks in the video, this conference seems like rushing to a conclusion. For sure, the faculty needs to say something about what happened. They should take a stance... but so soon after? No way have they given Jude a proper chance to explain himself. What if his comments were taken out of context? And why is Jude not here himself?

His absence troubles her, and Ditte wonders if he has been notified about the press conference. She feels uncomfortable for not having spoken up earlier. But who knows what she'd be getting herself into, and by extension her family? That spokesperson Nina was right in that regard. It was better not to become guilty by association, especially as she doesn't know the ins and outs yet.

By now, Eric is going completely off track and is reading out parts of his paper. Nina tries to catch his eye. Abandoning all subtlety, she's signing at her watch, and at some point makes a throat-slitting gesture. Only when she finally waves her arm in the air like she's about to lasso him to drag him off stage, Eric nods at her.

The Dean is visibly annoyed by being interrupted, and more so by the fact it has been noticed by the journalists. Out of breath from the chains of sentences he has been weaving together for the past hour, he exhales loudly into the microphone.

Then, he finishes it off in a tone much too avid for his final message, 'Therefore, we have dismissed Prrriòr summarily, we will now answer—'

As a barrage of questions erupts, Ditte's heart races.

§

Ditte and Jude are standing in front of a military bunker complex amid farmland and woods. The outer walls of the fortress are overgrown with ivy and riddled with bullet holes. Small brown wrens hop and fly in and out of the tangle of climbers on the tarnished reinforced concrete. Apart from a few wilted ones, the ivy leaves look artificially green for the time of the year. Although the air is filled with the promise of snow, Ditte doubts it will deliver on it. There hasn't been one flake of snow so far this winter and while it is chilly today, it isn't freezing. Ditte tries to follow the birds' movements, but they are too quick for the human eye to capture. It's like watching a stop-motion video.

Jude's partner Alexander called her this morning, two weeks after the press conference, to return her stream of messages and calls, which were enraged at first but grew more concerned the longer she didn't hear back.

Alexander begged her to take Jude out—'He just sits on the couch, Ditte. Doesn't say a thing. I know it's a lot to ask. You're his best friend, or you were. If you don't want to do it for him, can you please do it for me? The kids?'

Still unsure what to think of the entire situation, Ditte hesitated but finally gave in to Alexander's plea, seeing it as a chance to get clarification. She suggested coming here for a walk, across the border in Belgium. It's a stone's throw from Maastricht, and at the same time far enough not to bump into any colleagues or students.

'Did you know that this is where the Second World War started in Western Europe?' she asks him.

Jude doesn't respond to her question. It doesn't stop her from talking, as she has done during the past hour to avoid awkward silences. Mostly chitchat, segueing from one topic into the next. She hasn't figured out yet how to ask him if he believes the things he said in the video.

Moreover, Ditte wants to give her friend a chance to tell the story on his terms. Most of all, she's afraid she will yell at him when bringing it up. The video is so lurid.

She looks sideways at him. His green eyes are blood-shot and dart uneasily back and forth. His hair and short beard, normally shiny black symbols of his decency, are dull and unkempt. He exhales loudly, sending one breathing cloud after another into the cold air less than a split second apart. His generally already light complexion is ghostlike.

She tries to catch his eyes, but he avoids her gaze. Instead, he stares at the pancake restaurant behind her. She has just told him the grain mill in which it's located was hit by a Stuka dive-bomber in 1940, and even mimicked the eerie sound of it—'miiiiiiiiiiiiiouwww'. Up close, you can see tiny bomb shards in the wall. War and pancakes...

It's unfortunate the little restaurant is closed this chilly morning. Sharing a coffee or perhaps something stronger would've helped them to warm up to each other.

Ditte resumes her story, 'The fortification was believed to be impregnable. It took the Germans fifteen minutes. You know how they did it? Gliders. Can you believe that? They used gliders instead of motorised planes. An almost silent takeover at sunrise. Well apart from some gunfire and the explosions of hollow charges. They used those to penetrate the thick steel armour. First time they were—'

'Oh shut up, Ditte!' Jude shouts at her, his fists clenched. Behind him, the wrens fly up startled, twittering indignantly. 'Stop the cheerful charade. You must be furious with me. But I didn't do it! I would never say that. It's not me. It's a fake! The problem is, I can't prove it. It looks bloody real and I can't blame anyone for not believing me.'

Jude's usually piglet-pink cheeks are fiery red. Could it be a fake? There was indeed something off about the entire video. Ditte couldn't put her finger on it before, but she had sensed it. She feels somewhat relieved. Of course, it's a fake.

'I do,' she exclaims with sudden conviction. 'I believe you, Jude.'

'You'll speak up for me then?' He watches her expectantly, his voice trembling with hope.

Ditte averts her eyes. She's willing to support him but to risk her career, their livelihood? There's no evidence it's a fake, and she has a family to take care of. She struggles to find the right words, 'I have to think of my children...my job, I...But I believe you...'

'But I believe you. Well, isn't that nice for you!' Jude's parody is tense with restrained fury and painfully catches her cowardice. Then he breaks. 'Can you hold me?'

While it finally starts to snow, Ditte hurries towards him.

»«

CHAPTER 4

MARTIN

The blood-red painted letters on the wall of the open-plan living and dining room in Prior's house are at least one metre tall. The thick ferocious spray breathes the rage of its maker. For a moment, Martin is convinced the furiously tinted accusation is directed at him:

MCP

He flinches and closes his eyes. When he opens his eyes again the paint is still maiming the delicate flowers on the wallpaper. *MCP.* Male Chauvinist Pig. He tries to swallow down the sharp wave of panic hitting the back of his throat. It tastes bitter.

It hadn't been difficult to find Prior's address online. The detached white family house turned out to be situated in the south of the city. It's relatively close to where

Zac lives. Martin must've passed it a dozen times before without knowing. The dense pine trees in the front garden hide it well from uninvited stares from the street. The ride from his dorm to his professor's place was a mere ten minutes, but his legs had been burning with dread before he mounted his bike and it had felt like an hour. He made it though.

He is here to make amends, to put everything right again. Martin decided to do anything Prior will ask him. He'll sign any paper. Although it will certainly mean the end of his studies, he will even agree to make a public statement. Martin is painfully aware his desired career as a filmmaker will come to an end before it has started. If that's what's needed to undo what he has wrought...

He appears to be too late. If he hadn't known better, he would've sworn to be on the set of one of those drug and gang series he liked to watch when he was a few years younger. *Breaking Bad, Better Call Saul, Narcos, El Chapo, Cocaine Coast...*All of those shows ended the same, with people and places trashed to pieces.

There are glass splinters from the smashed front window everywhere. Careful not to trip—he doesn't want to cut himself—Martin tries to tiptoe around the fragments. They still crunch and snap underneath the soles of his brown boots. The brick with which the window has been shattered lies next to one of the four dining chairs, which are on their backs, three with their legs broken.

Except for a small portrait of a black-haired girl in a dark jumper, all paintings have been ripped from the walls. Although the portrait is still in its place, it has been gashed. The cut runs across the girl's skin from the corner of her mouth to her earlobe.

Martin leans in to read the inscription on the bronze plaque, which is screwed tightly into its frame: *De Maagd* by M. Borremans. The name sounds familiar, but not familiar enough for him to know if it's a valuable piece. He hopes it isn't an original. The painting is done in a style that reminds him of the Dutch old masters. The artist, however, gave it a modern twist—two laser beams, painted in white, blast from the girl's blank eyes.

The family photos, which Prior and his partner must have selected carefully once, have been knocked off the warm walnut sideboard. Martin bends over to pick up a frame from the herringbone parquet floor. Jude, his husband, and their three children, two boys and a girl, smile back at him through the dirt of a footprint on the glass. The boys look like they're six, maybe seven, possibly twins. The little girl cannot be more than three years old. She's smiling awkwardly into the camera and holds Jude's hand firmly.

Martin's heart is in his throat. Did they get away in time? What if they got injured, or worse? He places a hand against the wall to balance himself and staggers to the family sofa. It is slashed to shreds and bleeding down-stuffing. When he drops onto one of its seats, feathers fly up into the air.

Why has he waited for more than a week? Why didn't he come here earlier? He tugs at a little piece of loose skin from his cracked cuticles. A drop of blood wells up. He has recently started to bite his nails and the skin around it again. A nervous tick he thought he'd successfully given up on years ago. Eveline finds it repulsive. Martin can't resist it, although she looks at his hands with disgust.

He wishes Zac had come with him. Martin had asked him to, and as expected, he declined. Zac even poked his finger into his chest—'Confess all you like. But shut the hell up about me.' The violent way in which the house is trashed would have strengthened Zac's beliefs. Good he didn't come then. The unrepentant coward, with a friend like that...

He and Zac were only having a laugh when Martin made that bloody video a couple of weeks ago. It was a stupid dare. It had been the last evening before the Christmas break. They were having drinks in the fraternity's pub when Zac proudly showed him and Elon a clip he had made with the app *Fake It*. He had pasted the head of a female fellow student on the body of a porn actress. Martin laughed furtively at Zac's attempt and boasted about the superior quality of the deep fakes he could produce himself. His two friends weren't interested in what he had to say and kept playing the video on Zac's phone.

As Martin lived closer to the pub, Zac crashed at his place that night. When he opened the door, an unpleasant, sweltering heat poured out of the room. It had been an exceptionally warm day. The heating in his room was, however, controlled centrally by an anything but smart system.

It expected winter to be, well, winter.

Martin carefully hung his leather jacket on the coat hook on the inside of his door, opened the window and turned on the ceiling fan. The single cold drink he could offer Zac, besides vodka, was the bottle of prosecco in his fridge. It was a mere cheap house brand, as he couldn't afford anything else, but sparkles were sparkles. He had kept it for a special occasion and decided this was a night to remember. They had survived the first semester after all. The foam squirted out of the bottle when he filled two coffee mugs.

Zac downed his drink before Martin could raise his cup to make a toast. As his friend helped himself to a refill, he begged Martin the question with which it would all go down, calling him out on what he had bragged about in the pub. 'Time to put your dick where your mouth is. How's what you do different from what I did with the app?'

Martin laughed. 'Put my dick where my mouth is, eh? Well, in a video by me, that dick and mouth would be one hundred per cent na-tu-ral. *As real as a donut, motherfucker.* Most apps suck. Yes, the looks are there, but how a specific person tilts his head or lisps...And the expression of emotions, don't get me started. You need a human touch for that. That's where I come in and—'

'The master of programmed emotions?' Zac joked

But Martin wouldn't let Zac deter him. If Zac thought he was bluffing, he was about to be proven wrong. He knew this stuff better than Zac. 'I can make a video convincing. And if it's credible, no one is ever going to find out it isn't real. With the software I use, no digital fingerprints, no hashtag discrepancies.'

'Big talk, my friend. But that's all it is, talk, innit? You'll need to do one now,' Zac demanded. 'Who shall we pick?'

'How about one of the Hemsworth brothers?' Martin suggested. 'Chris perhaps?'

He was already browsing for footage when Zac interrupted him exuberantly. 'No, no, wait. Do Prior. That'll be a blast. There's enough stuff online for you to work with.'

Martin messed around with it for quite a while. He had a hard time concentrating. Even with the window open, the fan merely moved hot air around. The alcohol didn't help either. He mopped the sweat on his brow with the back of his forearm. Luckily, there was half a pizza left in his fridge from the day before. Carbs and fat to outweigh the alcohol, to gain the focus needed.

After three tasteless slices of cold chewy dough, set cheese, and tomato paste, he felt ready to finish it. 'What will we make him say?'

Zac was working down the rest of the pizza on the small yellow couch, his legs dangling over an armrest. He got up, threw the crust of the last slice back into the cardboard pizza box, and watched over Martin's shoulder in sweaty proximity. He was breathing down his neck. 'Hmmm, I'm in the mood for something vile.'

'As usual.' Martin chuckled.

'Let's...' Zac unfolded his plan.

Martin was taken aback by his friend's suggestion. 'Seriously? No, Zac. I can't make him say *that*.'

Zac clucked like a chicken. 'I didn't take you for a pussy, Martin. Come on, it's a joke. If we gonna do this, we should get all the way out. Or are you perhaps not as good as you claim? Too much of a challenge, eh?'

Martin took a large slug of prosecco. The wine tasted sour but made his cheeks burn feverishly. He would show him what he was made of. If Zac wanted it foul, foul was what he got, the foulest. 'Challenge accepted.'

After half an hour he turned the screen to Zac. 'What about this?'

'Let me see.' Zac's booming laugh thundered through his room. 'Wow, Martin. You weren't bluffing. I'm impressed. That looks absolutely legit.'

The lace curtains in front of the shattered window in Prior's house bulge. Martin gazes at them without seeing. He's gnawing at the remains of the ruined nails on his left hand, then starts fidgeting with the zipper of his jacket. How could he have been so stupid? That he made it was one thing. Why did he let Zac post it?

He should've taken his initial gut feeling seriously, but his friend had persuaded him to do otherwise. Zac had bolstered his ego, saying it was too good not to share with the world. He had persuaded him there was nothing to worry about. It was so over the top that people would immediately see it was a joke, his friend had argued convincingly. Besides, the alcohol had clouded Martin's judgment. He hadn't been himself, which wasn't an excuse. Still, if only he had been sober.

What should he do? In an attempt to wipe out his anxious thoughts, Martin runs his right hand through his hair. Fast. Briskly. Some feathers from the inside of the cut couch whirl upwards again. Their unexpected movement startles him, but not as much as the biting voice flying through the living room a split second later.

'What are you doing here?'

Martin turns around so abruptly that the feathers closest to him twirl in mid-air. He's half-expecting to see Prior or his ghost. Instead, it's his history professor. Ditte something...he doesn't recall her last name. Like most professors in Maastricht, she invites students to call her by her first name. Prior never allowed it.

Ditte is standing in the staircase opening. She is wearing a pair of jeans and a red hooded sweater, quite different from the silk blouses and woollen dresses she wears at university. In her arms, she's holding a plastic hamper filled with children's clothes and toys. On top, there's a pink, stuffed hare. There are white fluffy tassels on the tips of its long erect ears. Dishevelled by the chaos around him, Martin gawps at the hare. It's threadbare and its once black nose is tattered.

Ditte squints her eyes. 'Martin Hermans?'

For a moment, Martin simply sits there, and glassily stares at her with his mouth open, like a gaping wound.

'Are they...are they ok?' he finally manages to ask.

Distraught for the response he holds his breath.

'Yes, luckily they weren't home. They were visiting family in England..'

Martin exhales, relieved. They're alive and safe. He doesn't want to think about what could've happened. It didn't, mercifully.

Ditte puts the hamper down on the floor with a dull thud. 'Why would you care?' There's scorn in her eyes.

Suddenly, Martin realises she suspects him of something. Of gloating at least. Perhaps she even thinks he is one of the vandals. He could confide in her. This could be his moment to come clean. Maybe Ditte knows what to do to fix this mess. She seems to be someone who knows how to get things done.

Yet with the relics of uncontrolled vigilantes around him, he starts to panic. What if Ditte turns him in for inciting hatred and violence? Or worse, what if his confession leads to the mob finding out and coming after him? Those people have no scruples. If they learn he's involved, that those fabricated statements came out of his sick mind...*Audiences like to see the bad guys get their comeuppance.* No, he'll have to keep it to himself.

Martin almost trips over the lies rushing out of his mouth. 'I...I simply do. Believe me, I have nothing to do with this mess. He's my professor. I love his work. I hope to be like him someday.'

Ditte doesn't look completely convinced. It must be written on his forehead that he *is* responsible. Still, he's merely partially so. He's responsible in a limited way, and not directly. *He* didn't use any violence.

She casts him a long, searching look. 'Didn't you see the video?'

A tangle of thoughts cuts off his breath. What should he say? That he didn't watch it? That's hardly credible. Everyone in the faculty has. Could she possibly know he's the maker? Would Zac have told her? No, his friend has turned out to be an unreliable nobody, but he wouldn't do that. Ratting on him would imply risking his own skin as well.

Martin squeezes out a story. Something about people being allowed to make mistakes and that, who knows, it's a fake. With that last sentence, he hits the right chord. Ditte nods, defeated. He feels relieved and guilty at the same time. Perhaps it would've been better if she had caught him out.

In the awkward silence following, he brushes some glass splinters aside with the side of his right foot, pondering what would be a good moment to leave.

'Do you need a hand?' he asks instead, pointing at the hamper. He could bite his tongue. Why does he offer to help? The longer he stays here, the more likely he's to get into trouble.

'Would you? I could use the break. It's not that much work anymore. I almost got everything.' Ditte reaches for her phone in the back pocket of her jeans. 'I have a list with things Jude wants me to send over to England. They won't come back soon after this. The police advised them not to. If you give me your number, I'll send it to you. I've gone through almost all the rooms. I was about to do his office on the second floor when I heard you.'

Martin gets up from the couch and straightens his jacket with both hands. She casts him a thankful smile as she sits down. With his phone in his hand, Martin climbs the stairs to the first and then the second floor. He stops on the doorstep of the office. He should turn around and run away from this place as far as possible, but Ditte is waiting for him downstairs. Finally, after a minute or so, realising the way forward is the fastest way out, he walks into the office.

He is surprised by its neatness—the vandals have apparently not reached this part of the house—and by its simple décor. There are a few photos of Prior shaking hands with various famous actors on a basic grey office desk. A folded piece of paper under one of its legs stops it from wobbling. In the corner of the room, a couple of stacked banana boxes rest against an almost empty book-case.

Ok, let's see. Martin glances at the list on his phone. The pictures and two books. Is that all? He looks around the room and can't suppress his curiosity. Although minutes before, he wanted to flee in a hurry, he's now intrigued. How often does one get to set foot in the sanctuary of one's idol?

He opens the desk's drawers. Empty. Perhaps the police took whatever used to be in there as evidence. What about the boxes? He peeks through the half-opened cardboard lids of the top one. He cannot believe his eyes, is that—?

'Can you find everything?' Ditte's voice travels up the staircase.

Martin quickly gathers the pictures and grabs the two books from the shelf. 'Yes, all set,' he yells back and closes the office door behind him.

He'll come back for that box later, tonight.

§

At night, the devastation of Prior's house terrifies Martin even more. He tells himself to man up, to toughen up. He can do this. No, he *needs* to do this to lift the feeling of guilt weighing him down, to restore some of what's left of Prior's reputation without putting himself in serious danger. Coming clean isn't an option, but this he can pull off. He lifts the top banana box from the pile in the corner of Prior's office and puts it on the desk.

Martin got the idea when he glanced into the box earlier that day, seeing what he believed to be the DVD cover of Prior's first movie. He has a public screening of Prior's films in mind. That way people can experience them first-hand and see for themselves how worthwhile they are. He knows it's barely a drop in a bucket, but it'll be a start.

In a short time, Prior's films have become extremely hard to come by. Martin has a copy of one of his later movies, a gift from his father and the only DVD he owns. He hasn't played it in ages. The last time he tried watching it, was together with his dad. The image turned out jumpy and froze every few seconds. The sound was awful. Although Martin had treated the disk with utmost care, it had got scratched somehow. Those silvery things were so fragile.

These days, he doesn't own a DVD player. Why would he? Why would anyone? If he wants to see a movie, he can stream it for free whenever he wants, if not legally then illegally, and the quality is generally much better. Of course, he could download Prior's pictures from the web too. But since his fake video has gone viral, any illicit online action, however small, scares him. And so his plan completely depends on the content of the closed box in front of him.

'I don't think this is a good idea, Martin,' Eveline hisses next to him.

'I think it's FAN-TAS-TIC,' Martin pronounces every syllable of the last word to be convincing. It sounds as if he's wilfully mocking her, picking a fight. Perhaps he is.

'Shhhh, not so loud,' Eveline whispers.

It wouldn't be wise to draw attention indeed. He and Eveline are technically trespassing. It's a wonder Eveline is still here. Martin only told her about his idea minutes before, while he was cycling with her sitting on the bike's horizontal rod between his legs. They were about to hit the town for a night out when he suggested the detour.

He hasn't shared the whole truth, the reason why this is so important to him. Martin will have to at some point. He almost confessed in *Lumière* the other day. But it hadn't been the right time. Besides, he's dreading the moment. Every time they touch the subject of Prior, they end up in an argument.

'Can I have some light here, Eveline? No, not like that. Give me the torch, I'll do it myself.'

His eyes are watering. Dust, old hairs, and bits of dead bugs, which he frees up by going through the box, float down around him, clotted together, as dandelion puffballs in spring. Luckily, he had thought of putting on his new puffer coat and not his dad's jacket. The puffer was cheap and one in a million, the leather jacket irreplaceable. He wouldn't mind if the coat got dirty or torn; the jacket, however...

Martin rifles through the box's contents. Not only is he proved right about the DVD of Prior's first film *The Detainees* being in there, but there's a load of other films as well. Most of them directed by Prior. Some of them rare extended editions, unreleased director's cuts and raw versions. Those aren't even on the web. This is a goldmine.

'I don't like it. I'm sorry, I don't. We shouldn't be here,' Eveline frets.

'Ev—'

'No, don't interrupt me. *You* may think they're amazing, but those films are more or less out of bounds. For good reasons, if you ask me. And how and where on earth are you going to do this? You're biting off more than you can chew. So typical.'

Martin doesn't react and starts to take the DVDs out of the box, organising them in neat piles. The iconic blue and yellow drawing on the banana box of a woman in a ruffled dress and fruit hat is faded. That picture used to raise his spirits once, take him back to his childhood, the time spent with his father.

It had been only the two of them, him and his dad. His mum had died when he was a little less than a year old. His dad rarely spoke about her and Martin never inquired. He hadn't known her, so he never missed her.

His father used to be fond of Prior's work too. Particularly of *The Insurgents* in which local Columbian workers kick American plantation owners out of their country. Prior used the banana company's original jingle—the one with the fake thick Latin-American accent— as a soundbite to a hilarious fighting scene.

Martin doesn't think it's Prior's best work, far from it. But he cherishes the memory of his father before his dad got ill three years ago. It started with a stupid sinus infection, nothing major. But none of the antibiotics they gave him worked. Finally, it spread to his lungs. A mere five months after the first cough, his dad passed away, just two weeks before Martin's nineteenth birthday.

He shared his sentimental attachment to the song with Eveline once. Yet his girlfriend only gave him a heartfelt rant about how the jingle, the logo and the brand name of the company were part of a carefully planned strategy to veil the bloodstained, patriarchal, racist and colonial history of the Western banana industry—'Using any of it, even ironically, perpetuates this, Martin. The death and suffering of thousands of people isn't a joke.'

Martin knows she is right in principle, but now the

image cheers him up nonetheless. With every film title that goes through his hands, the torch clamped under his chin, he's more convinced of his idea. It's the proper thing to do and he's the one who should do it. No matter what Eveline thinks.

Ok, he's taking the films without permission, but it isn't stealing. He's borrowing them, for a good cause, to do right. Besides, if they stay here, unattended, uncared for, they'll surely be damaged or destroyed. With him, they're safe. He'll take care of them until people get to their senses and Prior can return.

Below his breath, but hard enough for Eveline to recognise the words, he starts to sing, '*I'm Chiquita Banana, and I've come to say...*'

§

It's been three months since Martin had his idea for a film night with Prior's work. Tonight, it'll finally be realised. The conference room he has booked for the occasion is stuffy and its atmosphere torrid. Martin has tried to open the windows, but they're all screwed shut.

He and Eveline have worked all morning trying to get everything up and running for the film screening. Hopefully the first of many to come. His girlfriend is operating the player, which had been at the bottom of the box in Prior's office. Martin stands near the projector, ready to focus it manually if needed. He is getting agitated and hungry. They should get something to eat. A decent meal is probably too much to hope for in this rundown hotel wedged between the motorway and Maastricht airport.

The windows are bare and look out onto the runway, which is empty apart from two small planes, probably private ones. When he unpacked that mouldy box with DVDs for the first time in Prior's house, he had imagined something with more grandeur. The faculty's lecture hall would've been perfect, but out of the question for obvious reasons. *Lumière* didn't want to be associated with Prior either. It had 'quality standards to live up to'. Online screening wasn't an alternative, not with this old technology. Besides, Martin didn't want to stick his head too visibly above the online parapet. Not after what had happened to Prior. The hotels in the city centre were too expensive, so this nearly abandoned hotel had been his single option. No standards to uphold here.

Martin is glad Eveline has come with him. Not that it has been easy to persuade her. Luckily, he had the book-in-his-junk-card up his sleeve. She still felt indebted enough to him after that well-aimed throw with one of his novels. Casually rubbing his crotch, he'd put on a painful grimace and bend over a little, before pleading with her.

Of course, it also helped that enough time had passed. Most of the dust over Prior had settled. Zac had been right about that—it would eventually blow over. Martin could have known. However hard you try to push it down, quality always floats to the surface. Like oil. And slick as oil they are, those films by Prior.

Eveline isn't here for the movie or for Prior though. She's here to support him, and even that's under protest.

Nevertheless, she *is* wearing the short maroon skirt she knows he likes. If *that* isn't a sure expression of solidarity...

Martin relies on tonight's film, *The Detainees—the director's first cut,* to turn his girlfriend around completely, to convince her he's right about his hero's work. The heist story with a strong female cast never got boring. Brutal, honest, and relevant to this day. A clear indictment. A game changer. A masterpiece. And, most importantly, an open attack on misogyny. Eveline *must* like that.

All seats sold out in advance. There were forty. Martin couldn't cram in more chairs. They were cheap too— *It's a deal. It's a steal. It's the sale of the fucking century.* Nonetheless, he was glad to find out he's not the only one thinking Prior's work is cutting-edge. After tonight, Eveline will have to agree to that as well. But then he needs to be able to show it.

It had been a challenge to find a projector he could connect to Prior's old DVD player. One that came with the right cable, a *Syndicat des Constructeurs d'Appareils Radiorécepteurs et Téléviseurs cable* or, plainly put, a *SCART.* Martin combed every inch of each online marketplace to locate one. He took the train all the way to Brussels to pick it up.

The woman who sold it to him ripped him off, for sure. It was hard to understand her, her fast speaking rate, the Brussels accent—'Péritel. C'est une péritel. Rare. Précieux,' the woman had repeated, before babbling something about a 'Euroconnector'.

For a moment, he believed he had made the whole

trip in vain, yet after consulting some obscure, dead online forum, he eventually figured out it all boiled down to the same thing. Péritel, euroconnector, scart, fart, whatever. *What's in a name,* anyway? Luckily, he gets to live most of his life unplugged.

Martin checks whether the cable is properly connected before Eveline presses the play button again, for the zillionth time. The hum the machine has been making accelerates, suggesting something is about to happen. Still, the screen remains white as snow, apart from the shadows of two hairs on the lens.

'Is it supposed to make that sound, Martin?'

Martin sighs. 'How should I know?'

'Maybe we put the disk in wrong?' Eveline picks up the worn DVD case of *The Matrix,* with which they have been testing the machinery to read the description on the back. The Brussels lady had thrown the film in with the projector. Eveline tosses it back on the table. 'It doesn't say anything. Should the label go up or down?'

'Up. How did you put it in?'

She's bent over the player. 'I don't know. I can't get it to open again.'

He rushes over and hits the open button. A weird whir, nothing else. Has she done it wrong on purpose? He can't help but think so.

Martin is studying the glowing yellow symbols on the player when an unfamiliar voice pierces the dry air in the room. 'Hello?'

He looks up, bewildered. A delivery woman is

standing in front of the projector. He didn't hear her coming in and by the look of her, neither did Eveline.

'I called a couple of times, no one answered,' the woman explains herself.

Martin blinks and tries to adjust his eyes to the harsh light beam. The woman is still luminous. In her black stretch trousers, long-sleeve top with polo neck, and equally black gloves, she might as well have walked or flown straight out of the world of *Marvel*. Although, on second look, she takes more after one of those characters from *The Matrix*. The male lead was Neo. What was the female character's name again? Triplet, Trilogy, Triplex? Anyway, this woman is a somewhat impatient version of her. The razor-sharp cut, dark hair is tightly parted in the middle, framing her regular features and pale, flawless skin.

She unclips her phone from her belt and unfolds it. 'I have a package for, ah, here, I have it, Martin Hermans?'

'Uh, that's me, but I—'

'Ok. Let's get on with this. I get paid by the piece.'

'I didn't order anything.'

'Well, you are Martin Hermans, aren't you?'

'Can you not arrange this with the people at the reception desk?'

'No, it's a recorded delivery with acknowledgement by receipt.'

'Miss, I don't—'

'It's Mix.'

'What?'

'Not Miss, not Misses, and no, not Mister either. I choose to be addressed as Mix. It's written as mx.'

Martin squats in front of the machine and pushes the buttons again. He knows he shouldn't assume people's pronouns and he didn't mean to. Why does she have to make a deal out of it? He thought of the *Matrix* when seeing her, *them*, for goodness sake. When it came to crossing gender boundaries that film was quite progressive for its time. His *intentions* are good. He can feel Eveline's eyes burning in his back. She won't let this slide.

He sighs and gets up to apologise. 'Yeah, of course, sorry, mix it is then.'

'Well, you should've asked. But thank you. And the package is yours. Whether you ordered it isn't my business. I'm not taking it back. Sign here please.'

He doesn't have time for this. He needs to get that player to work. Martin places his right index finger on the oval signature box on the device the deliverer is holding out to him and scribbles down something looking remotely like his signature.

'Where do you want it to go? I'll need some space to manoeuvre.'

Martin waves that it doesn't matter. He'll sort it out later. First things first. Would it help to turn everything off and on completely? To unplug and reboot? He pulls the plugs from their sockets, plugs them back in. A brief silence follows. Then the same whir, this time accompanied by a percussive sound, as if there's something stuck in there.

New symbols are lightening up on the display. He has no idea what they mean. One resembles a flower, a boxy one. It could also be a cogwheel. Are there real cogs in there? It would explain the ticking. He groans and takes out his phone. Maybe he'll find a solution online.

Martin is opening the *SCART Plug Fan Club*'s site, after futilely browsing through some Wiki pages, when a rumble surges through the room. The sudden noise, as loud as thunder, completely overtakes him. In a reflex, he raises his arms. His hands protectively hover above his head. Did the DVD player explode? Only when the sound has already died, he realises that it wasn't coming from the machine, but from behind him.

Shaken, Martin turns around, in no way prepared for the scene unfolding. Dozens of dildos and vibrators in an immense variety of colours, shapes and materials. Pink, red, green, blue, gold, silver...Plastic, metal, glass, wood... Some are as small as a little finger, others as huge as a forearm.

'Scarcely the beginning.' The deliverer wheels out an empty handcart. 'After this one, four more cartloads.'

Had it been a film scene, Martin would've considered it hilarious, but it's different when it's real and the joke is on you.

Eveline, however, doubles over with laughter, tears rolling down her cheeks. 'Oh my Gawd.'

Martin is too dumbfounded to say, let alone do anything. Stunned, he watches the ever-increasing heap of sex toys.

'That's it.' The delivery person smiles contentedly at the pile after having dropped off the fifth load.

The insurmountable heap is so unsettling. He should be yelling to take those things out of here, but he feels completely out of his depth. 'Eh, they haven't been used, have they?'

The deliverer picks up a realistically shaped, transparent dildo with a gloved hand. 'Well, who's to say? This one might be. Perhaps if you smell, you can tell...?'

In the background, Eveline shrieks, 'Oh stop it, I'll wet myself.'

The delivery person grins and hands Martin a card in a square, blue envelope. 'This comes with them.'

Congratulations
It's a boy
STOP Patriarchy
Stop Permeating Prior
~G*RRRLS (Dutch Division)~

Martin doesn't know how long he has been staring at the card. When he comes back to his senses, the deliverer is gone and Eveline is finally done laughing. She's entertaining herself by making a shadow figure on the screen with two dildos and the light of the projector. It resembles a peace sign.

'Look, Martin, now *that*'s a proper bunny,' his girlfriend smirks.

Feeling anger welling up in his chest, Martin

brusquely slams his flat hand on top of the ticking and buzzing DVD player. To his surprise, the machine kicks in and the silhouette of the dildos gives way to Keanu Reeves reflected in the silver sunglasses of Laurence Fishburn. Fishburn's dark voice fills up the room:

After this, there is no turning back. You take the blue pill—the story ends...You take the red pill—you stay in Wonderland and I show you how deep the rabbit hole goes.

Eveline wraps her arms around his neck and smiles at him, amused. 'And you, Mister Hermans, can take the red or the blue vibrator. Let's go eat something. It finally seems to work and all that laughter made me hungry.'

§

Martin winces when he touches the dildos with his bare hands and gags. He has no choice but to pick them up. Otherwise, he'll have to request people to climb over them when they enter the room.

He had asked for a pair of disposable gloves at the reception desk. The woman behind the counter claimed they didn't have any. They must have them somewhere, what hotel doesn't have any cleaning materials? He's sure she took one look at him, realised he was the guy who had more than a thousand artificial dicks delivered, and decided not to give them to him. Who knows what he'll use the gloves for, she must have thought.

By the time the doorway is cleared, Martin is perspiring heavily. Luckily, there is still some time to clean his hands in the hotel's restroom. He scrubs them vigorously and repeatedly and uses an obscene amount of green soap from the automatic metal dispenser.

After the fifth attempt, his skin is burning, but he hasn't got rid of the synthetic sex smell. He needs to go back. It's a quarter to six already. He checks his face in the mirror, wipes his hair from his sweaty forehead—*Confidence! That's the attitude*—and rinses his hands one last time.

When he returns to the conference room, his palms and fingers still slightly wet, Eveline is standing at its entrance. His girlfriend is pointing the arrived moviegoers to their chairs without much enthusiasm. In one hand, she's holding the cardboard cup of black coffee Martin bought her from the vending machine in the hotel lounge.

Most people queuing are men, ranging from their early twenties to their mid-fifties, but there are a few women as well. Martin had been a little afraid of only white, older men showing up, which would have put off Eveline more. Content with the relatively varied audience, he joins her on the threshold.

'Finally. There you are. I'm not sure if you remember, but this is *your* event. And I'm not your assistant, but your girlfriend,' Eveline bites at him.

Pointing his head to the pile of dildos in the back, Martin softly rebuts Eveline's accusation, 'I had to clean my hands first…*that* wasn't part of the plan, you know. However—'

But just when he is about to thank his girlfriend for jumping in, Martin is interrupted by a group of young men waiting in line. Most likely students, who are making "witty" comments about the sex toys. One of them, the tallest and beefiest, even dares to target Eveline. He has strikingly ice-blue eyes, cold and callous, and he glares at her to measure the effect of his distasteful words. 'I bet *you* tested every one of them.'

Martin knows he should come to his girlfriend's defence. He should say something. Eveline doesn't blink, but she must be boiling inside. Still, he doesn't want to cause a fuss, let alone start a fight. Not tonight. And that muscle will take him out in no time.

He smirks uncomfortably and waves the men over to check their tickets. Unimpeded and still joking, they pass to take their seats.

All the while, Eveline has silently gazed at her cup of watered-down coffee. Her voice is sharp from frustration when she finally speaks, 'I'm going to need something stronger to get through this. I'm off to the hotel's bar, be back when it starts.'

As she briskly walks away, her claret skirt flutters like a war flag.

§

'What is this rubbish?' They aren't halfway through the film when a man in the final row shouts.

Martin had just started to relax. He was enjoying the movie after the commotion earlier that day. Now this again. Some idiot who thinks it's a good idea to interrupt the film.

Not at any given moment, but right in the middle of the most seminal scene. The one in which the hostage-takers—all women—are turning on the heat on the men they are holding captive, who have slut-shamed them and other women by sharing sexual images without their consent. They force the men to perform a striptease, which they record to put online.

Martin turns around to signal to the shouting man to sit down when someone else raises his voice, 'This isn't what I came out here for.'

Then a third voice soars above the film's dialogue, 'Yeah, I didn't pay for this.'

Martin shifts uncomfortably in his chair. He doubles up his fists, gets up and pauses the film. The beam from the projector strikes his face, like a lamp at the beginning of a police interrogation. *The usual suspect*, that's who he is, for everyone apparently.

'Ok, yes, as I made clear before the start, this is the original director's cut—'

'It's completely different. I cannot make heads or tails of this. And what happened to that hot actress?' The man in the back, the one who got up first, shoves his oar in again.

Martin realises it is the student who offended Eveline earlier. In the dusk, his eyes appear to emit light.

'You mean Daisy Violet? Prior shot the scenes with her later, because of commercial reasons, because the production compa—'

'So she isn't in it? Why would anyone wanna watch it then?'

Irritated, Martin protests, but the man doesn't listen and shouts again, 'The way I see it, you either give us the genuine stuff or our money.'

The air is thickening up with sounds of agreement and restrained violence, like an overheated bag of popcorn. Martin can smell it: burnt and caramelised.

He cannot afford to pay everyone back. All the money went into the equipment and this sorry excuse for a conference meeting room. He glances at Eveline, who's shaking her head, her arms folded across her chest. He didn't bring the cut they are asking for. There's no way out. He'll have to pay. Although he has no idea where to get the money from.

His voice cracks when he gives in dolefully. 'Ok, I understand where you are coming from. I have your contact details. I'll make sure you all get your money soon.'

Luckily, the audience members buy into it. However still loudly complaining, one by one, they slowly leave the room. Martin pretends not to listen and leans over the player to shut it down completely, his back turned to the room, to the leaving people, to Eveline.

»«

CHAPTER 5

EVELINE

Eveline has been running her left hand through Martin's thick hair, fondling its lovely unruliness, while swotting non-stop for hours.

They always prepare for exams together in Martin's room. Her place isn't exactly a stimulating study environment. She lives with three other students in what once used to be a terraced home for a family of four, with ample space to avoid each other. Yet two of her roommates study music—trumpet and opera. In the days before exam week, the house turns into a cacophony of up and downbeats, hooting and screeching under the pretext of art.

By comparison, this dorm is a sanctuary. Eveline is sitting in the corner of Martin's more-or-less yellow couch, reading an article on her iPad. There's a small crack in the glass. She's saving up from her mum's allowance to buy the latest version. Two more months and she'll have enough money. For now, the broken device will have to do.

She has balanced the tablet on the sofa's armrest, right beneath the glaring floor lamp. The light is connected to the home battery on the lowest bookshelf. It is powered by a small solar panel in the windowsill. Martin's best friend Zac cobbled it together with a lot of grey duct tape, but it works. The lamp came on automatically about half an hour ago as the dusk set in.

A golden TUC biscuit wrapper on the floor glows brightly in its light. Eveline wolfed all the salty crackers three hours ago, including the extra twenty per cent mentioned on the package. She could use the energy. On top of her regular tests, she has an exam for an elective honours course in legal psychology. She needs to pass it if she wants to graduate Cum Laude this year. Yet the material on her screen is scholarly tough. She has to work hard to understand it fully.

Martin is lying next to her, curled up and half-asleep. His head is resting on the cushion with the clapper board print, a present from her for his twenty-second birthday last July. He must be tired. Most of his nights have become sleepless. Martin goes to bed too late or not at all.

Her boyfriend is already done with his exams. He only had to submit two papers and he finished them well before the deadline. Eveline doubts if Martin made an effort. He never does. Always just putting in the bare minimum. But she's not going to pressure him as she usually does. She's not sure how that'll go down. He has been restless since that failed movie night weeks ago. They have been at each other's throats, or at least he at hers, ever since.

Eveline feels for him. She empathises with his disappointment. But Martin won't see her point of view. On the behaviour of the men in the room. On the film itself, or the parts she saw. He won't take a word of criticism. And whenever he runs out of valid arguments, he tries to out-shout her. He doesn't care where they are—in the privacy of their rooms, a bar, or the middle of the street—his clamours are equally deafening.

He is worried, of course. So far, Martin hasn't been able to pay anyone back. Eveline offered to loan him the money, which she could spare easily. The new iPad could wait. But Martin wouldn't have it. Too proud as usual, he said it was his problem to solve, not hers.

He hasn't been successful in doing so. Some of his creditors have been harassing him on social media up to the point he couldn't cope anymore. Probably those students who believed they were being funny. To escape them, he shut down his TikTok and Insta. He even gave up on his beloved X account or whatever its name was now. Eveline doesn't get why he had it in the first place anyway. It isn't something for their generation. His self-chosen death on social media doesn't help much. He is still on edge.

Tired of the stubborn repetitive pattern of their hostilities, she avoids the topic altogether now. She simply wants them to go back to how it was, how they were in the beginning: on the same page.

Eveline can't simply turn her back on him and forget how well they got along once. How he understood her and what she wanted. For one, he had immediately grasped why the open relationship was important to her. All that patriarchal drama about Prior must be because of his father; because he had liked the films. She refuses to believe that's who Martin is, at least not deep down.

Her new strategy seems to work. It's a relief to be in each other's presence again without arguing. She stares out of the window, which Martin had left ajar earlier that evening to ventilate the room. A warm breeze caresses her forehead. It's getting dark.

Eveline focuses her attention back on the sentences on her tablet—*Deception is a successful or unsuccessful attempt, without forewarning, to create in another a belief that the communicator considers untrue.*

'Something to drink?' Martin mumbles, half yawning, waking from his nap.

Eveline raises her index finger to indicate she needs another minute. She has almost finished the page. 'OK done. What is it?'

'Coffee? Water?' Martin sits up, stretches his arms and cracks his knuckles. The sound crawls down Eveline's back and makes her shiver.

'No, thank you. I'm fine.'

Martin picks up the water bottle, which has been standing on the blue metal tray table in front of the couch. Gulping greedily, he points at her tablet. With the back of his hand, he wipes some stray drops from his chin. The skin of his palm appears dry and the lines on his fingertips look deeper than usual.

'Anything good?'

He's probably asking it because he feels obliged somehow. Her boyfriend's whole mind has been so focused on Prior. Nothing else interests him anymore. Not his studies, not his fraternity. His friend Elon tried. He came over a couple of times when Eveline was there as well, inviting Martin to go out for drinks. Martin's repeated refusals had been so decisive that Elon finally gave up. Zac must have too. She hasn't seen his best friend in ages.

Worst of all, sex has been off the cards. They have some, yet it's barely worth the name. It's as if Martin isn't there, and though he comes, he doesn't bother to make sure she does.

She sighs. 'It's dense but the bits on police interviewing are interesting.'

'Eh, what?' Martin turns his lean body questioningly towards her. His sudden attention surprises her. It's been so long since he's been drawn to something other than that stupid Professor Prick. For a moment, she's taken aback.

'Go on,' Martin encourages her. He sounds genuine. Maybe they can finally move beyond it.

Eveline quickly scrolls and swipes through the text on her tablet. Her hand is greasy from caressing Martin's hair and her fingertips leave behind semi-transparent imprints on the touch screen—circular lines of sebum and hair oil. Looking for something to captivate him, her eyes fly over the authors' names, the title, the summary, the keywords...

'It deals with common misconceptions of lying and nonverbal cues.'

The curious glow in Martin's eyes dims a bit upon hearing the academic jargon.

Eveline searches her mind to forge the right connection. 'Okay, how do I explain this? Hmm...ah, police interrogations in movies. Bet you've seen plenty of those?'

'Well, obviously.' Her boyfriend sounds amused, as she hoped he would—jackpot.

'If an interrogated suspect in a film sweats a lot or averts his gaze, what does that mean?'

'Well, that he is guilty.' Martin raises his left eyebrow, convinced of being right. 'Or that he's hiding something at the least.'

'That's what we're led to believe by movies, aren't we? And it's also what the police think in real life. They've been influenced by films and series too. But it's complete *nonsense.*' Eveline raises her voice to stress the last word. 'Perspiring or fidgeting...it doesn't mean a thing.'

Martin's green-brown eyes cloud with slight disbelief.

'It's true,' Eveline persists. 'Counterintuitive as it may seem. When interrogated, liars aren't more anxious than people who tell the truth. Most people break out in sweat when they're accused. Even if they didn't do anything wrong.'

'Ok. What does give it away then?' Martin finally

takes her seriously.

'Not much. It's best to focus on the content of what somebody tells you and always in light of the evidence. The staff at our faculty have been training the local police in this. Cool, eh?'

'Very. Can you show me where it says...Wait, let me...' Impatient, Martin reaches past her to lift the tablet from the armrest.

For the next half an hour, he is stuck to the screen, while Eveline strokes the dark hair on the nape of his bowed neck, twirling it around her fingers.

§

It's nine a.m., unusually early for a visit to the supermarket. Normally, Eveline decides what to make for dinner in the late afternoon or early evening, but she wants to clear the day for further uninterrupted study, and she needs a more solid meal than yesterday. Crackers aren't going to cut it.

Martin has come along as well. Eveline insisted. She thought it would be good for him to get out of his room. But he has been dragging himself past the racks of the small inner-city grocery store, his eyes locked on his phone, while nervously moving the zipper of his ridiculously oversized leather jacket up and down with his free hand.

Perhaps a proper meal will do him good. She at least is craving one. Yes, nutrition is what they need. No one is upbeat on an empty stomach. Eveline knows good food can help prevent depression.

'What do you reckon? A curry?'

'Hmhm,' Martin responds absentmindedly.

She picks up a plantain from the vegetable aisle in the middle of the store—too yellow, not ripe enough—and puts it back down. Spinach and chickpeas then. And coriander, lots of it. Martin loves the fresh citrus-like flavour of it as much as she does. Maybe the punchy taste of his favourite herb will finally wake him up, and help him to see things in perspective. Coconut milk, ginger. Where's the red curry paste? Oh that's right, all the way in the back. She'll get it later. What else?

Martin shambles along.

'Which rice do you want? Basmati or jasmine?'

'No...' he moans.

'Oh, no rice? They have naan too.'

'Huh, no, I mean this.' Martin points to his phone.

Eveline groans. 'What is it?'

'They're going to sue.'

Eveline turns to him questioningly, expecting and dreading what's to come next. Martin's eyes blaze like a wildfire out of control. His hair is tangled. He has been rubbing his hand through it like a madman.

'Prior, of course,' Martin exclaims, his voice rough from outrage. Of course, there you had it. No matter how much she had tried to dance around it, here it was. Again. As usual, Martin raves on, 'His films. Some institute for gender equality wants scenes taken out if they're ever shown again. They wanna take it to court. I didn't know that was possible. Is there legal ground for that? Prior has already responded. See?' Martin pushes his phone in Eveline's face. 'Prior is not gonna cave though. He's refusing to attend a trial in the Netherlands.'

Eveline shrugs. 'Ok.'

'Ok?'

'Let's not get into this, Martin,' Eveline soothes, but she sounds slightly more tersely than she intended.

'Ah no, you can't do that. Now you have to speak your mind.'

Eveline clenches her teeth. The muscles in her jaws twitch. She speaks quietly, yet some of her pent-up anger creeps through the silences between her words. 'Well, if you insist...I think it might not be a bad idea to take some scenes out...Especially given Prior's statements in that video.'

'That shouldn't be used as an excuse for censorship,' Martin replies obstinately, his nostrils flared.

'It isn't censorship if those films offend and harm so many people, is it, Martin?' Eveline tries to reason with him but knows it's futile.

'To limit what can or cannot be said, done or shown in the arts...it's undemocratic. It needs to sto—'

'How is it undemocratic?' He has asked for her opinion, so he is going to get it, whether he likes to or not. 'He gets an honest and transparent trial, if it gets to that. It's not like he's...like that man in Germany the other day, beaten to death because he was accused of something on social media, what was it for again? Anyway, it turned out to be false, it wasn't him. No, I don't think we take it far enough. We need *more* rules. People shouldn't be allowed to go around offending others and telling lies without re-percussions. Besides, nobody wants to watch those movies anymore anyway, except for misogynists. We have seen *that* at your movie night.'

'Screw you, Eveline! You know *I do*!' Martin has gradually been raising his voice and some other customers in the supermarket have stopped to watch them.

She has stepped out of line, she knows. But for him to show her such disrespect after she has been so patient for such a long time, he might as well have hit her in the stomach.

Eveline puts down the shopping basket at Martin's feet. Painfully aware of the gazing bystanders, she leans forward to hiss the words in his ear, 'Screw you? Did you really say 'screw you' to me? Well, screw you too then. Cook your own food.'

Martin keeps persisting. 'You don't understand. I'm responsible, Eveline, for Prior—'

'You're bloody right you're responsible,' she interjects angrily. 'It's people like you that Prior made his films for. As a bigoted straight, white guy you're part of the problem.'

The remark is apparently not harsh or honest enough to stop him. Martin keeps begging her to listen, to hear him out.

It's the last drop. She has had enough. Ignoring his pleas, she turns her back on him and walks down the aisle to leave the shop.

§

Eveline has parked her blue Gazelle bike in the bicycle rack near the university library. The combined sounds of crying babies and excited toddlers coming from the house next to it are deafening. The library is located in an old, cobbled street with stately nineteenth-century mansions no one lives in anymore. They've been turned into homes for companies, offices for university employees, and a day care facility, which for some reason Eveline has never noticed before.

She rarely visits the library, but she cannot stand to be around Martin after this morning's fight in the grocery store. His room is no longer an option for studying.

Most children in the day care are trapped in cots in front of the high windows. A two-year-old presses his snotty nose against the glass and smears his yellow-green booger all over it. The boy takes a step back to judge the result from a distance and beams with pride. Eveline laughs at the sight and waves at him. Too preoccupied with marvelling at his work—he *made* that—he doesn't detect her.

The child rubs his hand over the snot, the fine art of finger-painting. For some reason, he's disappointed with the outcome. He doesn't attempt to alter or clean it. Instead, he studies his smutty fingers, squeezing his eyes together. His nose all wrinkled, he starts to scream so loud and unexpectedly it startles Eveline.

She quickly removes her satchel from under her bike's carrier straps. The number of study desks in the library is limited. She'll have to hurry if she wants a spot. It's already hard enough to secure one early in the morning, especially right before exam week. Some students go as far as to camp in front of the door, with sleeping bags and everything. Now, at two p.m., it's next to impossible, but she has to try.

Kiara is coming over to the library as well. Her friend has promised to help her to ace legal psychology. Being in law, Kiara took a quite similar course last semester. Eveline messaged her this morning to meet her at the bike stand instead of Martin's dorm.

There's no sign of her. She checks her phone and sends her another message. Kiara replies immediately— *Running a bit late. See you inside. OK?*

Eveline exhales, relieved. Kiara hasn't forgotten. Wasting no further time, she heads for the library, walking through the vertically barred gate in the brick rampart encircling the building. The tips of the steel gate sticks are covered with pieces of coloured glass and are wrought to interlock in an arch. It's meant to be a reminder of the stained-glass panels in the many churches scattered across the city. Currently, it looks as twisted as her relationship with Martin.

The throng of students in front of the library's transparent sliding doors isn't visible from the street, but on the other side of the bulwark, there's no denying it. This is futile. She might as well admit her defeat.

Eveline walks back through the gate to sit down on a sun-beaten, wooden bench underneath the lime trees on the median strip of the wide cobbled street. There she waits for Kiara, her cracked tablet in her lap, the second e-chapter of *Finding the Truth in the Courtroom* opened.

The noise from the nursery behind her goes on relentlessly. Its charm is now completely lost on her. Those brats are getting more unruly by the minute.

Eveline stares intensely at the words on her tablet—*For decades, experts in memory have been testifying in court about the factors that affect the accuracy of eyewitness accounts...In the early nineties, a defendant, Tom, was convicted of capital murder.*

After her fifth failed attempt to read the introduction to the chapter, Eveline looks up in time to see Kiara arriving. Her friend is parking her bicycle against the day care facility instead of in the bike rack, chaining it to the drainpipe. She's about to walk through the gate to the library when Eveline waves and yells Kiara over to the bench.

A minute later, her friend flops down next to her. After the obligatory kisses on the cheek, of which one lands in the air, Kiara glances down at the tablet on Eveline's lap. She has dyed her curls red-purple this time. The colour is so bright it would've looked ridiculous on any other person but her. Her friend smells sharply of the henna dye she used, and Eveline suppresses a sneeze.

Kiara rhythmically taps on the tablet's screen with one of her freshly painted nails, the colour of which matches her hair.

'*Misinformation in the Courtroom,*' Kiara reads out the chapter's title. 'We went over that one too. It's good.'

'I can't get my head around it,' Eveline answers muffled, the sneeze in the back of her nose. She places her bag on the bench and rifles through its contents. She is sure she put a pack of tissues in there. Where is it? Her lipsticks, her emergency package of tampons, a travel-sized tube of sunscreen...no tissues. She takes some empty chewing gum wrappings out of her bag and throws them in the metal bin right next to the bench.

Kiara starts talking about the chapter, 'If I remember correctly, it begins with a story about a man who's on death row for murder.'

'Tom. The man's name is Tom,' Eveline adds.

'Could be. Anyway. His conviction was based on an eyewitness account only. But that's unimportant.'

Eveline rubs her nose on her forearm. The matter-of-fact way in which Kiara deems a life, two lives, insignificant, confuses her. Can murder and death ever be irrelevant?

Her friend must have sensed her hesitation, as she sets out to explain her brash claim, 'Sure, to this Tom guy and the person who got killed, it's deathly relevant. Although come to think of it, the latter can't care anymore.' Kiara laughs heartily at her own joke. She has a dark sense of humour. One of the things Eveline likes about her friend.

Still grinning, Kiara resumes her explanation. 'The

Tom case, that's a way to attract the reader's attention. The authors actually aim to provide an overview of scientific insights concerning misinformation.'

'What do they mean by misinformation?' Eveline is still sniffing and searches the pockets of her dress for a handkerchief. Not finding one, she wipes her nose on the inside of the skirt of her dress.

'Very simply put, misinformation is all faulty information an eyewitness receives after a crime has taken place.'

'Like?'

'Oh, it can be anything. The colour of a jacket, the weapon, the perpetrator's sex...Any detail, however minor, can when altered change the entire memory of an incident or a person. Social media is a huge problem there. Within minutes after a crime, witnesses have been exposed to online rumours, photos and videos, fake and real. I'd love to hear how you think one should deal with this in court. What's the soon-to-be psychologist's take?'

Eveline has been listening with half an ear. Her mind drifted off to Martin again, to his lousy behaviour. It takes a minute before she realises Kiara is waiting for a response.

'Social media? Eh..', Eveline stammers.

Kiara examines her, concerned. 'Eveline, what's going on?'

'We had another fight.'

'You and Martin?'

Eveline smooths the yellow cotton fabric of her skirt. 'He's acting so stupid lately. Ever since that thing with his teacher.'

'The one who got fired for that video?'

'Yeah, have you seen it? It's so vile. I think it serves him right.'

'What's Martin so worked up about then?'

'He thinks it's unfair. I don't see why. I mean what that man did is—'

Completely absorbed by their conversation, Eveline only notices Zac when he's less than a metre away from their bench. He greets her enthusiastically.

Eveline suppresses a smile. Martin once told her Zac fancies her. He needn't have. She knew when she first met him.

As always, Zac is wearing a sleeveless shirt with a deep V-neck. A stuffed grocery bag dangles from his right shoulder. Small drops of sweat glisten on his mildly hairy chest. She's a bit worried he might have overheard them talking about Martin. If so, Zac doesn't give it away.

Contrasting sharply with the eagerness with which he previously spoke to her, he addresses Kiara in an uninterested voice, 'And you are?'

Annoyed, Kiara presses her lips together, gearing up to make a snappy comeback.

Eveline isn't in the mood for another argument, and she interrupts before her friend can have a go at him, 'You've met Kiara before, Zac. We went out together with you and Martin once. Don't you remember?'

'Vaguely. Probably had too much to drink then.' He looks around, unmistakably searching for Martin. Where she goes, Martin follows, he must think.

'He's not with me,' Eveline responds to his scanning of the environment. 'We had a falling-out.'

'Oh?' Zac sounds concerned and content at the same time.

Eveline lifts a hand to shield her eyes from the sun as she tries to catch his eyes. 'Can I ask you something, Zac? I'd understand if you don't wanna talk about it, as he's your friend and all, but have you noticed anything different about Martin?'

He pensively bites his lower lip. 'To be honest...I've been avoiding him. Did he tell you what happened? Between us?'

She shakes her head. Next to her, Kiara is leaning in to pick up every word.

'Nothing at all?' Zac seems to find it unbelievable.

'No, no, nothing. Why, what happened?'

'Are you sure you wanna know?' Zac smiles playfully.

'Now you *definitely* gotta tell me,' Eveline flirts back—she wants to find out what Martin has been hiding from her.

'Don't get me wrong. I'm not afraid of Martin. But the way he has been talking to me, telling me to shut up. Anyway, some weeks ago, he pulled me into one of the faculty's corridors and smashed me against the wall, because I didn't agree with him on Prior's films.'

Kiara whistles through her teeth.

'Noooh.' Eveline inhales, astonished. 'That doesn't

sound like his usual self...'

'His usual self...,' Zac muses, his eyes looking remarkably cobalt and determined. 'Who's to tell, maybe this *is* his usual self. You know what they say about people in times of crisis.'

From the corner of her eye, Eveline can see Kiara nodding in agreement.

Eveline is still digesting what he has told her when Zac changes the topic. 'Why are you studying here?'

'I'm sorry?'

He points at the building behind her. 'Why aren't you in the library?'

'Oh, well, too late, you know. It was packed when we arrived.'

'Ah, if you want to, you can study at my place,' he quickly invites her, obviously pleased to have a legitimate reason to do so. 'It's super chill. My flatmate, Jens, you met him once I think, he hasn't yet returned from Germany.'

'Yes, things aren't going well there, are they?'

Zac shrugs to indicate he doesn't know what to make of it, or that he doesn't care. 'Anyway, Eveline?' He raises his light eyebrows expectantly.

Before she can politely decline, Kiara interrupts their conversation, 'I gotta go, I'm afraid.'

As her friend leans over to kiss her goodbye, Kiara whispers something in her ear. With the sounds of the toddlers in the background, Eveline has a hard time making out what it is. 'Have fun' perhaps, but it could also have been 'run'.

Confused, she watches her friend cycle down the street a minute later. Eveline is already reaching for her phone to send her a message, when Kiara watches over her shoulder before biking around the corner, goofily rolling her eyes and sticking out her tongue. Eveline laughs, 'have fun' for sure, and puts her phone down to turn back to Zac, who's waiting for her to respond.

It's clear what Kiara thinks she should do, but being Martin's best friend, Zac has been off-limits. She eyes him up and down. He's the opposite of Martin in almost every way—shoulder-long blond curly hair tied up together in a bun at his neck, bronzed skin, a tall, muscular build, and big strong hands. Most of all, he has a blithe vibe. As if nothing and no one can ever knock him down. He's precisely what she needs. Besides, she has already made up her mind about Martin. As they will no longer be a couple soon, she wouldn't be doing anything wrong. The rules have changed.

Zac holds up his bag with groceries. Parsley leaves are sticking out of it. 'Well? There's a free meal in it. What do you say?'

'Ok. Let me get my bike.'

§

Standing still on the threshold of Zac's room, Eveline weighs the strange decor, stumped. Martin's best friend turned out to live close to the library. The dorm was on the other side of the city park in the *Sint Pieter* area, in a street behind the police station.

During the short walk, Zac had been talking and asking questions non-stop, about his studies, about her studies, and which books and music she likes. At the moment, he's silent, taking in her reaction to what she's seeing. There's a huge roll-top bath with four silvery, mermaid-shaped feet on the carpeted floor in the middle of the room. His bed, a single, is cramped right next to it.

Eveline walks inside and bends over the bath, still perplexed. She runs her fingers over the arched porcelain rim.

'Does it work?'

'Certainly.' Zac turns on the brass standing tap next to it and the warm water flows out like a waterfall, clouds of steam rising. Next, he reaches for the bottle of soap on the little bamboo rack at the foot of his bed and pours a generous amount of emerald liquid into the water. It foams intensely and fills up the room with a sage and rosemary odour.

When Zac takes off his shirt, his muscles flex with his movements. 'Shall we?'

Eveline can't help but smile at the twinkle in his eyes. She takes off her dress and underwear as rapidly as possible, hoping he doesn't notice the faded sports top and the ragged pair of knickers she's wearing. She isn't exactly prepared for this.

She swiftly lowers herself into the tub. The water is so hot it makes the skin on her feet and legs blush. When two seconds later, Zac joins her, the water spills over the brim and clatters onto the navy carpet, leaving dark marks looking like Rorschach tests.

He blows some soap froth in her direction.

She observes him, amused. 'Something tells me there's a story behind this.'

He grins. 'How did you guess? This isn't allowed of course. The landlord had no idea. I installed the tub myself. There's only a shower in the shared bathroom and I prefer a bath.'

Zac holds a hand up in defence. 'I know, I know. It isn't sustainable. But who cares? The world is going to the dogs anyway. One might as well get a little comfortable. I carried the tub up the stairs when Jens was away for a weekend to visit his family in Germany. It's not as heavy as it looks, it's made of fibreglass, then I...'

Zac pauses and watches her chest. The froth has receded and her breasts are fully visible.

Her nipples harden, yet Eveline wants him to finish his story first. She's intrigued. 'Go on.'

'Then I...I connected the tap to the hot water boiler, and after two days of work, I could take my first bath. When I got out, however, after an hour or so, I realised I had forgotten about—'

'Oh my God, the drain!' Eveline exclaims.

'Yes, the drain indeed. I've installed it in the meantime. Back then, I had to find another way to clear the tub. I got to it with a bucket at first, which was inefficiently slow. So I decided to haul the tub to the bathroom and empty it in the shower. I nearly had made it, but when I tried to cram it through the bathroom door, it tipped over. Any idea how many litres fit in a tub? I poured out a whopping seventy-five of them on the landing. They rushed down the staircase with enormous speed.'

Zac smirks. 'In an attempt to stop it, I threw myself in front of it. I don't know what I was thinking. It was water. One can't stop water. And of course, right at that moment, Jens came home. When he opened the front door... He was soaking wet. And *swearing*. I've never heard a German swear like that.'

Eveline laughs loudly. His anecdote isn't *that* hilarious, but it has been such a long while since she enjoyed herself.

§

Eveline is running late. She has already messaged Kiara that the night with Zac had indeed been lots of fun. More than that, they couldn't keep their hands off each other this morning either. She could have broken it off with Martin through a text or video message. It would've been a lot easier, but unfitting for such a long-term liaison. Like the relationship, the break-up deserves to be an experience. And so, she's meeting Martin in person.

She messaged Martin to meet her at ten a.m. on the terrace of *Café Zuid* on the edge of *Plein 1992*. Kiara once told her the square was called after the year in which the *Maastricht Treaty* was signed, the EU's foundation document. The neutral ground will hopefully keep him from throwing too much of a tantrum.

Martin has already arrived when she does. Of course

he has, it must already be half past ten by now. He looks horrible—unshaven, his hair in every direction, dark bags under the reddened orbits of his green-brown eyes. He's sitting on a cosy cushioned porch swing for two with a view of the river. His tired jacket hangs loosely over his hunched shoulders.

She's absolutely not going to sit with him in that swing thing. Eveline pulls up a patio chair next to the wicker table in front of him instead. There's a cup of coffee on its glass top.

Martin smiles pleadingly. 'I ordered you a double espresso.'

How hard can it be to remember she takes her brew with lots of milk? Espresso? Really? She's annoyed by so much inconsiderateness. She wants to end this quick and clean, however, so she doesn't say a thing. Eveline swallows some of the bitter, already cold beverage and also eats the dry complimentary gingerbread cookie. She hasn't had breakfast.

Martin is having a lager instead of coffee. He catches her disapproving sideways peek at his drink. 'Breakfast for champs. More wheat than cereals,' he jokes uncomfortably. 'I'm so glad to see you, Eveline. Our last fight...' He coughs. 'You look good.'

This is going to be harder than she anticipated. How could he not have got the cue, the major cue, the cue which could mean one thing only—*We need to talk!* That had been the start of the message she left him. Anyone would immediately understand what it means. Except for him of course, the so-called future filmmaker. Or perhaps he's hoping for a Hollywood ending against all odds? He's an incurable romantic. She needs to rip off the band-aid fast.

Her words cut through the space between them. 'We're not here to make things up, Martin.'

'Of course, you're right. Let's forget about the fight.' He raises his hands in surrender and laughs relieved. 'So, what do you wanna do tonight? A movie perhaps?'

'You're not getting it. That's not what I mean. It's over Martin, *we* are, *us*.'

His smile turns frozen-thin.

Eveline nervously turns her cup on its saucer. 'Martin? Do you understand me?'

'But I love you!' Her soon to be ex-boyfriend sounds horror-struck.

'I know, Martin. I think I do too, but I can't, no, I don't *want* to do this anymore. And neither should you.'

'Why not? Why now? I know it hasn't been going well lately, but we can get through that, be better. I'll be better,' he desperately weaves together promises.

'That won't be enough, Martin. We're too different.'

'Isn't that a good thing? Differences keep it interesting.'

'Some maybe, not all, Martin.'

'Are you talking about our fights about Prior?'

'That too. They're symptomatic I guess, of the opposing ideas we hold.'

'No, they aren't. And you wouldn't think so either if

you knew the truth. You'd see we're on the same side.'

'I doubt th—'

With a bang, Martin hits the glass top of the little wicker table, knocking over Eveline's cup. While the tar-thick coffee drips from the table onto the cobblestoned terrace, he points to his chest and shouts, 'I made it!'

His interruption is almost triumphant, as if he's telling her he has won something. Eveline is not sure what he's getting at.

'What do you mean...you made it?'

'*I* made that video of Prior. It's a deep fake,' Martin declares, his eyes darkened by hope.

This time, it's her turn to be confused. As the meaning of his words slowly sinks in, anger builds up in her chest until she's finally seething. The crowded terrace doesn't stop her from yelling and ranting at him, what an idiot he is, a coward, and above all, a liar.

'That poor man! Why haven't you done anything to help him?'

Ashamed, he gazes at his hands, which are resting defeated in his lap. 'I tried to, I did. Honestly. But it was too late.'

'Too late? It's never too late. You can always do something. He got sued. You can't stand by and let it happen. You should go to the police and tell them what you did.'

Martin wrings his hands, obviously uncomfortable with her suggestion. 'I...I'm not sure if...Do you think that's necessary? It might not come to an actual trial. You thought so too, remember? Besides, I'm not sure if...if it'll undo what has already happened to him.'

If he thinks she'll let him wiggle his way out of this, he's messing with the wrong person. Eveline gets out of her chair. Sitting there in the ridiculously large swing seat, Martin appears small, pitiful. A familiar twinge of sympathy makes her grasp for air, but that doesn't stop her from dealing him her ultimatum before she walks away.

She thrusts her face into his to make sure he gets her threat from the first to the last syllable.

'If you don't get your ass to the police, I will. And that'll be much worse for you. Be bloody sure about that.'

»«

CHAPTER 6

MARTIN

The couple at the table close to his seat is watching him as if he's a dangerous criminal, or worse, a wife-beater. Eveline made quite a fuss before she left the terrace. They must've overheard the things she yelled at him.

The pair is overly fancy dressed. The man is wearing a dark suit, the woman a tweed dress in nearly the same white-golden colour as her pinned-up hair. She disapprovingly pulls down the corners of her painted fake smile.

Martin turns up the frayed collar of his coat to avoid their looks. Has Eveline actually left him? Are they really through? Dazed, he clamps his hand around his beer as if it's a lifebuoy.

He raises the half-full glass intending to down it, but instead starts to blubber into the pilsner. The tears run freely down his cheeks and a heartfelt curse rolls over his lips. The suited man from the table next to him snorts derisively.

Martin snuffles and finally manages to finish his beer. It isn't enough to wash away the lump in his throat. He needs another drink. Scanning the ordering code on the top of the table, he selects the Alfa Spring Bock and pays upfront with his banking app.

Waiting for his beer, Martin stares over the Meuse. The river's water glistens in the strong late morning sun. There's a family of mallards struggling against the current and a lonely swan sits on the shore in the shade underneath a willow tree. A male, by the look of the knob on his red beak.

Without a word, a waiter in a tightly wrapped, black apron removes Eveline's knocked-over espresso cup and wipes the tabletop clean. He picks up Martin's empty beer glass and replaces it with a full round one on a stem. Fine bubbles rise in the orange liquid and foam flows over the brim. The red and white beer company's logo is printed on it—a family crest with three goose heads. Decapitated birds.

Martin slurps from the overflowing glass. From the corner of his eye, he sees how the woman waives the waiter over with her hand. The pearl bracelet on her wrist moves along ostentatiously. He turns his back to the couple and reaches for his beer.

'Young man?' After talking to the woman, the waiter walked back over to him. He's pointing to the glass in his hand. 'I think you've had enough.'

Martin is surprised by the way the man addresses him. It's only his second beer. He isn't drunk, he's not bothering anyone. Well, he has been crying, and every once in a while a curse has escaped him, but he can't see why that would be offensive.

'I think it's better if you'd go home.' The waiter uses the type of soothing voice negotiators in movies bring into play when talking with hostage takers. What has the woman said to him?

'But I paid for it,' Martin starts to argue.

'We'll transfer it back to you. Please leave calmly.'

'I'd like to finish my drink.'

'We don't want this to get uncomfortable, do we?' The waiter nods in the direction of one of his colleagues, who's standing in the middle of the terrace, three metres away from them. The man is extremely broad-shouldered, his white shirt stretched almost to the point of tearing. *He surely eats dumbbells for breakfast.* Not someone you'd want to run into in the dark. Let alone bug by daylight.

Intimidated, Martin hastily tries to stand up. But instead of getting out of the swing chair, he sets it off rocking. The waiter folds his arms tightly across his chest and observes him as if he's a childish idiot. Martin tries to stand up again, but something is detaining him. He must have got caught in the chair's iron mesh.

'Young man...' The waiter is getting impatient.

'I can't. My jacket got stuck.'

'Now, please!' the man commands, while his *Hulk*-like colleague gets closer.

Panicking, Martin tries to tear himself free. His jacket rips. He doesn't see it happening, he feels it, but most of all, he hears it—the sound of tearing leather is crushing.

Martin stumbles off the terrace past the contently smiling couple. Around the corner, beyond a remnant part of the medieval city wall, he stops. Carefully, he inspects his coat, running his finger over the pliant leather, cherishing some hope he was mistaken. But his finger gets caught in the slit.

Shattered by the damage done to his father's jacket, Martin doesn't notice the persistent pinging of his mobile at first. As it carries on unabated, it finally draws his attention. He checks his phone. One after another insult rolls over his screen, sending a surge of panic through his body.

He believed he'd covered all his online tracks. His social media accounts were dead and he made sure his personal information was nowhere to be found. But apparently, the internet indeed doesn't forget. Some of the people he still owed money must have found his phone number somewhere. He can only hope they haven't got his address too.

With a ping, another message pops up on the neon-green display. Martin gasps. A threat instead of a mere insult this time—*You had enough time. Now YOU will pay* 😺😺😺

§

Martin has been leaning against the wall across from Ditte's office for at least ten minutes, if not fifteen. He simply had gone to the scheduled meeting with Ditte after receiving the messages. It seemed the safest option. He didn't dare to go home and he didn't know where else to go instead.

He made the appointment to discuss his paper last week. Ditte failed him, although he did everything right. He ran the spelling and grammar check, stuck to the right number of words, and included a bibliography of sources, formatted according to the latest APA guidelines, as requested.

It's a good paper. Just the title itself is already brilliant—*The Irrelevance of Accuracy in Filmic Intertextual References. The Case of the Second World War.*

It must be a mistake. And if his work is that bad—it isn't, it can't be—she could've cut him some slack. After all, he helped her. He carried Prior's things, including the heavy stuff, to her car. That should count for something.

The fact that Eveline left him one-and-a-half hours ago is still sinking in. Martin glances at the cut in his coat. It isn't too big. Perhaps he can glue it together. His eyes are welling up again. There's no room for tears. This isn't the right moment. He straightens his shoulders and takes his paper out of his backpack.

He tries to decipher Ditte's handwritten notes once more. She must be the last professor who wants work submitted on paper. Well, at least she doesn't use automated feedback like most of his teachers, he should give her that, but her handwriting is illegible. The letters dance before his eyes.

What's taking her so long? Ditte is supposed to meet

him at noon, but it's currently well after. Distressed, Martin wanders about in front of her door. He can hear her high voice on the other side. She's talking to someone, a man, but he cannot make out a word either is saying.

Martin is growing impatient, yet he doesn't dare to interrupt them to let her know he's here. The note with letters in black marker on her door is clear—*Please wait to be called in. Do not knock!*

His body is weighing him down, he's tired. He can feel it in his legs. Martin considers sitting down on the checkerboard-patterned tiled floor, but he feels undignified enough as it is. Besides, who knows how much longer it'll take, he might as well get a bit more comfortable.

Martin walks over to one of the burgundy sitting booths against the wall further down from her office. He flops down on the padded, studded sofa, the paper in his hand, his backpack next to him on the seat. Although the leather feels cool, it doesn't quieten him down.

It must be the hall's red colour that's working him up too. Hallways should be painted taupe. Brad Pitt was right when saying *that* in *Ocean's Eleven—Taupe is a soothing colour.* With the threats and insults from the men he still owed money for the failed movie screening appearing on his phone, he'd almost forgotten about Eveline giving him an ultimatum. Staring at the red paint on the wall, it comes back to him. She threatened to take matters into her own hands first thing tomorrow morning.

Will she follow through? She did sound serious. He's never seen her taking anything that seriously. What is he doing here? What's the point of hiding, if he'll have to turn himself in to the authorities today anyway? He's postponing the inevitable execution. And if he's going to be executed anyway, then better by the police than by a derailed mob.

Martin swings his backpack over his shoulder and stands up unsteadily. His legs rubbery, he walks down the hallway, towards the exit.

At the moment he passes Ditte's door, it swings open. Shaky as he is, Martin doesn't manage to step aside in time and bumps straight into the person coming out of the office.

'Hoh, mate, careful. I know I'm irresistible, but no need to jump me.' Zac grins, pushing him back.

Zac's touch feels too familiar. His smell brings back memories as well, Gauloises blue, and something else which Martin can't readily identify. Something sweeter. He hasn't seen or spoken to Zac since he cornered him. Martin hates him for it, but he misses him too.

'How else do I get a hold of you?' Martin replies. 'I sent you an invite—'

Zac brushes some imaginary dust from his shirt. '—to your movie night. I know, I know. Couldn't make it, bro. Nothing personal.'

Martin grunts, it's definitely personal to him. 'Well, you missed out on the event of the year.'

Zac examines him sceptically. Martin isn't sure how long he can uphold the lie and changes the topic, pointing to the open office door, 'So, you also failed?'

'No, why no.' Zac laughs. 'Ditte is looking for a student assistant. I was asking about the job. *You* did, Martin?'

The idea clearly whets Zac's pleasure. Martin is about to issue a denial—it wouldn't be untrue, not really, the failure is a mistake—but catches Zac glancing at the paper in his hand. His poor grade is in full sight.

Martin grins uncomfortably, rolls his essay into a tube and taps it against his tie. Seemingly nonchalant, he runs his other hand through his hair.

Then, unknowingly saving him from any further embarrassment, Ditte calls him in. But before Martin can escape into her office, Zac quickly drops another question, his blue eyes gleaming devilishly. 'How's Eveline?'

Keen to get away from Zac as fast as possible, Martin pretends he doesn't hear him. Zac has always had a thing for Eveline. Let's hope he doesn't see an opportunity when he hears they've broken up. He couldn't bear the thought of them getting together.

§

'—and that's another historical inaccuracy,' Ditte taps the paper with a short fingernail.

His professor has opened a window, but the room remains stuffy. Her perfume is pungent and smells like overripe oranges. They're sitting next to each other at her ergonomic workstation, almost shoulder to shoulder—the office is too small for an extra meeting table. Martin hasn't taken off his jacket and his leather sleeve brushes against the silk fabric of her white blouse. His paper lies between them.

'Right there. In the second paragraph. You need to get your facts straight, Martin. Your argument is interesting, but you need to substantiate it. You can't simply make claims.'

They have been going over his paper for at least half an hour, circling the same points. Martin is having a hard time concentrating on what she's saying. He'd like to leave, but she's intent on making him understand. It looks like Ditte will make him stay until she's convinced he does.

'You didn't use a chatbot, did you?'

He feels his cheeks reddening with insult. That she'd think he could sink so low. 'No, of course not!'

'It's just…Well, the lack of clear references to literature from the course made me think of how a chatbot would typically write such a paper.'

He shrugs. 'I didn't use one,'

'Good. Then make sure to add proper references when you revise your paper for the resit. And Martin, don't use words like 'proof' either. We can never absolutely prove something.'

He's growing ever more frustrated. Ok, true, he can't think straight now, but *this* isn't making any sense at all.

'You want me to be more factual and you're telling me I cannot prove something *at the same time*?'

Ditte swallows a sigh and patiently repeats what she has already said twice before, 'Academic writing is about being specific, precise, to be clear about how you've reached your conclusions. You need to get the information on which you build your argument out in the open and it should be correct. At the same time, nothing can ever be proven beyond dispute. Academics make mistakes too. Besides, there are no absolute universal truths. Remember what I told you in my lecture?'

Martin gazes at her finger on his paper. There are blue ink spots on its skin. He needs to be truthful, and there are no truths? What is she talking about?

'Ehh…?'

'About creating *situated knowledge*? That's why hedging is so important,' Ditte persists stoically.

'Hedging?' Martin wipes some sweat from his neck.

'To be cautious, to build in safeguards. Sweeping statements like yours…far too risky. You're overplaying your hand. Instead, you should use words that leave room for doubt, like might and may, can and could, probably, possibly.'

'Ok, fine.' Martin throws in the towel. 'But you also said my paper is original. That's worth more than a minor linguistic issue.'

'It isn't minor, Martin. Besides, although it is interesting and yes, potentially relevant, you haven't used any in-text references. Unless it's widely shared knowledge, every idea, every thought that isn't originally yours should be referenced in the text. The idea counts, of course it does. The execution is—'

The knock on Ditte's office door is loud, insistent, and welcome as far as Martin is concerned. He's fed up arguing with her. What does she know? She's no artist, like him, like Prior. He wonders whether she's truly an intellectual. She sounds like a bureaucrat, talking about all the formal requirements he hasn't met. Besides, he has other, more important things to worry about.

'One moment.' Irritated, Ditte gets up to yank the door open. 'Can you not read? Oh, hi, Gus, sorry, I took you for a student. How can I—'

'Have you seen the news? Oh Ditte, it's horrifying. I can't believe it.'

Gus teaches film history and is the type that wants to be popular. As usual, he's wearing the latest pair of Nikes and a sports jacket. He's known for taking the students out for a drink after class in the bar across from the faculty. He pays for the first round and sometimes a second. Martin used to like him too, but not anymore. Not since his class on the history of the villain.

Martin had enjoyed Gus's lecture at first. Effortlessly, he dropped one after another one-liner and they rang so true—*'Film is an emotion machine'*, *'We don't just watch films, we feel them, we embody them.'*

Gus played some old iconic clips, including the infamous 'gay' scene from the 2012 Bond movie *Skyfall*. Martin believed it a fantastic choice. That film has the best villain ever. Javier Bardem is so convincing when he partly unbuttons Daniel Craig's shirt, touches his neck and chest, the inside of his legs, talking in a dirty accent with soft t's and rolled r's—*You and me, you see, we are the last two rats, we can either eat each other...hmmm...or eat everyone else.* The sexual attraction between the two men is credible and thick. And that horrific moment later in the film, when he takes out his denture, and his misshapen jaw and rotten teeth are in full sight. Undeniably a villain for the history books.

As it turned out, that wasn't why Gus had shown it. He instead aimed to illustrate what he considered to be 'a foul archetype', which portrays the villain typically as 'other', as queer, non-Western, or disabled.

'Luckily, most films nowadays figure different villains,' Gus drove home his point. 'The new crook is the straight, white, cis-gender male. And his signature feature is to complain about how hard it has become to be him.' Gus clicked his tongue and shook his head after saying the word 'hard', clearly thinking such self-pity was petty.

The female students around Martin started to laugh, and Martin couldn't curtail himself. He raised his voice before he raised his hand. 'You think that's a good development?'

'Yes, of course.' Gus smiled condescendingly, to go on with zeal, sensing the crowd was eating out his hand. 'It questions those in power. Come on, Martin. You aren't one of those men who's afraid to take a good, honest look at themselves, are you? Are you such a snowflake?'

The sneers hidden in the form of questions incensed Martin immensely. He had wanted to make a come-back, but the eyes of his female fellow students burning in his back kept him from it.

Trapped in Ditte's office with Gus blocking the doorway, Martin hopes he won't bring the discussion back up. Gus strikes him as the kind of person who'd do that. Someone who'd milk it, to prove himself right again in front of a different audience, a colleague this time. But Gus doesn't notice him.

Instead, his teacher rushes over to the desk, brusquely shoving Martin's paper to the side, and bends over the keyboard of Ditte's laptop. Ditte also seems to have forgotten Martin is there. She pulls up her chair to watch whatever Gus is about to conjure up with a couple of clicks.

The next moment, wedged in between his professors, Martin stares into the blue light of Ditte's computer in disbelief, engulfed by images of uncontrolled riots.

Crying children, water cannons blowing women off the roads, knocked over cars...Berlin, Dresden, and, closer to the Dutch border, Cologne and Aachen...all of them burning.

§

Martin is back in the disturbingly red hallway. The escape from Ditte's office turned out to be easier than he had thought. He slowly wheeled his chair back to leave quietly, without saying a word. Ditte and Gus were too captivated by the broadcast to notice. They probably still haven't realised he's gone.

What he saw on the screen is horrible, but it hasn't made Martin forget about his problems. The images added to his anxiety at first, then it dawned on him the breaking news could be the solution to his problems. *It's shocking but positively shocking.* Everyone has forgotten about Prior, or they will soon. They'll leave him and his family alone. The worst is over. What Martin did was hardly a small feat in a world on fire. Eveline will have to acknowledge his fake video pales in comparison.

He takes out his phone to call her. *It's a bingo,* for sure, it must be. His heart jumps when he hears her soft voice. Maybe she'll also have him back, who knows?

'Yes?'

'Have you seen the news?' Martin can barely conceal his excitement.

'About Germany? Yes, of course.'

'With such dreadful things going on, so close to the border, I mean...you, I...'

Eveline groans, irritated. 'That doesn't change a thing. We're over, Martin. And if you don't turn yourself in today, *I'll* take care of it.'

The cold, callous reminder of her threat cuts his breath away. Before he can plead with her, Eveline has already disconnected.

Distressed, Martin checks the time on his phone: nearly three p.m. That doesn't give him a lot of time. Hopefully, the police will be mild on him.

§

Martin has already walked past the police station twice. Its curved white walls and reflective windows remind him of the *Panopticon.* From the street, he can only see the mirror image of himself. It's impossible to make out if there's somebody on the inside looking at him.

Last semester, they had to read the work of a French philosopher about the *Panopticon*. A lot of confusing theoretical babble about power and knowledge. You could leave that to the French. All he gathered from it, at least he thinks he has, is that it's a design for a prison in which the guards can see the inmates. The inmates, however, can't catch a glimpse of them. Because the prisoners are never sure if they're observed, they'll eventually always behave well, watched or not. That's the idea at least.

It's beyond Martin as to why they had to know this. What use was it for film analysis? Anyway, the *Panopticon*, that's what the station reminds him of. *La visibilité est un piège*. The transparency is the cage.

There are hardly any police cars on the terrain. The border with Germany is a mere thirty kilometres from here. The police must've hurriedly left to help their colleagues there. Not that they've succeeded at preventing chaos so far. Within a few hours, Maastricht is already crowded with refugees. One German-license-plated car after another is passing on the busy thoroughfare in front of the police building.

The men, women, and children in them clearly left in a hurry. The vehicles are filled to the roof with all sorts of hastily-grabbed-together things, from cutlery, china and clothes, to paintings, books, toys, bedding, plants and guitars. Everything they could get their hands on has been thrown in, crammed in hastily. Some chock full estate cars have stopped at the side of the road, on the edge of the city park. On the curbs there are families with children, letting off built-up energy and frustration after hours in the car.

Martin already felt anxious. The frantic traffic and his nervous pacing up and down have also made him dizzy. He turns into the usually quiet side street next to the police building. The street turns out to be partially blocked for the shooting of a local crime series. The crew's van is half-parked on the sidewalk. On it, there are large white letters against a blue and red background: *Flikken Maastricht*.

Everyone here carries on working imperturbably, ignoring the turmoil a hundred metres away. Time is money. The show must go on. The camera and sound crew are checking their equipment. Actors are waiting for the director to call their cue.

Martin has observed them filming in the city before. The director takes a bit after Tarantino. Not in terms of accomplishments, but in appearance—the same thin, fleshy lips, the same position of the eyes in relation to the nose, the same hair. Only his chin is less pronounced and his eyes are blue instead of brown.

The series itself isn't anything special. It is a typical whodunit, with the female inspector generally outsmarting the male one, suppressed romantic feelings between the two, and the usual chase and gun scenes. It has been running for ages however.

Martin needs to calm down first before setting foot inside the police station. He might as well watch the start of the recording. Maybe he'll learn something new. Not that he'll ever be able to apply that knowledge...

Martin sits down on the empty sidewalk, in front of the orange-striped barrier tape. He can see some of the action from here if he peeks through the clothing racks next to the crew's van. The actor playing the female inspector is wearing a mermaid costume instead of her usual police attire. The powerful scaly tail swishes behind her, as she walks across the set. Her small breasts are firmly cupped by two large blush-coloured seashells, held up by sisal twine, which visibly cuts into her back's flesh.

The other actors are wearing costumes as well. There's a Snow White and a Prince Charming, someone in a Santa suit, and a clown. When a small marching band starts to play a renowned local song, Martin understands they're re-enacting the annual carnival parade Maastricht is famous for. The inspector is to catch a crook amidst the celebrating crowd without getting noticed.

Martin doesn't get why the female lead lowers herself to something like that. Does she need the money? He hasn't seen her popping up on the big screen recently. Her last proper film is from years ago. It was set in the future. She had played an android, designed to control her owners' life, to keep them in check. Alexa was her name, not the actor's, the robot's. Martin doesn't recall the woman's name; the prospect of possibly being arrested preoccupies him too much.

Trying not to think about it, he focuses on his breathing, like his father taught him when he was a small child. He used to have regular panic attacks and he'd start to hyperventilate for no apparent reason. It made his father feel extremely guilty. He somehow believed it was because Martin didn't have a mother anymore. Luckily, he grew out of it, or at least he thought so. Yet here he is, wheezing again.

Martin lets his breath flow deep down into his belly and breathes out gently. In through his nose, out through his mouth. He repeats the exercise, over and over, rhythmically. Slowly the breathing starts to come naturally and his mind turns blank, like in a trance.

He comes to his senses again an hour later when the director belts out 'Cut!'. Martin rubs his eyes. He's no longer dizzy and he also is less anxious. Feeling more secure, he gets up. Brushing the street dust from the back of his jacket and his jeans, he fixes his eyes on the big steel handle on the police building's glass door in the distance.

Time to show his mettle. The third time's the charm. Who knows, maybe Eveline will have him back after this, if he does what she believes to be the right thing. And if he has to do time, she'll *have* to visit him in prison. She'll have been the one to have put him there in the end.

Martin throws one last glance over his shoulder to find himself looking right at the naked back of the leading woman actor. She is changing for the next scene behind the film crew's van, untying the knot in the sisal rope on her back.

Not knowing what to do, afraid she might spot him and think he's secretly watching her, Martin holds dead still. Nonetheless she turns and stares directly at him. Did he make a sound?

As he feared, she starts to yell.

'Pervert!'

Her shrill voice hurts his ears.

'No, no, don't worry,' Martin hastens to say, making a reassuring gesture with both of his hands.

But the woman persists in screaming. When her cries alarm the rest of the crew, Martin decides to make a run for it. He flees across the main street without looking, deftly dodging the cars with German refugees, ignoring the honking, after which he dashes into the confines of the city park. After several minutes, he stops and inspects his surroundings.

Nobody has followed him. Panting, he drops down on a brown-stained park bench. He knows the park well. Martin likes to come there when he needs to think, which goes better without distracting city sounds. They filter through but are muffled enough by the lime, plane and magnolia trees, or otherwise overridden by the quacks and shrieks from the wild ducks, swans and greylag geese.

The bench is situated opposite a concrete pit in which, according to the inscription on a wooden board, they once kept live bears. Currently, it serves as a stage for a collection of bronze statues of deceased animals. Bears in Maastricht...It's an idea for a film script he has been playing around with. To set the bears loose, allow them to get even with the city. *Grizzly Man meets Maastricht*, or something along those lines.

Also now the park feels safe. Martin is anxious to leave it. He checks the opening hours of the police office on his phone. They don't close until ten. He'll wait then, at least until the film crew is definitely gone. What he has done is bad enough. No need to add a complaint for sexually transgressive behaviour. The sun goes down around eight, that'll be a much safer time.

He sets the alarm on his phone and curls up on the bench using his backpack and his jacket as a pillow. A nap will do him good.

§

Martin is lying on his stomach on the ground next to the bench when he wakes up, disoriented. His left cheek is glued to the tarmac of the path running through to the city park. There's blood running down his forehead and nose, into his mouth.

The metal taste of it conjures up strangely warm memories at first. He's six or seven and waiting outside his father's office.

His dad rented a small workspace in the old *Sphinx* Tower, a short walk from his school. Martin spent most of his late afternoons there. Sometimes his father allowed him to sit at his desk, on his big swivel chair, and showed him the latest commercial he'd been working on. Stills, video, sound and programming language would come together in a seamless flow of attraction.

Most times, however, Martin waited on the dust-covered vinyl floor of the waiting room down the hallway. He'd gaze at a TV, sucking on the zipper of his training jacket. Ticking the tab against the inside of his upper teeth with the tip of his tongue, he'd indulge in its iron flavour.

Mixed up, Martin tries to get up. He barely manages to lift his bludgeoned head. His ears are ringing and drumming. He wipes some grit off his cheek and chin, and tries to open his eyes. His eyelids are swollen and stuck shut, but he can peek through them. He's nowhere near his father's office. Instead, he looks right into the dead eyes of a bronze giraffe.

The park. It all comes back to him, he's in the park. Like him, the giraffe is lying flat on its stomach. Next to its head is a statue of a young woman. She's wearing high heels, an elegant long ball gown and elbow-length gloves. She's tenderly stroking the animal's neck, trying to console it in vain.

He could use someone to comfort him too. *Eveline!* She'll have to be sympathetic when she sees what they've done to him.

Martin lowers himself back down and tries to reach for the phone in his left pocket. Some red-coloured saliva drops to the ground as he moves. The intensity of the pain, shooting through his stone-chipped, embossed skin, scares him.

How bad is he wounded? He breathes in and out. Not too deep, his ribs hurt too much. What else? He carefully examines his chest and abdomen, then his head. All his muscles are tight and sore, like the day after a fall from a staircase or a bicycle. Some warm blood, not that much, he'll survive. *Well, at least he will not die without any scars.*

He didn't see them coming, not truly. Martin could merely make out some shapes—it was already a bit dusky. They had said nothing, except for one obliterating loud call—'Here he is. Let's give him what he deserves!' Then, almost immediately, the first kick, from behind.

He doubts it was someone from the film crew. Although recorded in Maastricht, the "deep south" of the Netherlands, the director, the actors and technicians involved are all from up north. This voice had sounded far too lilting, too local. The g's were too soft, the l's and the h's not thick enough.

No, it must have been some of the men from the movie night. It feels as if they split his head in two. Down on the ground, they'd gone for his back, his stomach. He had covered his head with his hands and forearms. How many had there been? Five? six? Could be more, could be less.

Half upright, leaning on his forearms, Martin looks around. His bag is nowhere in sight. They must've taken it. But that's the least of it. He can't see his jacket anywhere. No, no, no, let it not be true. Not his dad's coat. Martin lifts his head as far as possible, to the point of almost overstretching his sore neck, but there's no trace of it. He moans.

Wiping his hand over his running nose, he has another go at his phone. Eveline, he should try to call Eveline. Finally, he manages to pry it from his pocket. With unsteady bloodstained fingers, he selects her number. It's the last-called.

'Ebvvbeli? I need your h—' His tongue is thick and swollen from the beating.

A gender-neutral robotic voice interrupts him, 'Please leave your name and number after the...'

Damnit.

Before he can say anything, Martin receives another blow to his head. They must've come back to finish him off. The ringing in his ear is deafening now, but despite the pain he manages to catch a glimpse of one of his attackers. His eyes are bluer than he remembered them to be; the man who affronted Eveline. The guy readies to lash out again, this time with his foot. He makes a little dribble before taking his shot as if he's about to shoot a penalty in a soccer match.

Martin raises his arms to shield himself from the impact, but he's too slow. The foot hits him right in his face and he hears the bridge of his nose break. After another well-placed attack, this time in his stomach, he loses consciousness again.

»«

CHAPTER 7

DITTE

'Mama, look.'

Ditte looks up, distraught. It's already dark outside. Neither she nor Jeppe has thought of turning on the lights in their living room. Her daughter Louna is sitting at her feet on the round, milk-coloured woollen rug. She's in her pyjamas, the blue ones with the rainbowfish print.

With a chubby finger, Louna proudly points at the tower she has built. Wooden, painted blocks in black, red and yellow. 'Look mama, like the flags.'

How long has Louna been there? Ditte hadn't noticed Louna had slipped out of her bed and had come back down. Jeppe hadn't either. He has fallen asleep on the shorter right side of their lilac corner sofa. Ditte is sitting on the left one. The position he's in doesn't appear comfortable. Still half upright, his head is tilted to one side with a loose cushion propped under his back.

§

As Ditte hurried back home from her office, after seeing the news, she'd first called Jeppe, then her parents in Copenhagen to make sure they were ok.

Despite her bad experiences with the Dean, she'd never regretted leaving Denmark, but she would've loved to have lived closer to her parents, especially now. And true, the size and bustle of Copenhagen outshines Maastricht.

Still, in Copenhagen, she'd always felt like an outsider, which was, like the rest of Denmark, mostly white. People there treated her like a curiosity. They'd gaze at her until they got to know her. It had been like that as long as she could remember, from primary school onwards at least, where she'd been the single black girl among the pink-skinned and ridiculously blond kids.

Not only the people made her uneasy, but the culture itself as well. The paintings in museums barely showed women like her. With the statues in the streets she couldn't identify either. Ditte vividly recalls the disappointment when she had seen the bronze little mermaid in the city's harbour and understood it didn't resemble her in any way.

She was six years old at the time and she must've seen the bronze-green figurine many times before that. They had lived relatively close to the harbour after all, but she had no recollection of it prior to that moment. Her mum had been reading her the fairy tales from Hans

Christian Andersen. They had just finished *Den Lille Havfrue* better known as *The Little Mermaid*, which Ditte had enjoyed. The book's edition her mother had chosen didn't contain any pictures and in her imagination, the mermaid looked nothing like the sculpture, which was so obviously modelled after a white woman.

It was perhaps not the individual statue that had offended her that much, but the realisation that sunk in over the years afterwards—that she or people like her weren't culturally visible. The televised Disney version that figured a black mermaid, which she saw years later as an adult and by then mother, was too little too late to change that.

Maastricht has its share of white-people-statues and white-people-art too. In that sense, it isn't so different from Copenhagen. Perhaps it's worse, but it's located more centrally in Europe. On top of that, it's the place where the European Union was once founded. As a result, the university offers most programmes in English, and its staff and students, although the majority still Caucasian, are at least from around the world.

All in all, Ditte likes living in Maastricht. But when hearing her father's voice on the phone earlier today, for a moment she wished she hadn't moved. Her dad tried to reassure her it would all be fine, and that at least they were all ok now.

Her father hadn't succeeded in convincing her, and Ditte felt anxious when she walked through their home's back door. Instead of the lasagne she had planned to make from scratch—she always cooks on Thursdays—she chose something quick. A pasta with spinach, done in a quarter of an hour. Simply a matter of boiling water and adding some pepper and cream cheese. Student food.

After dinner, they put the kids to bed earlier than usual, at seven instead of seven-thirty. Jeppe cut the bedtime ritual down to one story. The children had been remarkably cooperative as if they sensed their parents' apprehension. Ditte had turned on the news and so they commenced several sweaty hours of nervous switching between *Die Tagesschau* on *ZDF*, the Dutch *Journaal* on *Nederland 1*, the Danish *Nyheder* on *DR1*, and the reels on *BBC World*.

The tone of the different anchors was equally shocked and the images were the same on all four channels: unrelenting violence in the streets, the *Bundeskanzler*—although it's unclear if he still is—urging people not to believe everything they read online, and opposition parties demanding the government resign because of exactly that information.

The cause of it all is online leaked reports, the exact origin and status of which is unclear. They target a failed migration policy, accusing the German government of having allowed criminals—murderers, convicted rapists, paedophiles even—to enter the country. It has knowingly welcomed them as citizens and let them have their way.

The full names of the allegedly so-called refugees, their home addresses, and the details of the responsible politicians are on the streets. And in those streets, the harsh law of retaliation reigns. People have been dragged from their homes in front of their crying relatives, and their houses have been set on fire.

Innocent people, according to the *Bundeskanzler*, victims of fake news, an act of cunning by trolling armies—Russian, British, who's to say, maybe German, perhaps there isn't even a country or person behind it but rather derailed, run-down chatbots—to take advantage of the immigration problems that had already divided the country.

Normally an epitome of stoicism, the sixty-something *Kanzler* is desperate and he flails his arms furiously in the air. There are sweat stains in his salmon-pink shirt, especially under the armpits. The soft flesh of his cheeks wrinkles angrily as he addresses the rioters and pleads with them to stop.

Most German, Dutch, Danish and British journalists on the news have been repeating his mantra. *Unschuldig, onschuldig, uskildig, innocent.* To no avail yet. The violence, the unrest, it hasn't stopped. The police and the army have been deployed. They too are riven. Or is it no longer clear who's in command? Agents and soldiers in navy and dark green uniforms have mostly stood by and watched.

§

Ditte strokes Louna's toffee-coloured curls. Nothing fit for the eyes and ears of a three-year-old. If all of it already causes *her* to panic, how would it affect a toddler?

She finally responds to her daughter, who's eagerly waiting for a compliment on the block tower she has built,

'Nice, Louna. I think it's the highest I've ever seen. But you should be in bed. Come, you can play some more tomorrow.'

Ditte forces a little smile and bends over to pick up her daughter under her arms, gently. Almost immediately, Louna clamps her legs around Ditte's hips, folds her hands around her neck, and rests her head on her shoulder. She knows the drill, the routine.

Ditte uses one hand to support her child and wraps the other around the stair's sturdy bannister. She always holds onto it firmly when carrying one of the kids upstairs. Once, she fell with Louna in her arms, when she was only a baby. From top to bottom, Ditte hit every hard-wooden step, until she was black and blue. Luckily, Louna didn't have a scratch. Ditte had turned her body to shield her daughter from the impacts. For Louna it had been a fun ride, she had laughed her lungs out all the way down.

She puts her daughter back in her cot. Louna is growing out of it. Maybe she can make some time to visit the furniture store near her work during her lunch break tomorrow and order a new bed. A regular one without bars. Those haven't stopped Louna anyway. For about a year, she has been managing to climb out. The little daredevil.

Jeppe is awake when she returns to the living room. He has closed the blackout curtains and switched from the Dutch news to the Danish one on DR1. A different border, but the same kind of hallucinatory footage, with in the left corner of the screen the date of today.

Somehow Ditte knows the date will be etched in their minds for years to come. It's one of those days of which everyone knows where they were and what they were doing when they heard the news. Like nine-eleven, *le treize novembre, tweeëntwintig maart,* and February twenty-four.

Her husband doesn't say a thing, nor does she. They've already said everything—they have voiced their shock and disbelief more than once. It's late, she has to go to bed. She has to teach at half past eight tomorrow morning. A workshop in a first-year course about archival research.

Yet Ditte cannot tear herself away from the repeated shots, alert to the minutest changes in the continuous loops, to any detail that could indicate a different outcome, a different story than this one.

»«

PART II

Two Decades Later
Maastricht, the Netherlands

*What one seems to want in art, in experiencing it,
is the same thing that is necessary for its creation,
a self-forgetful, perfectly useless concentration.*
(Letter from Elizabeth Bishop to Anne Stevenson)

CHAPTER 8

EVELINE

The song on Eveline's crackling car radio is old but familiar. *Rebellion.* Not the original by Arcade Fire of course, but the more recent instrumental version. Music is one of the few things still allowed in the Netherlands, but only if stripped of its lyrics.

Ever since the European Union had fallen apart two decades ago, the Dutch government has been imposing ever-stricter regulations. They are supposed to combat fake news, which brought Germany and then the EU to its knees.

Naturally, the use of the internet had been restricted first. More recently, fiction became suspect too. Up to the point that also song lyrics were no longer allowed. Lyrics are too much akin to fiction after all. They rearrange life while life is to be lived as it is.

Not that the Dutch government is very stringent in

enforcing that rule. It remains the Netherlands. A policy of relative tolerance abounds when it comes to the privacy of one's home. In the public domain, there are two official exceptions. The national anthem is one of them. Hardly anyone knows the words anyway. After the first two lines, everyone sort of mumbles along, finally belting it out again upon the relief of having made it to the last bit. And then there are the chants and songs of the football clubs, provided they aren't offensive. You have to give the people something.

Eveline turns up the volume. How old had she been when she first heard the song? Twelve, thirteen? Something like that. Whatever her precise age, she played it on repeat. The verses echo in the back of her head, conjured up by the sounds of instruments on the radio: *Sleeping is giving in...Every time you close your eyes...Lies, Lies.* She is careful not to sing them out loud. Rules are rules, as far as she is concerned.

Eveline takes a sharp turn and parks the nearly dead car in the space restricted for top management behind the local refugee centre where she works as Head of Permits. She hates the car. They could own a self-driving vehicle. It doesn't have to be a transparent, spherical model. They could pick one from the retro range as well. She's high enough up the tree for that.

Yet Zac refuses to give it up. He built it himself. Zac ordered the car kit from the Dutch manufacturer in Zutphen fifteen years ago. *The ultimate boy's dream you can afford,* or more accurately, that *she* can afford. She's the one who pays the bills. It took Zac two years to finish it. He spent hours working out the details, endlessly pondering the type of fenders, the gear stick, the body's colour, and other choices of parts of which Eveline didn't know the name. That's not why he doesn't want to let the car go though. It's because it reminds him of a life long gone.

As the sound of the slamming door echoes over the nearly empty parking lot, Eveline opens the boot and reaches for her black briefcase. She only sees the dent on the car's side as she closes the boot again. The paint is chipped and the silver-toned body revealed. Was that damage already there when she got into the car this morning? She didn't notice it then, but she'd been pressed for time as she first had to drop off Wolfke at school.

Her daughter is old enough to go there on her own. Though still in secondary education, she *is* nineteen. She should have been in college already, but Wolfke didn't pass her final exams last year. Eveline found out her daughter had been cutting classes recently. It will be a waste if Wolfke is held back once more. She's too smart and she will certainly get bored. Moreover, as Head of Permits, Eveline has a reputation to uphold. By extension, so does her daughter. Hence Eveline decided to drive her to school for the rest of the year.

She runs a finger over the deep scratches in the varnish. They are too deep for her not to have heard or felt something if it happened while she drove. It can't be her fault. No, it must've been Zac. She sighs and sets course to the refugee centre.

The old name of the building where the centre is located is still vaguely visible above the entrance—*Lumière*. Instead of elegant and flowing, the letters are straight, thick and business-like. Especially in the first years on her job, Eveline found it difficult to work in what used to be Martin's favourite movie theatre. No more *Her*, no films at all. Here or in any other cinema in the country for that matter. Luckily, Martin didn't have to witness that.

The wall next to the entrance has been sprayed with pink paint again. The words are nearly legible. Probably an old movie quote, like the ones before. Eveline rubs her thumb over the graffiti. The paint won't come off easily. She must remember to ask her assistant Yaya to call a cleaning company later, to get rid of the small act of resistance.

Eveline can't help thinking it's typically something Martin would do. But it can't be him. According to the police, she was the last person he had tried to contact. Weeks after his disappearance two decades ago, they found his phone in a garbage bin in the city park. The police played his voice message on her mobile. She hadn't noticed it was on there before the police pointed it out. Hardly anyone left voice messages back then, let alone listened to them. For years, the sounds would echo in her mind. Dull thuds of violence and Martin muffled screaming her name.

She had cherished some hope he would return. He didn't and so she moved on with Zac. She had to. Eveline used to find comfort in her relationship with Zac. He didn't take life as seriously as Martin, which was what she needed then. Even more so after the EU fell apart. It was all so terribly frightening. The past years, however, it hasn't gone that well between the two of them. Their relationship has started to feel like the pebbles in their garden— smooth, but hard and cold.

Besides, the older Wolfke gets, the more she looks like Martin. With her blonde hair and high cheekbones, Wolfke still is largely identical to herself at her age. Initially, the only things reminding her of Martin were her hands and her eyes. But as she grew up, she started to talk and move more like him too. Zac knows, of course. He probably knew all along.

As Eveline enters the refugee centre, her heels click decisively on the hall's concrete floor. With her briefcase clenched under her arm, she crosses over to the stuffy interview room where she will be working today. One of the former cinema rooms. It's called the red room, after the rouged colour of the panelled walls and floor. It used to be a deep cherry. They also have a blue and a purple room, which are smaller and shabbier. Eveline prefers this one. The rows of chairs and the film screen have been taken out, and it is the least run down. Its large size makes an impact on the refugees too.

The only two still working spotlights in the red room turn on gently when the sensor detects her movement. The room is empty, apart from a large desk with a steel-based table lamp and three chairs. Two black swivel ones for her and Yaya, and a small plastic folded one for the interviewees. The latter was once bright white. It has turned pale yellow from years of cold sweat.

As Head of Permits, Eveline is responsible for the interviewing of refugees who come in—mostly Germans—as well as the final decisions on their fate. There are hardly any surprises at this stage. The cases have been meticulously checked beforehand by Yaya. Although the talks are often not much more than a formality, Eveline prepares them carefully.

Sitting down behind the desk, she takes her laptop out of her rectangular briefcase. She folds it open in one movement, before putting it down on the desktop. It takes a while before the computer is up and running. She has to log in several times, with multiple passwords and a fingerprint scan. Even then, she still has to wait minutes. Eveline uses her spare time to redirect the table lamp at its flexible gooseneck, making sure the light will strike the person sitting in the foldable chair later at face level.

Finally, she can access the *Gratis Overheids Feiten Applicatie Check Service,* GOFACS. Or, as her daughter would laughingly say, GOFARTS. The freely available governmental information and fact-checking system crashes more than half the time.

'Ready, Eveline?' Her assistant Yaya has walked in almost imperceptibly. Yaya was speaking softly, almost whispering, but the nearly empty cinema room worked like an echo chamber. It sounded as if she was shouting. Although they have been working together for years, Eveline is still slightly startled by the effect of the room on her assistant's voice. As well as by the fact that Yaya simply seems to materialise behind her, next to her, or in this case, right in front of her.

'Almost. Two today, right?' Eveline inquires, while knowing very well there are indeed just two cases to be handled, unlike the first years, when there were numerous women and men, whole families, trying to get in. Lately, the numbers have been steeply declining in Maastricht, but the national figures have remained strangely stable. Eveline is wise enough not to remark on that. It's what the government reports say, so it must be true.

Yaya inspects the GOFACS application on her TOM. Like regular internet, regular cell phones aren't allowed. Everyone is to use the government-approved TOM—the *Toegestane OverheidsMobiel*. The oval phone is difficult to handle and ridiculously slow as well. It takes Yaya several seconds to find the information.

'Yes, two indeed. The first one is Schulze, from Aachen.'

'Ok, bring him in in fifteen minutes,' Eveline orders, while opening the right file.

§

Eveline is glancing over the report's conclusion—a clear dismissal—when her assistant enters with the refugee. Yaya sits him down on the yellowed plastic chair.

'Eveline?' the man stutters.

Confused, Eveline looks up from her laptop. How does he know her name?

The refugee is a tall slender man with a blond-grey

beard. He's wearing a black shirt, jeans two sizes too big for him and worn trainers, probably charity hand-me-downs. His face doesn't ring a bell, but when she glances down at his hands, their familiarity strikes her. She knows those hands.

Eveline examines him again. She can barely believe she let him touch her once. He has changed so much. There's fear in his bloodshot eyes. He has put on weight and his hairline has receded considerably, but it's him.

'Rrrrraoy?' she blurts. Startled by her outburst, Eveline restrains herself. She averts her gaze to the blushed wall behind him. That she slept with him once two decades ago shouldn't affect her work. It was a meaningless fling, nothing more. Composed and collected is what she should remain. She can do this, she's a professional.

Eveline straightens her shoulders and opens the meeting according to standard procedure as if Roy is merely the next anonymous case to be handled. 'Mister Schulze, this is the last step in your asylum procedure. A final chance to explain why we should permit you to stay in the Netherlands. The interview will last fifteen to thirty minutes. No longer. It's important you tell the truth, the facts. Nothing more, nothing less. Is that clear?'

'Yes, Eveli—'

'Good, your full name please.'

'Eh...Roy Rodolf Rodhi Schulze, but Ev—'

Eveline fires the next set of questions without pausing. 'Nationality German? Age forty-four?'

Roy nods but doesn't respond to her questions when

he speaks. 'I was an exchange student. The bartending was a side job.'

'I guessed. I mean, yes, that's in your file.' Eveline fixes her eyes on the blinking cursor on her screen. Luckily, Yaya doesn't seem to notice her slip-up. Composed, she should remain composed. She quickly carries on. 'According to what I have here, to what you have stated before, you immediately returned to Germany when the union collapsed. Correct?'

'Yes.' Roy nervously rubs his sweaty hands over the chair's plastic armrests, producing eerie squeaking noises.

'You must have known what was going on in Germany…The upsurge of nationalistic feelings and the riots, fuelled by fake news. The start of the end of the EU…Many Germans tried to get into the Netherlands…' Eveline stammers then pauses. She remembers the chaos, the mistrust, and the looming threat of those days intensely. The panic in the eyes of the German exiles, hundreds if not more. Allegedly the result of Russian fake news. Although it was unclear if it had indeed been Russian. It could've been British as well. Speculations abounded.

The Dutch hastily put up actual borders rather than the paper ones that used to exist. Provisionally at first, by putting shipping containers on the roads from and to Germany. But soon there were fences, concrete walls, and barbed wire. On the main roads: police and military patrols, and smart cameras to control the stream of refugees. To this day, no one is allowed to enter the country without official authorisation. Leaving isn't that difficult, but getting back...

Yaya, who has been sitting behind them taking notes, coughs. Eveline should go on. Yet she struggles to. She gazes at the panelled wall again, hoping for its familiar colour to comfort her. The middle panel appears darker than the two outer ones. Is it the lighting? Or has the paint on the other two faded more over the years? Why just those panels then? And how? The room never sees any sunlight.

Eveline barely manages to sound indifferent when asking Roy her next question. 'Mister Schulze, why did you return to Germany? You could have stayed in the Netherlands.'

'My mother was all alone.' Roy acts humble, submissive almost.

'And now you want to come back? Why this change? Your mother...How long ago was it again...?' Eveline pretends to search for information. It's part of her interrogation tactic; it helps to throw suspects off their course. 'Yes, here I have it. She passed ten years ago.'

Roy nervously rubs his palms together. His neck is covered with red blotches.

Eveline goes on mercilessly. 'Let me put it differently. Why should you be allowed to stay here?'

'It's not safe for me anymore in Germany. As a journalist, I revealed corruption by a higher official—'

Eveline waves her hand impatiently. 'Yes, yes, we know that. We need to know if you will fit here.'

'I do,' he exclaims with conviction. His words

bounce sharply off the walls. 'I lived here before.'

'Things have changed.' Eveline continues to grill him, once the echo of his words has faded away. She's supposed to. It's her role. It's all by the book, but she's having a hard time. 'You have no problems with our current regulation of the internet? The proctoring of its use?'

'No, no, not at all,' Roy hurries to say. 'Otherwise, it becomes a slippery slope, doesn't it? From facts to lies. The internet is a breeding ground for false information.'

Eveline has heard so many refugees proclaim the same before. They say whatever they have to. She feels for Roy however and she browses again through the documents Yaya has prepared. Could she go behind her assistant's back and change the status afterwards? Eveline has done it before, once, as a favour to her old friend Kiara. She cringes when she thinks of what she did. Eveline has been lucky it went unnoticed. No, she will do the proper thing, but with a heavy heart—she liked Roy back then. She'll abide by the procedures and keep going.

'Have you always thought this way?'

'Yes,' Roy responds rapidly.

Eveline knows better than to be led on by that. The speed with which someone provides information is no indicator of the truth. It is the evidence and the evidence alone that matters. Coherency between story and facts.

She opens a document in Roy's file—a student paper called *Freie Social Media für freie Meinungsäußerung*—and turns her laptop for him to see it. The screen's green-blue light highlights the expression of fear disfiguring his face.

She's about to pull the rug.

'Is this yours?' She opens another essay. 'And this one?'

Roy gawps at her as if she has dipped his dick in honey and staked it onto an anthill. 'How...'

'You never had any issues with our ideas?'

She has him confused.

'No, no, I don't, I didn't. I was young. Please Eveline, for old time's sake.'

Eveline can feel Yaya's eyes burning. The sound of her typing has stopped. Eveline briefly glances at Roy's hands. They're resting on his knees now, palms down, close to defeat. His fingers are fleshier, their skin is wrinkly, and they are more hairy than she remembers.

She suppresses a flicker of doubt. The official rule is she should decline a refugee if there is a reason or a technical possibility to do so. When it comes to Roy, the essays are a perfect ground for rejection.

Not wanting to raise red flags with Yaya she quickly rounds off the interview, ignoring his plea. 'Ok, thank you, Mister Schulze. Your asylum centre officer will inform you about the decision regarding your status in writing about a week after this interview. If a refugee or subsidiary protection status is granted, you will be released from the centre within two days. You will be automatically enrolled in the Alien Register and you will receive a residence and work permit for five years, the Q-permit. After these five years, you can apply for a P-permit, which is valid indefinitely. If the application for asylum is refused—and make sure to be prepared for that—you will be sent back on the same day.' Roy is crying now, but Eveline carries on reciting the bureaucratic information without flinching. 'In that case, you are allowed to take your personal belongings with you in a bag with a maximum size of forty by twenty by twenty-five centimetres and a maximum weight of three kilograms.'

§

It's well after sunset when they finally have dinner together that evening. Wolfke returned home late from school. She mumbled something about having missed the bus.

Eveline knows she's lying. Wolfke's head teacher contacted her at noon, during lunch break. She had ordered the month's special in the canteen, a lentil soup when his message popped up on her TOM. Wolfke was cutting classes again, despite Eveline having dropped her off right at the school's entrance. She had been fretting about Roy— had it indeed been the right decision? Was there nothing she could do?—when the news about her daughter shoved those concerns completely out of her mind.

Fuming and distraught, Eveline glares at Wolfke sitting in the half-shadow opposite her. Zac has turned on the pendulum lamp hanging above the chestnut dining table, but no other lights. Electricity is expensive and he needs a lot of it during the day. He's always working on some project in the house for which he needs power tools, a drill or something else. That's the downside of living in a monumental farmhouse. There's always another thing to be done. The renovation is never finished. On the other hand, at least he has something to do. Idle hands make idle minds, after all.

Wolfke is pushing her food around. It's the usual Tuesday dish, a quiche with cauliflower, sage and thyme from their garden. Eveline hasn't been this worried since she gave birth. She was twenty back then. Young, too young perhaps to have a child. She had chosen to keep it, which was *her* choice, no one else's.

Luckily, Zac had been by her side. Her mother hadn't been there, having quickly left the country for Brussels at the first sign of the change of regime. She didn't ask Eveline to go with her, as usual just thinking about herself. Not that Eveline would have gone. She doesn't like Belgium one bit. That county was an epitome of chaos already before the union collapsed, and with by now five official languages and sixteen different governments, disorder reigned completely. The EU had been the one thing that held the Belgian state and particularly Brussels together.

She visited it once after her mother had moved there and considered it abominable. The garbage on the pavements, the sprayed profanities on almost every building, the stench of piss travelling up from the subway stations... She and her mum haven't kept in touch since then. Just as well. Her mother's past singing career would make things unnecessarily complicated.

Eveline recalls the anxiety in the room when she delivered Wolfke, after nine hours of painful labour. It was the first day of the new year. Her daughter had been six weeks premature. Everyone was busy making sure she survived. When Eveline was finally allowed to see her, her inflamed skin should've appalled her, yet it didn't. During her studies, she had mainly read stories about attachment problems—baby blues, postpartum depression, psychosis. She was prepared for anything, but not for the utterly deep connection when she looked at her child.

At that moment, Eveline chose her name. It was an honest one, and it suited the wild light in her eyes. Moreover, she hoped it would ward off any falsehood she might have inherited from Martin. Animals don't lie after all. For the next eighteen years, they were as thick as thieves. The last year, her daughter has been slipping away. Should she have chosen a different name? Would it have helped?

Wolfke puts her fork down. Her fingers are thin, and her skin has the same fiery complexion as when she was born. It didn't disappear, as the nurse had reassured her it would.

Eveline tries to catch her daughter's eye before she raises her voice. 'Wolfke, I want you to tell me right now. Where have you been all day?'

Wolfke doesn't look up, let alone say anything. Frustrated, Eveline leans forward over the dining table, intending to grab her daughter by her chin. Doing so, she knocks over her glass—a cheap, local sauvignon blanc. She doesn't drink red. Not anymore. Not since Martin. Red was *his* drink. Besides, it's too expensive.

Wiping the wine from her blouse, she shouts at Wolfke, 'Go to your room and don't come down until you're ready to talk.'

Zac, who stayed out of the discussion, rubs the top of his head. He used to have long blond hair. Since he has started going bald at the back of his head, he shaves it all off.

His tone is reproachful. 'I'm not sure whether sending her to her room is the way to keep her on the right track, Eveline. She's nineteen.'

He uneasily smooths the folds in the blue plaid tablecloth. His hands have lost the reassuring ability they had when he touched her in the first years they were together. Eveline follows their movements with disdain.

'If you have a better idea, be my guest,' she snaps.

Ever since Zac had been stupid enough to pay a visit to an illicit website, she can't take him seriously anymore when it comes to seeing the importance of following rules. Eveline still has no idea how he bypassed the governmental firewall. She doesn't want to know. The reason he did it had been so trivial. To look up a film title he couldn't remember. He couldn't watch the stupid film anyway. Why bother about its name? As a result, his certificate of good conduct, which every Dutch citizen must present to be allowed to work, was revoked.

Not that this made much of a difference to his life. Given his background in film studies, Zac hadn't been able to secure a job before either. Certificate or no certificate, no employer wants to be burned hiring someone who once studied fiction and possibly even wished to become a filmmaker. A fabricator of stories. Of falsehoods. He was already marked.

Eveline eyes him suspiciously. Zac mindlessly chews on a bite of quiche. He hasn't said anything about the damage to the car. She expected him to bring it up, but he hasn't.

Finally, she breaks the silence. 'Are you ever going to tell me how it happened?'

'What?'

'The dent in the car.'

He answers with his mouth full. 'I have no idea what you are talking about.'

'Ah come on, Zac, don't take me for a fool.'

He must've known. Why else would he react so resigned? It's his precious car that got damaged.

'You think I'd lie? About something as petty as a little fender-bender?' He sounds offended. Eveline can tell he isn't, not genuinely.

She's disappointed he isn't open with her, and that he puts more energy in fibbing about the car than worrying about Wolfke. Eveline decides to give him the cold shoulder and finishes her dinner without saying another word.

»«

CHAPTER 9

LOU(NA)

Lou is sitting half upright on her double bed, blinking against the glow of the lamp on her bedside table. She has just flicked it on, alarmed by the sounds of someone pushing the bedroom door open.

Although the smoked-glass shade diffuses the light, it's too bright. Lou reaches for the switch to dim it. As her eyes adjust to the diminished glare, she scans the room. The coverlet of her duvet is dingy and the round mirror on the wall opposite is smudged with make-up. The rest doesn't look much better. There's a mountain of dirty clothes on the floor. Her mother is standing right next to it. She has let herself into her flat, again.

'That's not what the spare key is for, Mum.' Lou's voice is low and hoarse, the night of sleep weighing it down. Her alarm, which she had set at six a.m., is yet to go off. Even for her mother, this is extreme. Lou clears her throat before continuing her reprimand, she sounds raspy nonetheless. 'I've told you so many times not to—'

'I know, I know, emergencies only, but it's your twenty-third birthday, Louna!' her mother erupts cheerily. She walks over to hug her.

Her mum is wearing perfume. *La vie est belle*, unmistakably. A heady mixture of orange blossom and vanilla. From her last bottle. She only uses it on special occasions.

The familiar orangey-sweet smell travels up Lou's nose. Suppressing a sneeze, she attempts to push her mother away, yet a painful tug at her hair keeps her locked in the embrace. Their faces are a mere fifteen centimetres apart.

Lou tries to back away again, but another sharp sting shoots through her skull, drawing a short scream from her lips. 'Ow!'

Almost simultaneously her mother lets out a cry. 'Ouch, Louna, wait. One of my earrings got stuck in your curls. Careful, you'll tear my earlobe! I'll get it out. Don't move!'

Commanding her to sit still once more, her mum leans in to untangle the jewellery. Her breathing is unbearably loud.

'Got it!' her mum exclaims in the middle of a long, damp exhale, which was giving Lou goose bumps.

It must've taken her mother seconds, but it felt much longer. Lou rubs over the sore spot on her head. Laughing in relief, her mum sits down on the foot end of the bed and dangles the silver thread-like earring in front of her.

Lou silently stares at her, arms crossed. Not only is her mother wearing her special perfume, she's in her most festive dress as well—the silk cream one with gathered waistband. A multi-coloured scarf with a pied-de-poule print is knotted loosely around her neck and her eyelids are painted light-coral.

'Sorry for that, are you ok?'

Lou doesn't feel like reassuring her. She's mad at her, but the warmth of her mother's voice makes her nod nonetheless.

Her mum pushes the lock of hair in which the earring was caught back behind Lou's ear. 'Your curls are so dry. Don't you use the oil I got you?'

Lou still doesn't say anything.

After an awkward silence, her mother starts to chatter away, as she does when she doesn't know how to handle the situation, but then stops. Looking at Lou, she squints as if trying to decipher some hidden message. As her brows furrow, they cast shadows over her deep brown eyes.

In a split second, Lou understands what her mother is looking at. Shoot. Her shirt! Lou only wears the garment as pyjamas. No one has ever seen it on her. How was she to know her mum would show up unannounced in her apartment's bedroom this early, in what is supposed to be her private space? She quickly pulls up the duvet as high as possible, to cover up the shirt's print. It's a long-haired Tom Petty and a line from one of his songs—*she's a good girl, loves her mama.*

Has her mother read it? Let's hope not. Lou doesn't want to get her dad into trouble. Her parents had enough fights about her in the past. After finishing secondary education a couple of years ago, she didn't go to university and decided to start working instead. Her mum was furious, and considered it a waste, while her dad was more in tune with her frustrations about school. Ground for many heated discussions.

The T-shirt had been a gift from her father. Her dad used to collect vintage band shirts. Any band would do. Although he preferred the ones with Taylor Swift—'More Grammys than The Beatles', whatever and whoever those were—and Tom Petty indeed.

A few years ago, her mother had insisted on him giving up all the shirts with printed lyrics. Even a snippet of text meant they had to go. Her mum was such a snowflake. Sure, those were the new regulations, but as long as her dad didn't wear them, who'd know?

Lou doesn't get how her mum managed to convince her father. Yet she is glad he kept this one behind for her. Her dad knew how much she loved the top. Although she's merely familiar with the instrumental versions of Petty's work. She hasn't heard any of his songs with lyrics, at least not that she can remember. She had to promise her father, hand on her heart, never to put it on in public and *not* to tell her mother.

Clenching the duvet, Lou tries to read her mother. Her pupils are dilated and her mouth is contorted into a downward arc. Yes, her mum has seen it. She should nip this in the bud.

Without a moment's pause, Lou brings her decoy into action, 'You can't just walk in here, *Ditte*! What if I had a girl over?'

Her mother immediately turns red. Ha, she didn't see that one coming. It feels good to tell her off, using her first name. Lou knows how much her mum hates it when she does that.

'Which...wait...what...a girlfriend?' Her mother finally reacts in fits and starts. Her eyes are bulging. She resembles a fish out of water. 'If...if I happen to walk in, I'd be okay with that. You know that. A girlfriend, how lovely! Can I meet her?'

Lou sighs exasperatedly. 'This isn't about *you*, mum. It's about *my* privacy. *I* would mind!'

Careful to keep the shirt covered, Lou bends her knees and folds her arms around her legs. Her curly, caramel hair falls over her shoulders. She glares at her mother through mascara-clumped eyelashes—she hadn't felt like taking off her make-up before going to bed last evening. Her mum's eyebrows are still raised, but she appears a little less fish-like.

With her lips oddly puckered up as if she wants to kiss away the cold in the air between them, her mother stutters, 'Oh, ok...I understand, point taken...shall I make coffee? I brought cake. It's your favourite, with meringue and almonds. There's chocolate in it. Not much, but still, *real* chocolate, Louna.'

166

Lou is surprised her mother throws in the towel so quickly. Perhaps because it *is* her birthday. Her mum is already on her way to the kitchen when Lou puts up a final protest. It's pro forma, she knows her mother means well. Her mum must have gone to great lengths to get her hands on a cake with chocolate.

'No coffee,' Lou calls after her. 'I don't have any. Besides, I get more than my share at work. And Mum...no one calls me Louna anymore.'

Her mum pops her head through the door. 'Yes, of course, *Lou*. I'll make tea then, while you get dressed. Decently. *That,*' her mother levels her index finger at the still-covered shirt, 'will get you into trouble.'

§

Despite her mother's disappointment, Lou worked the cake down fast and hurriedly left for work. Her mum obviously wanted to spend more time with her. She'd gone to a lot of trouble. Besides the cake, she'd hung up spiralling garlands in the living room and got her a blue balloon shaped like a number twenty-three.

Lou considers dropping by after her shift to make it up to her. But right now, she has other things on her mind. Although she's not seeing anyone, she *does* have her eye on a young woman who's been visiting the coffee bar where Lou works. Lou wants to get there as soon as possible. She didn't waste time brushing her teeth and the slightly sickly sweetness of chocolate still lingers in her mouth. Today, she'll make her move. It's the second of February after all.

Double numbers, double chances and, on top, her birthday. Luck must be on her side.

The name of the coffee shop—*Bandito*—is etched on the glass door. Lou unlocks it. She doesn't enjoy her job as a barista much, but at least it's somewhat creative. Lou likes to make latte art, to make little petals and other shapes in the milk foam. There is, however, usually not enough time for that. It's generally too busy, especially when she has to work alone like she has the past weeks. Jerome, her boss and only colleague, has recently become a father, and he hasn't been around a lot lately.

Empty, the shop appears a little run down. The walls have lost their plaster in parts, showing off bricks and beams. The morning sun peeks through the glass part of the ceiling and paints dust stripes in the air above the wooden chairs and tables, their brown varnish chipped and worn. Although it's February, it's already humid inside. Lou can't remember the last time it was truly winter. Last year, there was not one day of frost.

The first thing she does is to switch on the espresso machine. It'll take an hour for it to heat up. Only then does she hang her parka on the coat stand next to the door, prying a hair elastic out of the pocket of her black jeans to tie her curls together in a high bun. She uses the metal fridge behind the counter as a mirror. Displeased with the cleanness of her topknot, she pulls at it and runs her fingers through her curtain fringe. Her hair works much better tousled. It looks more flirtatious that way.

She smiles at her reflection and turns around. The

large Arabica coffee plants in their baskets are a little wilted. The pointy oval leaves are curling at the tips. When she started to work here, Lou had expected them to smell like coffee, but they're oddly odourless. The plants only need a little water, about once every two weeks maximum. They don't like to stay wet, yet they seem very dry now.

Lou pokes her finger in the soil to check the moisture level. It comes out clean. They need a drink for sure. She runs the tap and fills up one of the metal pitchers. She'll give them a bit more than usual, a quarter pitcher each should do.

After the watering the plants, Lou starts on the soup. They make a fresh batch every day. It's what sets them apart from the other coffee bars in town. Besides dry goods, there's a pumpkin left in the pantry, and a few sad garlic bulbs and onions. She should call Jerome to see if he can pick some fresh veg from his garden tomorrow. Maybe leek or kale, if there is any left. If not, he should make sure to bring some of his conserving jars with pies or beans.

Lou scans the recipes, which Jerome has stuck on their note board with two refrigerator magnets—one with the text *I ♥ MAASTRICHT*, the other with a picture of a spherical architectural structure, which according to Jerome is the *Atomium*. Creamy cauliflower soup, mushroom and potato soup, celeriac and hazelnut soup, carrot and lentil...If she's not mistaken, they still have half a bag of red lentils and she doesn't have to soak those. Only give them a thorough rinse and cook them for about ten minutes. She can replace the carrot with pumpkin. Lentil and pumpkin soup it is then. Lou takes the recipe from the board.

Forty-five minutes later, the bar is filled with the sweet butterscotch smell of the pumpkin, which she quickly roasted and is now simmering in a pan with water. She'll add the lentils later.

She has five minutes before the bar opens, and she decides to make herself a macchiato. It's her birthday and if she limits it to one, Jerome will never know that she took a genuine drink. Lou is not allowed to use the good stuff. The *real* coffee is for the customers willing to pay for it, for the ones who can afford it. Most of them have to settle for Chikkocaf—a chicory and acorn surrogate mixture with synthetic caffeine. If they have a little bit more to spend, the half-half upgrade is also an option. For this, Lou is to scoop out the already-used coffee grounds to supplement the Chikkocaf.

She opens the bag with the real coffee, and grinds precisely enough beans for one portion, then carefully doses the fresh ground in the porta-filter. After inserting it into the machine, and having brewed the espresso, she cranks open the steam wand and dips the tip in the milk. Lou loves the soft popping sound it makes. During the rest of the day, combined noises of chattering and clattering china drown it out.

The coffee smells so authentic. Lou bends over the finished drink and inhales. Complex and full-bodied. She takes a small sip. The taste is every bit as good as the bouquet's promise. Unfortunately, she has to finish her stolen luxury quickly, and there certainly isn't any time to enjoy the macchiato's afterglow. The first clients arrive, and soon customers are lining up.

Every time the door opens, Lou looks up, hoping to see the young woman, but to her disappointment, it's always someone else: professors from the nearby university in need of caffeine to get through their morning lectures, shopkeepers on their lunch break, and the occasional stray businessperson in a grey suit demanding a double espresso on the go. Whoever they are, none of them notices her when placing their order, instead transfixed by their TOMs. Even the loud drumming each time she empties the filter in the knock box doesn't distract them.

By closing time, things have slowed down. It's unlikely the girl will be coming today. Lou has already rinsed the pitchers and is about to shut down the machine when she walks in after all. Her crush is wearing a navy-coloured school uniform, a backpack casually draped over her right shoulder. The skin on her cheeks is lightly freckled and there's a little dimple in her angular chin. Her half-long hair is cut irregularly.

It's not her beauty that throws Lou off. Normally she doesn't have a thing for blondes. It's her eyes. Not their colour, which is a greenish-brown, but their vibrancy. The girl looks right at her. Lou had been set on making her move, and now, she doesn't know what to say. Confused, she averts her gaze and pretends to rearrange the sacks of the surrogate mix. She wipes over the already clean worktop with a microfiber cloth.

Finally having mustered up enough courage, Lou turns to her. 'The usual? A flat white?'

'Yes please, the Chikkocaf.' The young woman glances at the analogue clock on the wall behind Lou, then points to the table near the window. 'Is it ok if I take a seat? I won't stay long. Only a couple of minutes.'

'Sure, no problem. I'll bring it over,' Lou replies, levelling the grind in the filter and gently, but forcefully, pressing it down with the wooden-handled tamper.

It takes Lou longer than usual to prepare the flat white. She wishes she hadn't treated herself to a real coffee this morning, so she could make the girl one. Lou doesn't dare to steal a second and she can't afford to pay for it. There isn't any used ground left to make a half-half either.

Although Lou has to use the surrogate, she wants the drink to be perfect. She gives the pitcher a thump on the counter and lightly swirls the milk around to smooth the foam. After having poured it on top of the hot espresso, she reviews it pensively. It needs something else, something more. Something that'll draw her attention.

Lou opens a drawer to take out the set with templates they sometimes use to pimp up a cappuccino. They'll work fine with a flat white too. She picks the stencil with three little punched-out stars. Holding it above the rich crema floating on the coffee, she dusts it with some loose instant substitute powder. The powder is their back-up option for when they've run out of everything else. Yes, much better.

Satisfied, Lou puts the white ceramic cup on its saucer. Her hand is shaking a little as she crosses the room to the table, but she manages not to spill anything when putting down the drink.

'On the house. It's my birthday. Lou, by the way.' She blurts the words out fast, soft, inaudible almost.

'What?'

'I'm Lou,' she repeats, rubbing her sweaty hand on the cleaning cloth, which she tucked in behind the waistband of her jeans.

'Ah, I see. I'm Wolfke.' The girl smiles and inspects her coffee. 'Wow, such nice flowers.'

'Stars.'

'They're beautiful. Thank you.'

Lost for what to say next, Lou points at Wolfke's uniform to state the obvious. 'You're still in school?'

'Well, sort of. I'm in my final year, for the second time, so I shouldn't be anymore. Your birthday, you said? But *you* should be the one getting presents then.'

Regaining some courage, Lou decides to go for a witty comeback. 'Indeed. Didn't you bring me something?'

Wolfke stares at her silently, her brows knitted. Oh, this is not going as she hoped. Didn't Wolfke get that... ?

Lou looks at her hands, which are stained from the surrogate. There's grind under her fingernails. 'That was a silly joke.'

Wolfke rubs her eyes as if waking up from a daydream. 'No, no, it wasn't, not at all. You know what, I *do* have something for you. *That*'s what I was thinking of. Wait. Come, sit down.'

While Lou pulls up another chair to take a seat next to her, Wolfke zips open the front pocket of her backpack. It's the same type as Lou had when she was in secondary school, which isn't surprising. The obligatory state school uniform comes with a matching blue bag. Wolfke's isn't entirely identical however. There are chalks and doodles on the inside of the flap that turn it into something different, a statement on its own.

Wolfke takes a small triangular piece of turquoise plastic out of the fumbled bag and leans in to put it in Lou's hand. She smells fresh and clean, like soap.

Her lips nearly touch Lou's ear, and her nipping breath strokes her cheek when she whispers, 'It's a plectrum.'

'I don't—'

'Well, you see, I knew that. That's the real gift. You'll get to learn.'

'And...and I can count on you for that?' Lou asks, hesitantly hopeful.

Wolfke rests her chin on her hand and tilts her head. 'I'm sure we can arrange something. But tell m—'

In an impulse, Lou leaps forward and brushes her lips against Wolfke's. She closes her eyes, and opens her mouth, softly searching around with the tip of her tongue. Wolfke's palm touches her chest.

It takes some seconds, before Lou realises Wolfke isn't responding to her kiss, but is trying to push her away. Lou retreats immediately to watch her anxiously.

Hints of confusion have blended in with the green-brown of Wolfke's eyes. 'Uuhh, I think this is a misunderstanding.'

As shame colours her cheeks, Lou starts to apologise, 'I'm so sorry. I thought...I'm sorry. Are you ok?'

Wolfke smiles, her eyes again a warm hazelnut. 'Don't worry. It's...you didn't ask and I don't know you yet and then...'

'You're right.' Lou cringes. How could she have done that indeed? What had she been thinking? She hadn't been, that was of course the whole problem. She could kick herself. If only the ground could open up and swallow her. At the same time, she understands Wolfke hasn't closed the door completely. *Yet*, she said, she doesn't know her *yet*. 'You gotta let me make up to you. I promise it'll be good. And that I'll behave.'

Wolfke laughs. 'What do you have in mind?'

§

The little restaurant is fancy. The sparse lighting, Lou decides, manages intimacy rather than frugality. Wolfke is stunning in its glow, wearing a vintage fake leather jacket over a bleached denim dress. Her backpack, which to Lou's surprise she brought as well, is standing between her feet. The round table for two is set with a lovingly ironed white tablecloth and napkins. There's a two-armed crystal candelabra standing in the middle, the base only slightly chipped.

Her mother made the reservation for her. Any restaurant is hard to get into without knowing people high up. As a professor, her mum has access to places others don't. At first, Lou had felt uncomfortable asking her mother for help, and for money to pay for the date. But her mum was so happy to be in on it. She'd reassured her it wasn't a problem at all. Her mother truly wasn't so bad.

Lou runs her fingers over the embossed blue and yellow logo of the restaurant on the menu: a stem cell and a pipette. They even have meat. Lab-grown of course. Lou can't remember the last time she had it, let alone if she'd liked it. They don't sell it in the shops. It's a wonder it's on the menu at all.

Her mum didn't hold back when she picked out the restaurant for them. She told Lou to order whatever they wanted, regardless of cost. Lou has stuck to what she knows though, ordering the beet salad with chopped walnuts, aniseed, and fennel. Wolfke, however, has gone for the burger.

The main courses arrive. Lou glances at the flesh on Wolfke's plate. It's floating in some sort of grey grease, not butter, that's for sure. Has it actually been cooked? Its red and white threads are visible. Lou is happy she ordered the salad. Technically nothing, nobody died. Yet the meat smells horrible, like blood and death.

'Do you want a bite?' Wolfke holds out her fork, a piece of burger spiked onto it.

Lou gazes at the disintegrating lump on the fork's end. It resembles a squashed ball of yarn. Lou is still nervous and doesn't know how to react instantly. She likes Wolfke a lot and she wants this to work out. After that failure of a kiss, she has to be at her best. She's been sitting on the edge of her padded dining chair all evening. Lou swallows. 'No, thank you. I'm good.'

Trying to get rid of the meat's carnal smell, she reaches for her glass of water. After several swigs, she resumes the conversation, 'So, you don't like school?'

'Some of it, but mostly not.' Wolfke cuts into the cultured beef. 'I go not to upset my mother. She found out I was skipping classes. How's your salad? This meat is unbelievably good.'

Chewing on her greens, Lou forms a circle with her thumb and index finger to make clear her dish is topnotch too.

Wolfke refills her glass with the red wine, something local and expensive. 'The classes are boring. I mean, take history. How many times are they going to tell us about fake news and how they put an end to it?'

Lou checks to make sure there's no one within hearing distance. 'I wonder if life wouldn't be more interesting without all of those restrictions, or certainly the ones which pertain to fiction. What do you think?'

Wolfke has stopped chewing and stares at her intensely, broodingly. The silence stretches uncomfortably.

Lou decides to quickly change the subject, retreating to safer ground, 'Dessert? They've got fresh strawberries.'

How could she have been so stupid? To hint at her doubts about the regulations? Has her mother not warned her many times? Not to hang her unconventional thoughts out there for everyone to see. But sitting across from

Wolfke, who she barely knows, she longs for the early years of her childhood, to the stories and their colourfulness, their promise of possibilities.

How she savoured the Danish fairy tales her father read to her. Her mum never did, she didn't like them. Lou did all the more. Every evening, she would beg—'again, again, again'—while her older sister Alma and younger brother Razi had lost interest already. Her dad gave in wholeheartedly, he loved his share of strong stories too, and she ate up every word.

Den Lille Havfrue was Lou's favourite. Not the sweet, Disneyfied version, but the one that ended tragically with the little mermaid dissolving in the sea. The first time her father read it to her, she was angry. She thought it unfair. After all that trouble, why did the mermaid not get the prince?—'Because she denies herself for somebody else,' her father explained. 'Never do that Lou. You'll dissolve, like a piece of soap in water.'

Lou was ten when he read his last fairy tale to her. It wasn't *Den Lille Havfrue*. Instead, he told a story about a girl who saved her brothers by knitting shirts out of stinging nettles, in complete silence, resisting the pain. When he had finished it, he delivered the message that this had been her final bedtime story. Lou cried her heart out. Her dad tried to calm her down. He urged her to see it as something positive, as a step to maturity. Yet she remained angry with him for months.

Later, she understood her dad was merely the messenger of a new government ruling limiting fiction further to include children's books, and indeed any story fancifully made up or invented. Her mother was far too fearfully law-abiding not to conform, and so bedtime stories came to an end.

But Lou couldn't resist the appeal fiction had on her, and instead secretly started to write stories of her own. She must have been seventeen when she was caught scribbling something down during calculus. Normally she wasn't so careless, but she couldn't resist the inspiration tugging at her that day.

The story dealt with a female scavenger who finds a mermaid. Instead of returning her to the sea, she takes the mermaid with her to keep her in the bathtub. At first, the mermaid seems to be doing fine. Then one morning, she floats inertly in the water, which has taken on a rainbow-ish hue.

Lou was working on the ending when her math teacher busted her and reported her misdeed to the head teacher and her parents. Her mum had been hysterical and her dad had been scared too, so she promised to suppress the thought of writing. She thus never worked out what the beachcomber did next—did she lament the mermaid's death? Did she love her? Perhaps she decided to sell the body to science, to be dissected and put on display in a museum, its genitals conserved in a pickle jar of formaldehyde.

Lou believed she'd successfully killed her attraction to fiction back then, but tonight it popped up, as a helium-filled balloon held underwater ultimately will. Well, that's it then. She has ruined the date for sure.

Wolfke is already reaching for her backpack. To Lou's surprise, she is smiling. 'No strawberries. Let's go to your place.'

§

Lou is sitting on her knees on her twin bed, while Wolfke is giving her directions on how to use the spray can and stencil. 'You have to hold it like this, very still. Press it down, harder, otherwise it becomes blurry.'

Wolfke has just confided in her that she understands what Lou had mentioned about the regulations in the restaurant. She went even further and told Lou that she does graffiti. Wolfke must trust her. She probably feels it too. Although strangers, it's like they've always known each other. When Wolfke opened her bag to show her the spray and the stencils, Lou instantly wanted to try it.

Her hand trembles a little when she presses the stencil against the wall. They are both still naked and Lou is a bit shaky from the sex they had, as well as from Wolfke's current closeness.

Although younger, Wolfke was surprisingly decisive in bed, yet never forgetting to check if she had Lou's consent. She asked Lou to lie down on her back like a stranded starfish—her legs stretched outwards, her arms above her head next to the pillow. She was so close Lou could take in all of her scents. Besides soap, Wolfke smelled of sebum and the Dutch liquorice sweets of which she'd worked down more than a handful on the way from the restaurant to her apartment. Luckily, the meat smell had evaporated.

When Wolfke gently pressed her cunt onto her mouth, it felt as if diving into a warm and welcoming sea. Lou resisted coming up for air for as long as she could. Wolfke's pubes covered her upper lip, tickling all of her senses. Licking her ever more savoury clit, Lou felt liberated. It was as if she was making love to Wolfke and herself at the same time. A duplication of pleasure she had never experienced before.

The spray can makes a sizzling sound and a fluorescent pink fills up the holes in the stencil. Lou considers the result on the white wall above the headboard. It's just one line, thin and barely visible, nevertheless, it's impressive:

Beautiful thing, the destruction of words

'Not bad for a first time, Lou,' Wolfke exclaims.

Lou blushes at Wolfke's compliment. Hiding her reddening cheeks behind her curly hair, she goes through the stack of templates. 'Where do you get them from?'

'The stencils? I make them. It's easy. I will show you h—'

'No, I mean the lines.'

'Oh, well, I have a book. I always carry it with me. Here, see.' Wolfke reaches deep into her backpack, takes out a small, fumbled paperback and hands it to her. The title is printed in elegant flowing letters—*Most Memorable Movie Scenes. A Hollywood Anthology*. 'It used to be my mum's.'

Lou flips through it. The pages are discoloured, the edges round and soft. Some sentences are underlined: _You had my curiosity. But now you have my attention. The past is just a story we tell ourselves. That's a bingo. If anyone orders a Merlot, I am leaving. I am not drinking any fucking Merlot_. On the first page, there is a handwritten inscription:

For Eveline

That's when you know you've found somebody really special.
When you can just shut the fuck up for a min-
ute and comfortably share a silence.
Love always,

Martin

'Your mum doesn't miss it?'

'Naahh. She doesn't know I have it. I snatched it from a pile of stuff she'd dragged out of the house because it had become illicit.'

Lou puts the book down and watches the dots of paint that have landed on Wolfke's naked body—on her forearms, her upper legs, her bosom, on her blonde hair as well. Wolfke presses the stencil against the wall and shakes the can to spray over it once more. The paint on her body dances in front of Lou's eyes. There's a small scar on the back of her left hand, close to her thumb, next to a dotted series of paint. Lou hadn't noticed it before.

'You see?' Wolfke speaks in a tenderly explaining tone. 'If you spray it twice, it comes out clearer.'

With the tips of her fingers, Lou touches the scar. 'Are you not scared when you do this out in the streets?'

Wolfke takes her hand. The cool touch of her fingers sends a shiver up and down her spine. 'Sometimes, but I'm careful.'

»«

CHAPTER 10

DITTE

Ditte is standing on the wooden dais. She's almost done with the last class of the day. The lecture theatre hasn't changed much in the more than two decades she has been teaching here. Its walls have been painted in a slightly different colour—eggshell instead of bright white—and the double wooden doors have been varnished dark blue instead of deep green.

The furniture has been replaced once. Yet it's nearly identical and by now, as run down to what was there previously. The edging of the fibreboard lectern has loosened, revealing the honeycomb-structured filling.

The nondescript artwork consisting of gymnast figurines is gone though, and they have taken down the framed poems from the walls too. Ditte misses the poems. They'd grown on her and became loyal companions. Their familiar layouts and their silent sounds and rhythms had turned the lecture hall into a welcoming space. At the start of long teaching days, they filled her with a warm and easy sensation. They made her feel at home. She still hadn't fully understood them. Perhaps that isn't the purpose of poetry anyway, to understand it completely. Perhaps it's more about what it does to you. Both physically and emotionally.

The poems have been replaced with photos of the Dean and other members of the board, wearing the newest academic attire. Eric looks ridiculous in his sequined burgundy robe and with the cap with frills and sparkles on top. Ditte has to wear the outfit too sometimes. Luckily, only during official ceremonies.

Her tongue is dry. She's been talking non-stop for the past forty-five minutes. Ditte pauses and reaches for the bottle of water on the tired lectern. As she drinks, she studies the students. The one right in front of her is resting her chin in her hands, her eyes half-closed. Others have nodded off completely, their heads awkwardly tilted to one side. A girl on the second row is lying with her arms and forehead flat down on top of her foldable desk. Ditte feels like doing the same. Like her students, she's fed up with the pre-cooked lessons she's obliged to teach. Every day the same unimaginative drag.

In the past, she had a hard time cramping everything she wanted to say into two hours. These days, she hardly needs more than fifty minutes to get through the materials. She doesn't have a say over the content anymore, it's dictated by the faculty's education committee.

Today, it's a monstrosity of a lecture on recent Dutch history. It lopsidedly deals with how the government coped so well with the EU's death. How it defended its population. And how important it is to maintain that protection, as the danger of false facts is ever-present.

Ditte has been racing through the slides to get to the end of the script as soon as possible. According to the teacher's instruction manual, she's supposed to finish by shaking her fist in the air, uttering the words 'Our vigilance shouldn't slacken'.

The only advantage of the new regime is that she doesn't have to worry anymore about her students using a chatbot to write their research papers. AI had been one of the first things to be forbidden.

At the time, she believed she'd been the lucky one. She was allowed to keep her job. Now she isn't too sure. Ditte remembers every detail of the day the Faculty of Film Studies was shut down to be replaced by a conventional history faculty.

Four years after Germany collapsed—and with it the EU—the then newly chosen Dutch Cabinet commanded universities to return to the core business of truth finding. The study of art, literature, theatre and film wasn't considered part of it, and state funding for these types of endeavours was cut severely.

There was criticism, of course, but academics aren't activists. They always put their research and students first. Moreover, the Netherlands was officially in a state of emergency. The right to rally was suspended and has been for most of the last two decades. Staff members at her own and at other targeted faculties expressed their dissatisfaction by wearing a two-by-two-centimetres red felt square, a homemade protest badge.

Ditte didn't wear the textile button. She couldn't believe then that matters would get out of hand the way and as fast as they did. But turning off the money tap was enough to turn rectors and Deans on their faculties. As a hunter sets his dog on his prey.

The letter she and her colleagues received in their e-mailbox that mid-summer, sixteen years ago, promised free support with finding a different job. The university would pay their salary for nine more months—a generous sop the length of a pregnancy.

The letter ended with a postscript in a much smaller font size: anyone who needed to pick up things from their office could do so that weekend between nine a.m. and five p.m. For safety reasons, the university would provide the moving boxes. Two per faculty member. They weren't allowed to bring their own crates or bags.

That Sunday, the waiting line outside the faculty had merely been a few metres long. Ditte had expected more colleagues, and at least a few protesting students. It had been clever of the board to choose the middle of the long, quiet summer vacation period for their announcement. Some fellow staff members in front of her were crying. Others hugged each other. Most of them gazed at the ground.

Jeppe had come along to help her and to offer moral support. He was holding her hand and squeezing it re-assuringly. Attempting to suppress her welling tears, Ditte looked over her shoulder, away from the emotional scenes in front of her, fixing her eyes on the Baroque relief on the outer wall. A poor decision. The relief—which has by now been removed for being too narrative, just like the po-ems—showed Amphitrite in a turbulent sea. She was be-ing taken against her will by Poseidon on a horse-drawn chariot. The helplessness of Amphitrite resonated with how Ditte felt.

Two broad-shouldered security men stood flanking the embossed mythical scene. Dressed in uniforms and equipped with tasers dangling from their black belts, they ogled Ditte from behind their reflecting sunglasses. One of them tapped his gummy club against his thigh in a casual, impatient fashion. As if he couldn't wait for her to break and misbehave.

Ditte intertwined her fingers firmer with Jeppe's. Clinched to him, she slowly moved ahead in the queue. Inside, transparent stackable boxes, each the size of a kitchen drawer, were piled up next to the reception desk. There was no trace of the familiar friendly receptionist Johnny. Instead, there were four tall men with safety boots from the clearance company the university had hired, and more security staff with clubs and tasers to make sure things ran smoothly.

Looking through the windowpanes, Ditte was sur-prised to see two shipping containers in the rear garden of the faculty. They'd been dropped on the withered lawn between the dry well and the mulberry trees. Someone had hammered wooden signs in the ground in front of their wide-opened doors, reading *Exam & Regulation Archive* and *Residual paper.*

Ditte watched how men and women from the clearance company pushed dollies with crates filled with books, binders and folders into them. The metal containers were painfully yellow, damaged and chipped by frequent use, and covered with profanities. On the long side of one, there was a drawing with Banksy aspirations of a young girl ripping pages out of a book and throwing them in the air, where they formed the shape of a flying bird.

'Next,' the man behind the reception desk shouted. He pushed two boxes against her chest without giving her a second look.

Had it not been for Jeppe, the plastic crates would surely have slipped out of her sweaty hands. He quickly helped her carry them up the spiral staircase to her air-conditioning-deprived office.

Her room was tucked away underneath the attic roof. The July sun made it stifling. Ditte opened the window to let in some air and placed the steel doorstop against the foot of the door to prevent it from shutting.

Jeppe put down the boxes between the things on her mouse-grey desk. His forehead was oily from the heat. 'Do you have the list, Ditte?'

She looked at Jeppe, confused.

'Of things you absolutely have to take with you?'

She started to panic. 'I think I left my phone on the

kitchen table.'

Jeppe put an arm around her shoulder. 'Don't worry. You'll know what you need when you see it.'

Ditte tried to pull herself together and looked around. Apart from her laptop, there was her e-notepad, her four e-pens and, of course, her old-fashioned paper notebooks. Some with pages as thin as tissue paper, others sturdy with leather, oxblood covers. She used them to write down ideas, but increasingly sparingly, aware of the scarcity of paper and the unsustainability of her habit.

The first crate was thus filled up quickly. Then she turned to her bookcase. The two steel racks, one metre wide each and a little more than two metres high, were peppered with pre-drilled screw holes. The collection they supported was a hotchpotch. Works related to her research stood next to gifts from friends and colleagues, and books she used for teaching. Two rows behind each other on each plank. No system. No alphabetic ordering.

Ditte started reading the titles to make a selection, but the words didn't get through. She began over again—*A Short History of Migration, Agonistic Memory and the Legacy of 20th Century Wars in Europe, Imagined Communities...*

Sensing her despair, Jeppe scratched his once fully red, now greying beard. 'Maybe it helps to get them out. To hold the books, to feel what they do to you?'

Reading and thinking hadn't worked so far, she might as well give it a try. She pulled a random book from the shelf. Its black cover was blank. No name. No title.

When Ditte opened it, it turned out to be a work of poetry: *Leaving. A Poem from the Time of the Virus.* Had it been a present? Had she borrowed it? She couldn't remember.

Ditte closed her eyes and ran her fingers over the cloth-bound spine, which was pliant. It had been handled and cherished by others before her. She smiled decisively. 'This one.'

After the first, it went fast. The second box was almost full and Ditte was about to reach for the books on the top shelf when the gritty, dark voice of the Dean broke her dedication. 'Ditte, can we talk for a minute?'

She wasn't expecting him. That he dared to show his face. Ditte almost felt assaulted.

'Eric,' she pronounced his name acrimoniously slowly and swivelled her hand in his direction to indicate he should get on with what he wanted to say.

He casually played with a golden cufflink in the buttonhole of his shirtsleeve, turning it around counterclockwise. 'Don't worry. I bring good news. We're starting a new faculty. No more film studies of course, but hard-core history. It'll most surely be approved by the national accreditation committee. They've already given us the green light, well unofficially. Anyway. We need teachers and thought of you. Our *true* historian.'

The Dean looked at the contents of her second box, his fingers sliding down the books' spines and backs. As he kept talking, he pulled out the book of poetry, and her Ben Elton novel, as well as her copy of *Alias Grace*. 'Your academic publications are spotless. In no way related to the artistic fabrications of the rest of the lot here. Well, what I mean to say is you've got a job if you decide to stay.'

Eric held out the books he had collected and blatantly looked at the office bin in the corner of her room, raising his right eyebrow to make the implied trade-off clear. Ditte was rendered as speechless and motionless as the stone Amphitrite near the faculty's entrance. She was about to knock the books out of his hands, but then her eyes struck the framed photo of her family on her desk, lying on its back.

It must've fallen over when Jeppe put the boxes on the table. The picture had been taken on the beach in West Jutland, Blåvand, near her parents' vacation cabin during a summer holiday. Razi hadn't been born yet. In the photo, Alma and Louna are sitting next to their grandfather near a puddle that remained behind at low tide. Her dad is putting a stick in the water to stir up the wildlife hiding underneath the wet sand grains, to point it out to the girls.

Ditte carefully put the picture upright again. Shaking and nauseous, she took a deep breath. Not looking at the Dean or Jeppe, she plunged forward. The books made a low, dull thud when they hit the bin's bottom.

There's a slight murmur in the back of the lecture hall. The students are getting restless. How long has she been standing there on the pulpit, reminiscing?

Ditte stares into the camera hanging at the back. All lectures are filmed and security officials carefully review all recorded classes.

Ditte is about to raise her fist in the air for the lecture's finale when the heat takes her by surprise. She turned fifty-seven last fall and has gone into menopause about four years ago. At a very late age, luckily. She's like her mum in that regard, who'd been fifty-three as well. Still, while her mother got through it within three years and with few complaints, there doesn't seem to come an end to her transition to the next life stage. The sweat from the hot flash runs over her back.

She quickly takes off her linen jacket and throws it on the stand next to her water bottle. There are dark stains in the fabric. Luckily, she's wearing a sleeveless dress underneath.

Ditte considers her jaded students and changes her mind. 'That's it for today. Out you go.' She sends them off without the obligatory final words.

She knows she'll hear about it. Eric will invite her to discuss her persistent lack of enthusiasm. But she can't bring herself to do it. She'll blame it on hormones. Misogynistic as he is, Eric will buy that. Ditte examines his headshot on the wall with spite. How she'd love to wipe out that winner's smile.

§

The ten-*denier* brown nylons won't come off. Ditte raced back home after her last class to get out of her sweaty clothes, but the tights have glued themselves to her legs. They turn into a second skin when she has had one of her hot flashes. She prefers not to wear them, to go to work barelegged. That would, however, be considered unprofessional.

She finally yanks her tights down with force. They've left a zigzagging mark in the soft flesh below her belly button. She'd pulled them up a lot higher this morning, but they slipped down. The nylons still look clean, yet they smell as foul as her mood. Ditte rolls them into a ball and throws them in the wicker laundry basket in the far corner of their bedroom before unzipping her linen dress. As the garment falls to the floor, it forms a beige circle around her ankles.

She doesn't take off her underwear, a pair of night-blue period panties. Ditte has started to wear them daily. Her menstruation has become extremely irregular. Though most of the time, she doesn't bleed for months on end, it sometimes takes her by surprise.

She lies down on top of the cool cotton bedding on her side of the king-sized bed. The warm late afternoon sun peeks through the half-closed curtains. Resting the back of her head in the palms of her hands, she closes her eyelids to block out the light.

Jeppe is sitting next to her on the bed, stroking her forehead with his thumb. Ditte didn't hear him coming in. She must have drifted off. The tone of his voice is caring. 'Everything ok?'

'I don't know. It's...' Annoyed, she pauses to tug down her panties. They have crawled up between her buttocks.

'What?'

Ditte doesn't want to worry him. She was madly in love with him once. After nearly three decades of living together, those passionate feelings have changed into something different. Not less, mind you.

Sometimes, they've been able to poke life back into the old fire. In the past, she could escape for shorter or longer periods by visiting colleagues abroad and going to conferences. Some time away from each other would be a sure way to revive the passion between them. Today it takes more effort.

Her last conference visit was nine years ago. It had been in Brussels. A city that, although nearby, she'd never visited before. No longer the centre of Europe, more than half of its massive office buildings had been empty when she arrived. Ditte was smitten nonetheless. Not only by the clashing contrasts of the architecture but also by the women.

In Maastricht, local women generally dressed in dark tones and wore high heels, even though the cobblestones on the sidewalks are unforgiving to women wearing them. Brussels had the same cobblestones, but the attire of most *Bruxelloises* was a diverse, incoherent mix of styles, combined with running shoes in bright colours.

The conference was held in a red brick building, a former brewery, on the edge of the Molenbeek district. Once a deprived area, it was at that time the greenest and cleanest part of the city. The place to be.

Ditte presented her then latest work, a paper entitled *Hard History: A Critique of Social Constructivism.* It was a call for returning to the idea of universal, objective knowledge, with immoderate statements like 'Facts aren't multi-interpretable, otherwise they wouldn't be facts'.

Her original argument had been less outspoken, more nuanced, but didn't withstand the ballot of the faculty's research panel. Every publication, conference contribution, speech or research proposal had to have its stamp of approval before leaving the faculty. Ditte had written rebuttal after rebuttal to the panel members. After the millionth policy-rigged message from them, she gave in. There was a limit to the amount of bureaucratic blah-blah-blah she could bear. When the submission deadline for the conference drew closer, she revised the presentation as requested.

Jeppe waves his hand in front of her. It smells like leek and onion; he must've been preparing dinner. 'Ditte?'

She blinks and fixes her eyes on him instead of the middle distance into which she was staring. Sweat is glistening in his beard. When did his hair turn completely white? Why does time seem to pass without her noticing to then confront her with things over and done? With no possibility of undoing them.

Ditte presses the heels of her hands on her eyes as if she can't believe what she's about to say next. 'It's...I used to love my work. To teach. To write. To travel...well, you know that's been off the table for a while. And the hoops they have us jump through. Fill out this form, don't write that, fill out that form, keep track of your hours, publish in those journals...Crudely three to one is the ratio currently. Three times as many staff members who write policy pieces as professors in the classroom.'

'Why don't you go do something else?' Jeppe asks cautiously, sensing the subject to be delicate. The only other career options with her background would be policy work or management. She'd go bananas in a month. As if he has read her mind, her husband adds, 'Or maybe do nothing for a while? I can get a job.'

'And what would you do?' She sounds tetchy, although she didn't intend to. Ditte knows it has been hard on Jeppe too.

She looks at one of his most recent paintings on their bedroom wall. Another cow from above. Realistic and politically unproblematic. Therefore, Jeppe is still allowed to paint and sell his art, but he doesn't dare to tackle any new themes, including the ones encouraged by the government. The guidelines for those are so detailed that a mistake is quickly made. Besides, they hardly leave room for artistic interpretation, which is why Jeppe doesn't want to work on them. As a result, he's stuck in an ever more depressing landscape with white and black dots in green isolation.

Jeppe never complains about the restrictions from the government. Not anymore. Not since he had to give up most of his band shirts and his beloved music albums. But she can tell he's struggling with the imposed limitations. Ditte sees it. Still, she doesn't dare to ask him about it. She cannot take on his grief as well. It's already costing her so much to stay upright. Ditte doesn't want to bother him with that, any more than he wants to burden her.

She shouldn't lash out at him. However, whatever job Jeppe will take on, he'll never make as much as she does. Their mortgage is high and far from being paid off. Razi is still living under their roof. It would be too unmooring. She cannot quit, not yet. Maybe in a couple of years.

Ditte wearily wipes some sweat from her forehead with the back of her hand. 'Sorry. You know me, just venting. There's no need for you to start looking for a job.'

'Will you get dressed then?' Jeppe gets up from the bed. 'For dinner? Remember?'

Ah, yes, how could she have forgotten? Lou and her new girlfriend are coming. It's the first time Lou brings somebody over to meet them. The girl must be something else.

§

Her hair wet from the cold shower, Ditte enters the living room dressed in floral shorts and a lavender T-shirt, the colours of which are only a little faded. The table is festively set. Jeppe used the crimson tablecloth. It used to be white once. He dyed it after they'd spilt red wine on it. He has taken out the fancy vintage cutlery as well. A present from her parents when they migrated to the Netherlands. The silver handles are shaped like fishtails. There are flowers on the table, the colours of which match her outfit. The scents of the pink honeysuckle and purple magnolia in the bouquet are almost overwhelming. Where did he find those at this time of the year?

Jeppe calls from the kitchen, 'They will be here soon. Can you light the candles?'

'It's still light outside.'

'Atmosphere, Ditte. They're not meant to light up the room,' Jeppe jokes—when it comes to daily life, he's as romantic as she is pragmatic. 'The matches are in the cupboard, the black one.'

Ditte goes through the drawers, digging through the collection of old phones, and other broken and obsolete devices. No matches, but there is a stack of photos at the bottom of the last drawer. Pictures from the past. Polaroids of her at a party at the faculty. In one, she's engaged in a visibly animated conversation with Jude. In another, she clings to his shoulder, screeching with laughter.

She hasn't spoken to Jude in years. Not since he decided to shoot campaign videos for the British Conservative Right. Having switched from strong-female-led movies to films with all-male casts after his return to London, his artistic work had already tipped to the conventional side, but with this, he went way over the line. She yelled at him for it during their last video call. They could still call abroad without special permission then. She didn't get how he could commit himself to such a party, to their intolerance.

Jude rudely interrupted her, accusing her of not having been there for him, of showing no backbone. The Conservatives at least had stood up for him. Even in the UK, he had been beleaguered by social media instigators who managed to keep the fire burning with their comments and memes. He owed the Conservative Right. They had defended him. Besides, he needed to do this for his family. To make their lives liveable again. To make a living at all. He'd expected that she, of all people, would understand.

Ditte didn't and still doesn't. In her perception, it's one thing not to speak up and look away, and quite another to actively take part.

The doorbell rings and Ditte quickly shuts the drawer, the photos safely out of sight. About some things one shouldn't think too long. The past won't come back.

She yells to Jeppe in the kitchen, 'I can't find the matches. Have a look, will you? I'll get the door.'

The girl in the doorway next to Lou is remarkably fair. She's much lighter than in the picture Lou showed her on her TOM. There are streaks of green in the brown irises of her eyes, which weren't visible in the photograph either. Despite the heat, Wolfke is wearing a discoloured vinyl jacket over a washed-out summer dress. She's carrying a guitar case on her back, which she puts down on the floor in one smooth movement. The skin on Wolfke's fingers is slightly red and rash-ridden, but the small hand feels cool and soft when Ditte shakes it.

§

They have finished the second course, roast romaine lettuce with tomato lentils, and are sipping on a bubbly frappé with lemon that Jeppe has served 'to refresh the palate'. He's gone all out to make a good impression, having spared no expense or effort. The food is exceptionally good.

Wolfke is sitting across from Ditte. Her elbow on the table, her hand under her chin, she's conversing engagingly with all of them. Ditte is pleased to see how relaxed Lou is around Wolfke. She is too. Wolfke's cheerful disposition and genuine interest in her and Jeppe are contagious.

Ditte has just asked her about her parents.

'My dad used to study film studies in Maastricht. Lou told me you worked for that faculty once. His name is Zac Bleecker. Did you meet him then?'

'Zac...I've known several students with that name. I might have. I'm not sure. It's been years.'

'My dad never talks about that period in his life. It must've been a fascinating time, from a historical perspective. What do you think?'

Ditte swallows her citrusy drink. Can she tell this girl how she feels? Better not. 'I think we should be careful not to romanticise the past. But what about you? You brought a guitar. You play?'

'I brought it because I'm teaching Lou how to. She's good alrea—'

'Really?' Jeppe sits up eagerly, looking at Lou in keen admiration. 'Let's hear!'

'No, no, no, Wolfke exaggerates.' Lou waves her hands crosswise in front of her chest.

But Wolfke is already on her way to the hall to fetch

her guitar. She returns pleadingly pouting and Lou gives in with a theatrical sigh. 'Ok then, but only one.'

'You need to tune it first,' Wolfke says, handing her the instrument.

Lou nods and reaches for her TOM, on which she must've installed a tuning app. She strums the strings and turns the guitar's pegs. When the phone produces a confirming ping, she readies to start playing.

From the first bars, Ditte recognises the song. *Apache* from *The Shadows* is immensely popular these days. The originally instrumental and thus perfectly safe piece from the 1960s is played on repeat in shops and other public places.

Jeppe and Wolfke drum on the table with their fingers to indicate the rhythm. Towards the end, Ditte can't curtail her enthusiasm either and joins in.

'More!' Jeppe shouts excitedly, when Lou has finished.

'I don't know other ones. At least not well enough.'

'Yes you do,' Wolfke exclaims. 'You can play your own.'

'No, no, I don't think that—'

'Come on,' Jeppe tries to persuade Lou. 'We're your parents. We won't judge.'

Lou wavers, but when her father blinks at her, the hesitant expression in her eyes gives way to a smiling one. 'Ok then.'

Before starting, Lou however first plucks at the top string. She listens intently, then reaches for her TOM to tune the guitar again.

'It's a new set of strings,' she explains. 'They detune quickly.'

As soon as the app has confirmed the instrument is good to go again, a simple EM-C-G scheme fills up the room. Ditte knows enough about music to recognise the basic chords. She had piano lessons as a child. Not that she was good at it. After several years, the frustrated tutor had advised her parents to let her quit. Strumming the same strings in a slow and more or less steady rhythm for a while, Lou adds a D to the three-chord sequence.

Then, to Ditte's shock and surprise, Lou starts to sing hesitantly. First a few words and phrases, next a complete verse, which she delivers with more conviction—*It's the story that blew me away. Can't believe they got nothing to say. All for nothing or nothing at all. Need some words just to carry on.*

The song lasts a little less than a minute, but the silence at the table afterwards lasts much longer. Jeppe puts his fork down. Nobody says a thing until Ditte can no longer restrain herself. 'Lou—'

Jeppe slides his chair back. 'Ditte, will you give me a hand with the dessert?'

Resolutely, Jeppe directs her into the kitchen and sits her down on a stick-backed chair at the kitchen table. They repainted the chairs last year, each one in a different colour—green, yellow, pink, red, orange and blue. Jeppe pours her a glass of wine from the opened bottle of Chardonnay in the fridge.

Ditte empties her cup, fuming with anger, then gazes into her glass, vexed. 'Shouldn't we start with the dessert?'

'It's a cheese platter.'

'Did you know?' Ditte eyeballs him furiously. If anyone could've known, it's Jeppe. And if he did, he should've told her.

'No, but don't make a big d—'

'She sang!'

'Come on Ditte, so many people sing in their homes. It's hardly a hanging matter.'

'Hmpf, if she sang an existing song, maybe, but Lou *wrote* this. That makes it an entirely different issue. And it isn't a simple love song. Those lyrics would be considered provocative.'

'Ok, yes, you're right. In principle. But Ditte, didn't you see how happy it makes her? As long as it remains between us, what harm can it do?'

Ditte struggles out of her chair. She's had too much to drink for this discussion. Her head aches and she wants to lie down.

»«

CHAPTER 11

EVELINE

Eveline wants to make sure Wolfke doesn't skip class-es again. She simply can't take Wolfke's word for it. Her daughter has broken too many promises. It's the middle of the night and Wolfke must be fast asleep. With Wofke's TOM in her dress pocket and a small silvery flashlight clamped in one hand, so she doesn't have to turn on the lights, Eveline climbs the stairs to her daughter's room.

She barely ever sets foot on the second floor under-neath the gabled roof. Somehow Eveline almost always manages to bump her head on the oak beams sticking out of the staircase walls.

She and Zac had overlooked the inconvenience when they bought the brick, former farmhouse five years ago, right after her promotion to Head of Permits. It is flanked by ugly 1970s concrete additions from the time when Maastricht was booming and the city overflowed its original borders, swallowing up independent villages around it. When the estate agent showed them around, they believed it would be a unique opportunity. The house has a large garden after all and there is a working well too. With fruit and veg not readily available and generally quite expensive, a potentially fertile plot isn't an unnecessary luxury.

Blinded by the land's potential, she and Zac immediately purchased the place without checking the inside, unaware of the struts' painful presence. The upper floor thus remained unused for years, until Wolfke claimed it for her eighteenth birthday.

Eveline exhales in relief, having made it to the landing uninjured. She clasps her hand around the Bakelite door handle and turns it smoothly. The floorboards creak as she walks inside the bedroom. Freezing, she points the flashlight down and studies the duvet-covered shape on the single bed in the corner of the room.

Nothing. Luckily, Wolfke is a deep sleeper.

Eveline doesn't like going behind her daughter's back. But it's the only way she can think of helping her out and putting her own mind at ease. Tracking Wolfke via the GOFACS on her TOM is the perfect and simplest way to find out about where she is. Still Wolfke always 'forgets' to take it with her. Like all young kids, her daughter regards a phone as uncool. She wants to be out of reach and, most importantly, untraceable.

If Eveline wants her peace of mind, she has to smuggle the TOM into her daughter's schoolbag. Wolfke takes the backpack with her wherever she goes. Never losing sight of it, she treats it like her talisman.

Eveline slightly raises the torch again. Careful not to shine any light near the bed, she searches for the bag. There! Next to the study desk underneath the large sky-light. The desk is actually a pine kitchen table which had been gathering dust in the attic when they moved into the house. The previous owners must've found it too much of a hassle to carry it down the narrow stairs, and left it behind. Eveline and Zac didn't bother either. The table remained forgotten and unused, waiting for Wolfke to find and repurpose it.

Prowling closer like a cat, careful not to make another sound, Eveline crosses the room. She places the back-pack on the desktop. It's a clear night with a bright yellow moon. And while it's still a bit dim inside, she doesn't need any artificial light to see enough for what she's about to do. She turns off the lamp, lays it down on the table and folds the flap of the backpack open. There are doodles on it. They seem to have been carved in with a needle first, after which Wolfke must've filled them up with markers.

Eveline pulls at the zipper, but it doesn't budge. The backpack's brushed fabric has got stuck in it. After some tugging, she manages to partially unzip it. She takes the phone out of the pocket of her dress and sticks her arm into the narrow opening as deep as possible. All the way down to her elbow. After all, she doesn't want Wolfke to notice the phone is in there. When plotting her strategy earlier, she'd considered cutting a hole in the lining and slipping the TOM into it. She abandoned that idea quickly. It would be too difficult and too noisy. Besides, if Wolfke were to find out, Eveline would never be able to talk her way out of it.

She digs around to hide the phone below the schoolbooks and slips her hand out. The moonlight strikes her fingers and she freezes at the sight of them. The crimson familiarity of the blushing spots of ink on her skin and nails sends a shiver down her body. Is it indeed the same pink colour? It can't be.

Anxiously, Eveline reaches for the switch of the reading lamp on the desk rather than her torch, not caring anymore whether she wakes Wolfke. She yanks the zipper open with so much force a few stitches pop, then turns the bag upside down.

Agape, she gazes at the contents. Although hiding in the half shadow of her bent-over body, the stencils and paint cans are visible. The cans are remarkably tiny, small enough to hide in a closed fist. Eveline studies the stencils. Looking at the cut-out phrases, she realises she has seen them many times before on public buildings across town. On the back of the central station. On the sides of the three bridges connecting the separated halves of the city. And on the walls of the place where she works, on *Lumière*. The painted letters made her think of Martin then. Never did she make the connection to her daughter, but the evidence is undeniably smudging the table.

She pushes the templates aside to examine the book that fell out of the bag as well. Eveline recognises it instantly as the Hollywood anthology Martin gave her on their second date—*Most Memorable Movie Scenes*. Wolfke must've taken it out of the trash when she got rid of it a couple of years ago. Eveline has been holding her breath all the time, now she respires loudly.

'Mum? What are you doing?' Wolfke sounds groggy, not fully awake yet. 'I'm trying to sleep. I have school tomorrow.'

'What's this?' Eveline turns around to challenge her daughter, the book firmly clenched in her hands.

Wolfke gapes at her, her eyes wide open. Eveline has awoken her now. Her daughter doesn't say anything. Choosing the wordless offensive instead, Wolfke crosses her arms in front of her chest. The skin on her fingers is irritated as usual. Its red colour contrasts sharply with the white scar on the back of her left hand.

The scar is a reminder of the currently illicit children's books Eveline used to read to her, when still permitted. *We gaan op berenjacht* and *Raad eens hoeveel ik van je hou* were Wolfke's favourites. Eveline doesn't remember which one exactly had given her daughter the nasty paper cut that got infected.

Wolfke forces her lips together until they vanish into a horizontal line. The teenager's proven recipe to flip the tables. It won't work this time.

'It is what I think it is, isn't it?' Eveline decides to ignore Wolfke's mute resistance. 'Well?'

'You always worry about nothing, *Mum*. Lou's mother is exactly the same. At least her dad understands us.'

Her daughter spits out the word 'mum' with disdain. As if it's the most unforgivable thing anyone can be. Mums: always overprotective, overbearing, fretting about everything. Mothers are not to be taken seriously, while fathers can do no wrong, even when they aren't present.

But that isn't what struck Eveline the most. It's the fact that Wolfke mentioned her girlfriend, which alarms her. She knew the girl was trouble the first time Wolfke went out with her. Wolfke didn't come home that night and Eveline had been worried sick.

Eveline clutches *Most Memorable Movie Scenes* more tightly. 'What do you mean by *us*? Does Lou have something to do with this?'

Ignoring her questions, Wolfke furiously gets out from under the bedding and stomps over to her desk. She starts stuffing her things into the backpack. Everything, except for the TOM, which she demonstratively leaves behind.

'Lou is like me. You don't understand,' Wolfke exclaims, swinging the bag over her right shoulder, then turning to Eveline to snatch the book from her hands.

Eveline doesn't let it go. Standing her ground, she gawks into her daughter's green-brown eyes. The emotion reflected in them is the same that Eveline has been trying to forget for decades. She understands it all too well. Better than Wolfke at least, who probably doesn't recognise the feeling for what it is. She and Martin didn't back then. Eveline wishes she'd been aware of it well before they started to hurt each other. It's too late for that, but perhaps she can spare her daughter the same fate.

'Lou put you up to this, didn't she? I knew it. I don't want you to see her again. Wolfke, do you hear me?'

But Wolfke doesn't listen. She runs down the stairs, her sleep-tousled hair dancing angrily on her shoulders. Still holding the book, Eveline goes after her, stumbling down the stairs, and hitting her head on one of the beams. When she finally makes it down with a nasty bump on her forehead, the front door is wide open and Wolfke's coat and sandals are missing from the wardrobe. Her daughter wanted to get away from her so eagerly she left in her pyjamas with a jacket thrown over them. Deflated by this and by what she has discovered, Eveline closes the door and sinks on the tile hall floor.

When Zac enters the hallway twenty minutes later—he must've heard them arguing and decided to lie low; he's so pathetic—she's tearing up the pages of *Most Memorable Movie Scenes*. One by one, film quote by film quote, Eveline rips them apart, to end with Martin's handwritten declaration of love.

§

Eveline is waiting for Kiara on the park bench across from a hyper-realistic sculpture of a charging bear. He's standing on his back feet with his gob wide open, his dangerous sharp teeth exposed. According to the sign, the bronze bear is a nearly exact replica of Jo, who was born here in captivity in 1968 and lived a caged life in the concrete bear pit until he was moved to a proper zoo in 1993. The artists' collective used 3D modelling to make the statue as realistic as possible, feeding an algorithm with all the pictures of the bear they could lay hands on, from every possible angle, to replicate almost every individual hair of Jo's fur.

There used to be a different statue in its place. Something with a giraffe, which is already strange in itself as giraffes were never kept here. The figurine had not merely been misleadingly false but also far too narrative and thus it was replaced by the bear. A logical and better choice, as far as Eveline is concerned.

She and Kiara bonded anew only recently. Their friendship had already been fading in university, and after graduation, their lives took completely different turns. While she had Wolfke to care for, Kiara started working as a legal assistant with the local police. They still met up, once or twice a year, usually on Wolfke's birthday. After her friend had climbed up to become chief of the regional police, they lost touch completely. They hadn't had a fight. They had enjoyed each other's company. But they started to move in different circles. That didn't change when Eveline made it to Head of Permits years later.

How surprised was Eveline when Kiara reached out for help three years ago? Eveline had been looking forward to an evening on her own. Zac and Wolfke were away together for the weekend, on a father-daughter hiking trip. Looking back, Kiara must've known this somehow. Her old friend suddenly showed up at her doorstep with a bottle of Aperol and prosecco. She had brought two large oranges too, an extraordinary treat.

Kiara had aged. There were new lines between her eyebrows and on her forehead—a *triangle of sadness,* or was it thought? She looked good nonetheless. Power suited her. She had dyed her big, loose curls in a plain pink blonde, which softened her expression. The light colour made her more imposing than the bright, darker shades she'd opted for in the past.

Kiara didn't get straight to the point, making Eveline and herself a drink in the kitchen first. She acted as if she'd been at their house for years, although it was her first visit.

'How is Wolfke?' Kiara was cutting the oranges into slices on a wooden board with a red-handled potato knife she'd found in a kitchen drawer.

'Oh, she's so lovely. Smart and beautiful. The last time you saw her...she must've been what, four? She's already fifteen now, a young woman. Wait, I'll show you some pictures.'

Eveline took out her TOM and scrolled through the dozens of pics. Wolfke feeding ducks in the park. Wolfke paddling in the city's public swimming pond. Wolfke in school uniform for her first day at primary school. In a different uniform for her first day in secondary school...

Kiara glanced at the various photos. 'She has a lot in common with you, but I can also see something of Martin in her.'

'Yes, I know.' Eveline smiled pained.

Eveline had confided in her friend when she found out she was pregnant and told her who Wolfke's real father was. She had to tell somebody.

Kiara took her hand and squeezed it reassuringly. 'She's beautiful and she's not him, she's her own person. By the look of her, she'll probably take after you anyway.'

'I need to share something with you too,' Kiara continued when Eveline wiped a welling tear from her eye. 'Can I trust you?'

Eveline smiled warmly at her friend. 'Of course you can.'

Eveline was so happy to see her again. She'd missed her and she was flattered Kiara came to her. Their friendship had meant something and it still did.

Kiara took a deep breath before speaking. 'I met someone. He's from Germany, originally. But he's decent. He is really. He has been here for almost five years. There seems to be something amiss with his file. I'm afraid he'll not get his permanent permit.'

'I'll have a look.' Eveline put her empty glass on a round cork coaster so it wouldn't leave any rings. She reached for her laptop, which had been lying on the kitchen table—she'd planned to get some work done over the weekend. After turning it on, she opened the library with secured files on her GOFACS. 'What's his name?'

'Stefan, Stefan Fischer.' Kiara poured Eveline another Aperol Spritz, adding not one but two slices of orange. The liquid looked black in the computer's blue light. Eveline drank it anyway.

She searched quickly, routinized. There were several people with the same name. Together they looked at the photos of the men on her screen.

'There. That's him.' Kiara pointed at the picture of a blond, bearded man. Not exactly the dark, tall and handsome type her girlfriend used to fall for.

Eveline opened the attached file and studied it meticulously. She'd developed a good eye for details. 'Hmmm, there's a mistake on the forms he filled in on arrival. It says here he entered the Netherlands on November the ninth. There he wrote it was September eleven.'

Eveline pointed out the difference to Kiara, 'See? Nine-eleven and eleven-nine. That'll be a problem.'

Her friend nodded. She wasn't surprised or upset like Eveline had expected her to be. Instead, she fixed her eyes intently and insistently on hers. Kiara coughed before placing her request in a soft voice. 'It doesn't have to be, does it, Eveline? You can change the numbers. Three digits, it's a triviality.'

The problem with trivialities was they were hardly ever that. They almost always pointed to something deeper. To something profoundly disturbing. When Eveline looked at her old friend, however, she could not divest herself of the urge to help.

Thinking back to how easily she had given in to Kiara, Eveline feels ashamed. It's the only time she has bent the rules. She has been extra strict about applying them since. No matter how bad she sometimes feels about it. Like recently with Roy. For her daughter, she's willing to deviate from them again. Maybe she'll be able to stop beating herself up once she has collected Kiara's debt. Especially if she can help Wolfke that way.

She scans the park and catches sight of her friend, who's walking up to her from a different direction than she expected. Kiara is a few metres away and already waving at Eveline enthusiastically. She's wearing a high-collared floral beige dress and mid-calf, brown lace-up boots with block heels. Her hair is still blonde-pink. She hasn't changed the colour over the last few years.

Approaching the bench, Kiara pulls her good old goofy face. She probably wants to cheer her up, she must appear worried. Eveline forces out a thin smile when Kiara bends over to hug her.

'How's Stefan?' Eveline inquires almost immediately, while Kiara sits down next to her.

Her friend peeks over her circular, black sunglasses and gives her a big smile. 'Good, good. Why do you want to know how he's doing? I assume there's a reason you want to meet up here?'

No wonder Kiara is with the police. She instantly picks up on the meaning of the location and Eveline's question. Eveline has never inquired about Stefan before. Not since she changed his status. That she does now means something.

Eveline observes the small group of wild geese that landed underneath some lonely lime trees. There's no one in sight. The nearest 'safety' camera is attached to a tree over five metres away. It's a secure spot for sharing secrets.

She still lowers her voice when putting her cards on the table. 'I want to talk to you about Wolfke. She's heading in the wrong direction.'

'What do you want me to do?'

§

Eveline parks the car in front of their home. When she turns off the engine, the vehicle makes an ominous rattling noise. Probably some part that is about to fall off. She shrugs. At the moment, even the car cannot bring her down. She feels so relieved. Kiara is on board! Surely, everything will be better soon.

She opens the front door and walks through the hallway into the living room. Wolfke should still be in school, but Zac is supposed to be in. He planned to do some work on the wooden floor in the living room, as several boards had come loose. They'd shrunk once too often during the drought last year. The room is, however, empty and Zac hasn't done anything.

Eveline walks into the kitchen. The sliding glass doors that give way to the garden are wide open. The kitchen would've been a dark hole without the big transparent panels. They had to use quadruple solar-resistant coated glass against the heat, which had been ridiculously expensive, but it was worth it. She is glad the competent authorities allowed them to put them in. Their house is listed as protected heritage. It's one of the few things they had been permitted to change. The beams in the staircase and attic, for instance, had to stay.

Zac is sitting outside on one of the wobbly, wired French chairs underneath the walnut tree. He's drinking a beer, straight out of the bottle. She hates it when he acts uncivilised. Eveline opens an upper kitchen cabinet and takes out his vintage Alfa beer glass. It's dusty from disuse. She considers giving it a quick rinse but cleans it with the kitchen towel instead. Though she would've used the tap connected to the underground basin with filtered rainwater, and not the one attached to the drinking water supply, they have to be frugal with the water.

Holding the glass by the stem, she steps into the garden and walks up to Zac over the pebbled path. His old grey shirt with a V-neck is sweaty and covered with splatters of fresh varnish in a hideous glossy turquoise. Nothing in their house has ever been painted over in *that* colour. And if she has a say—which she does—nothing ever will. Zac has probably been doing odd jobs somewhere else again.

Eveline suspects him of working illicitly on the side. He hasn't told her, of course. But besides the paint, there have been other pointers, such as strangers ringing at their door asking for him. She's not going to say anything about it now. One thing at a time. She has enough going on with Wolfke. Besides, she's too excited about her plan. She's convinced it'll work.

Eveline sits down in the chair next to Zac and holds the spherical glass out to him.

Reluctantly, he takes it from her and pours the rest of his beer into the glass. He takes a swig and wipes the foam from his upper lip. 'Lovely day, innit? Not too warm.'

Eveline hums absentmindedly, in her head going

over the details of her scheme.

Zac examines her face and laughs heartily. 'I know that expression. Though I must say I haven't seen it in a while. You're excited about something. Come on. Tell me.'

Eveline can't hold herself back. She knows she should. The fewer people who know, the better. But it's such a great idea. She wants to share it with him. Besides, although he doesn't show it, Zac must be worried too, at least somewhat.

'I have a solution for the problem with Wolfke,' she blurts out.

'I'm glad to hear you talked with her.'

'She doesn't want to talk with me, Zac. You know that. I spoke with Kiara today. She wants to help. Kiara and some colleagues from the police will scare Wolfke a bit. Don't worry. Wolfke won't find out I'm behind it. She won't remember Kiara. Wolfke only saw her a few times when she was a toddler. And if Kiara plays it well, Wolfke will blame her new girlfriend for it, who is a bad influence anyway.'

Zac gawks at her. The whites of his eyes are showing and his voice trembles with incomprehension. 'Are you crazy?'

It would perhaps have been too much to expect him to understand it fully, but Eveline didn't anticipate Zac to be so negative or to care that much. He hasn't been very involved in raising Wolfke. Sure, he has done his share of practical things—registering her for summer camps, driving her to and from them, washing and ironing clothes, cooking meals...Yet, when it comes to the important stuff, to teaching her morals and principles, he has always withdrawn.

'They're not going to arrest her officially.' She tries to sound conciliatory. 'They're merely taking her in for a couple of hours, off the record. That's all. Doing nothing isn't an option, Zac.'

He frowns resentfully. 'But still...to make her friend pay the price for it...What if somebody finds out? It'll be the end of the life we've built together.'

Ah, there it is: his true motivation. He fears it might have consequences for his all too comfortable life. He isn't at all that concerned about Wolfke. Once an opportunist always an opportunist.

'Ha, that's what it's all about, isn't it? You're merely trying to help yourself. Well, you're not gonna stop me from protecting my daughter. Besides, you aren't her *real* father.'

For two seconds, Zac glares at her. When he finally responds, his voice is charged with contempt and sarcasm. 'You gonna play it like that? Sure, you're "protecting" her. You're such a good mother, thinking about her daughter's well-being. Yeah right. *You're* the one who has been lying to her all her life.'

How does he dare to sling that accusation at her? She'd do anything for Wolfke. What good would it have done to tell her Martin is her biological father? A dad in name solely, who Wolfke would search for in vain. Her daughter doesn't need that grief to bring her down.

Eveline would love to hit Zac right in his sorry, smug face. But ever since she became a mother, she has learned to control her temper. No more throwing books around, and hitting men in their balls. While decades later, she can still picture Martin's twisted expression after she'd struck him with one.

Zac is, however, partially right. If her plan is uncovered, Eveline is in danger of being compromised. Her reputation, her position, their life...it would be all up for grabs. It's a huge gamble, but she's running a risk now, too. If someone finds out about her daughter's "art", the whole family will be tainted by association. To a lesser extent, Zac does have a point there. Yet, she *has* to do this. She misses Wolfke too much.

»«

CHAPTER 12

LOU

Lou is lying on her back on her bed. Her breathing sounds irregular. She's exhausted. She and Wolfke just made love, although it's far too warm. In fact, it's too hot to make any movement whatsoever. The only sensible thing to do on a blistering August day like this is to lie or sit dead still.

All shops, offices, and restaurants in Maastricht close between eleven in the morning and six in the evening for good reason. Social and work life come to a halt during the always-tropical days in July and August. The weather keeps everyone in a thrall, but Lou and Wolfke hadn't been able to curtail themselves.

Wolfke is recovering next to her, a hand's length away. The cotton sheets are crumpled up at the foot of the bed. It doesn't matter, they don't sleep under them anyway. Even a sheet is intolerable in this heat.

The curtains are drawn. Nobody in their right mind

lets the searing sun in at this time of the year. Although it's dim in the bedroom, Lou can discern the clutter in it. The elephant ear plant in the corner is withering. Two dead leaves are lying on the ground. Clothes are scattered across the floor: Wolfke's dress, Lou's pants and shirt, and several pairs of panties, which could belong to either of them.

It's been two weeks since Wolfke has moved in, exactly five months after their first date. Lou sometimes feels as if she herself is the one who did. It's not that Wolfke has taken over her place, nor that she behaves like its owner. On the contrary, Wolfke has been rather modest. She only brought one bag. Yet once Wolfke's feet had crossed the doorstep, the space immediately curved toward her. It welcomed her, enclosed her naturally. As if Lou's chairs and table, her shelves and pans, her shower and toilet decided Wolfke had belonged there all along.

Even before Wolfke moved in, they saw each other nearly every day. Wolfke would rush to Lou's work at *Bandito* after her classes. Anxious not to lose time, she'd throw her bike against the outer wall of the coffee shop. Lou experienced a similar kind of unrest. She couldn't explain it away nor could she determine its source. It was an inexplicable turbulence—untraceable and overpowering.

After their first date, Wolfke had given Lou her old beginner guitar, a cream-coloured acoustic western with steel strings. It was about a quarter size smaller than a regular one, fit for children's hands. Whenever the last customer had left *Bandito*, they would practise together.

Given the slim neck of the three-quarter guitar, Lou

struggled with getting the fingering right at first. But she picked up quickly under Wolfke's tutelage. Soon she felt confident enough to improvise with the basic chords. As the melodies formed, the verses came to her, uninvited.

The songs would stick with her for days and weeks, especially when they were still in the making. Her first song...Lou cringes when thinking of it. She knows the lyrics are quite sentimental, that's not why it makes her uncomfortable. It's the memory of the disappointment dripping from her mother's face when she sang it, which makes her feel like cowering.

Nonetheless, to this day, she still writes. Lou knows very well it's illicit. That she has to stop. But the bars which held her imagination captive have been lifted. She *has* to continue.

'Shall I get us some water from the fridge?' Wolfke interrupts her train of thought.

The sound of her voice is fresh and Lou drinks it in. She hums affirmatively.

Her girlfriend gets up from the bed and stretches her arms in the air. Her deft movements cause a light breeze in the desert-like air. There's sweat beading on every bit of her body. It trickles down her back in little streams.

Lou never sweats. Well, never, rarely and if, very little. Instead, to ward off the hot spells, her brown skin turns maroon. Starting with her cheeks, spreading over her forehead into her hairline, going down her neck, the blushed colour finally covers almost her entire body. A faulty mechanism. She always feels roasted rather than cooled down.

Wolfke leaves the bedroom slowly and purposefully. When she returns minutes later, she's holding one of the glass litre bottles. They filled and stacked them in the refrigerator this morning. Wolfke hands her the uncapped flask and curls up next to her.

Lou drinks slowly, the water is too cold to down.

Using her index finger, Wolfke draws imaginary lines on Lou's stomach, below her belly button. 'What do you think I drew?'

Wolfke's tickling touch has Lou feeling a bit drowsy. 'Hmmm, The sun? Or is it a house? I don't know. Can you draw again?'

'How on earth can something look like the sun *and* a house?' Her girlfriend lets out a tittering laugh while her hand slides down. Wolfke's fingertips dance in circles on the responsive swollen red clitoris underneath Lou's pubes.

Languidly quivering, Lou climaxes, a silent sigh lingering on her lips.

§

It was Lou's turn to get them water now. She stands in front of the opened fridge, a new bottle in her hand. She closes her eyes, indulges in the cold that pours from it.

Her girlfriend comes up behind her. Lou didn't hear her coming into the kitchen. She only notices her presence as Wolfke touches her shoulder with her left hand.

With her right, Wolfke points to the top shelf in the refrigerator, to the small rectangular and square packages. There are about twenty, wrapped in brown greaseproof paper. 'I've been meaning to ask you about those.'

'It's soap.'

'Soap?'

'I collect them. Here, look.' Tiptoeing, Lou reaches for the rearmost one. She unfolds the paper. The bar of soap is blue-green. Caught in the middle of the transparent mass is a small pinkish shell. 'This is my first. I get one or two every year. For Christmas or my birthday. They remind me of something significant my dad used to say.'

'You never use them?' Wolfke gazes at the stack.

'No, that would be a shame. They're handmade.' Lou smells the bar. It's as lavender as she remembered.

'Can we not use one? Please? I'd love to soap you.' Wolfke winks at her.

Lou hesitates. 'Well...ok then. But just because it's you.'

Wolfke giggles. 'I didn't know I was *that* dirty?'

Lou decides to go for it. She's going all in, no reservations. 'You're never dirty to me...You know I love you, don't you?'

Lou stares at Wolfke beseechingly. The tension in her chest builds up in anticipation, like the tightening of guitar strings. Wolfke doesn't smile anymore. Her girlfriend's eyes are a starry stillness, bearing away Lou's hope for vocally returned love.

In a couple of seconds, Wolfke pulls herself together

to be her buoyant self again. 'Ah...why put a label on what we feel for one another?'

Afraid of the awkward silence that will surely follow, Lou nods quickly. 'Ok, no labels.'

Lou tries to act casual. But inside her, the steel strings snap, lash after lash.

Wolfke doesn't notice or chooses not to, and holds up the soap. 'A shower, then?'

§

Lou stays in the shower long after Wolfke has got out. She washes and washes herself, over and over again, exhausting all available shower water for that week, until all the soap is used up. Lou wishes she simply could vanish with the violet froth into the shower drain. She feels so effaced by her yearning for Wolfke's stamp of approval.

Lou is about to wrap her long wet hair in the towel when someone insistently knocks on the front door of her apartment. Almost simultaneously there is a yelled command, 'Police. Open up!'

More bangs on the door follow, increasingly louder, combined with the persistent, presaging sound of the doorbell. Alarmed, Wolfke rushes back to the bathroom. Her eyes are as pale as her skin. Her hand shaking, Wolfke questioningly points to the door. Lou raises her shoulders. She doesn't know what's going on either. They've both been careful. Wolfke hasn't been doing any graffiti in public spaces for a while. And Lou hasn't been so foolish to sing her songs outside of the confines of her apartment.

Have the neighbours heard her? Did one of them rat out?

Thank goodness she insisted they'd find a proper hiding place for Wolfke's graffiti material. At first, Wolfke waved her concerns away, but after much discussion, she finally agreed for Lou to hide her stuff under a loose floorboard at *Bandito*, together with Lou's lyrics. The police won't find anything. They have nothing on them. She and Wolfke will be ok.

'Stay out of sight and let me take care of it. They don't know you're here too,' Lou whispers to Wolfke.

While her girlfriend sneaks back out of the bathroom and into the bedroom, another voice raises from behind the front door. This one is lighter, sharper. There must be more than one agent out there. 'Now! Or we will bust the door down.'

'A minute, please. I am not decent,' Lou yells from the bathroom door that opens onto the hallway of her apartment, her voice husky with fear, to realise her robe is on the clothing rack in the bedroom. The towel then. If she holds the ends together with one hand and if she doesn't stand up too straight, she will be able to cover up her intimate parts.

As Lou opens the door, she looks right into the blue irises of a middle-aged woman. The bile in them is so strong that it pushes Lou back into the hallway. The woman's hair is soft pink-blonde and her attire is misleadingly unofficial, consisting of a flower skirt and a short-sleeved collared blouse.

She's flanked by an agent in a traditional street uniform. The agent appears to be about the same age as Lou. It's hard to tell, given the large amount of make-up she's wearing. Bright red lipstick and blue eyeshade—the nation's colours. Her long hair is parted in the middle, and tied in a low ponytail with an orange ribbon.

Without saying anything, the pink-blonde woman, who's unmistakably in charge, holds out her TOM and starts to scan Lou's eyes to check her identity. The agent pushes past them into the apartment, where she opens the curtains one by one, letting in the burning evening sun.

A surge of panic bubbles up inside Lou's stomach. Wolfke! Lou immediately restrains herself. She should keep her cool to get them both through this. Yes, the agent will find Wolfke, but that's ok. Having a relationship isn't illegal.

The TOM bleeps twice and the woman swipes through the information on the screen. Almost simultaneously, the agent returns to the hall, dragging Wolfke along by her wrist.

Standing still in front of the woman, the agent exclaims triumphantly, 'Look what I found.'

The woman smiles and takes her time to inspect Wolfke from a short distance. Wolfke, however, fixes her eyes on the ground.

'Look at me, when I speak to you,' the woman commands.

Wolfke doesn't budge.

The woman waves at the agent, who immediately places a hand on Wolfke's shoulder, her fingers jabbing

229

into the flesh around her collarbone.

'Stand up,' the woman demands again.

The agent pulls with so much dogged determination and force that it must hurt. Red and white blotches appear on Wolfke's skin, next to the officer's dug-in fingers. Wolfke has no other choice and obstinately thrusts out her chin to the woman.

The woman smiles, content at the sight of the loot. '*A good girl*, right? Well, you don't look like a good girl to me.'

Only then does Lou realise Wolfke is wearing *her* pyjamas. Relieved as Lou had been about the graffiti materials and lyrics being out of sight, the shirt had completely slipped her mind. Wolfke must have grabbed whatever was closest to her to cover herself up.

'Like *she* told us,' the agent in uniform cheerfully points with her head in Lou's direction.

It takes a minute before Lou understands what the agent is implicating.

Wolfke, however, gets it right away. 'Lou?' She sounds dejected.

Lou struggles to answer as panic and despair reduce her voice to a pleading near-whisper. 'No, no, I didn't...You *must* believe me. She's lying.'

The agent pulls out a flex steel tie-wrap.

'You can't take her!' Lou intervenes futilely, sounding even softer than before. 'That shirt isn't hers. It's mine.'

Despite her confession, the agent straps Wolfke's hands tightly behind her back.

Transfixed, Lou can only gawp at the unfolding scene. She should've listened. Her mum was right, right, right, all along.

She wants to scream at the officials and cast them an indicting look. But her eyes feel hollow and the sounds are stuck in her chest.

»«

CHAPTER 13

DITTE

She will have to use the spare key. Lou won't like it, but Ditte has no choice. She rang the doorbell a couple of times, then knocked. But the door of Lou's apartment remained closed. Ditte has been messaging her daughter for two days without receiving an answer, so she's concerned. As a mother, she's allowed to be. If Lou is going to be mad at her for not respecting her privacy, so be it.

The key doesn't slide in easily, but Ditte knows the trick. She needs to pull the fire-resistant door slightly towards her, while simultaneously pushing the cylinder up with the key blade to be able to turn the key quickly.

When the door opens, an unexpectedly sweet smell hits her. It isn't the usual sweetness that lingers where adolescents dwell—the combined scents of unwashed young skin, pheromones, and mouldy sandwiches under the bed. Those are there too but mixed up with various other odours fighting for attention: chocolate, citrus, and something reminiscent of freshly mowed grass. The clashing dark-sweet and sour tones are perhaps lovely in themselves, but when combined in a too-strong bouquet, like now, rather stomach-turning.

Ditte hesitantly steps over the doorsill. It's afternoon, but the curtains are wide open. Everything bathes in blinding sunlight. Her eyes adjust to the golden glare that ricochets off the walls. The contours of the more-than-usual clutter gradually emerge out of the excruciating glow. She almost trips over the guitar, lying in the hallway. Its neck is snapped as if it is a victim of a rock concert that got out of hand—not that she has seen any of those in the past two decades.

Drawn by the percussive sound of the soft dripping shower, Ditte pushes open the bathroom door on her left. No one, merely more havoc. She picks up the hairbrush from the chevron-tiled floor. With the back of her hand, she pushes the toppled toilet brush upright. Holding on to one of the shower cubicle's panels, she leans forward to turn off the tap properly.

Ditte approaches the bedroom with caution. If Lou and Wolfke were having sex, she wouldn't want to embarrass them.

'Lou?' she says hesitantly, prepared to be scolded at any moment.

No response, also not the anticipated chastisement.

Ditte peeks in, straining her neck, trying to stay out of sight of whoever might be in there. In the corner, next to the bed, there's a knocked-down elephant ear plant on the ground. The leaves are bleached to a brown as light as parchment. No Lou.

Ditte felt worried yet now she moves up a gear into a motherly state of fear reserved for acute danger. When the kids were younger, the usual anxiety popped up when they ran a high fever. Or when they crossed the streets without looking out for fast-driving traffic coming their way. And of course, it was there to accompany Lou's nightly parasomnia attacks. When she was under ten, her daughter suffered from what the paediatrician called night terrors or sleep terrors.

Whatever the right name was, it meant Lou would scream incessantly for half an hour during the night once or twice a week. She would be extremely upset, shakily pointing at an empty corner in the room, exclaiming 'there, there, there', seeing something or someone that wasn't present.

The first time it happened, it felt like a nightmare to Ditte and Jeppe. It was so incredibly alarming. It wasn't harmful, said the doctor they had rushed to see the next day. He reassured them that while Lou might seem awake during the fits, she wouldn't have any recollection of them, as she was asleep, even though her eyes were wide open.

Night terrors were relatively common in young children, the paediatrician claimed. It had something to do with the brain's development and eventually, Lou would grow out of it. In the meantime, there was nothing they could do, besides waiting and making sure Lou didn't hurt herself. Indeed, it didn't bother Lou. She didn't remember any of it, as the doctor had said. Ditte did all the more.

Rushing from the bedroom to the living room, Ditte yells out Lou's name. She couldn't care less about receiving a rebuke. She'd be relieved to get one. There's no one there either. Yet the smell, that sickening floral scent, is getting stronger. There's something feral about it. Where's it coming from?

Ditte walks through the sweltering chamber. The jeans-blue sofa is bathing in the sun. One of the curtains has been pulled roughly from the railing. It's half torn. She tries to shut a sheet that is more or less in line to block some light, but it doesn't budge. There's nothing here that explains the smell either, but it is more intense on this end of the room, near the kitchen. She almost gags. It must come from in there. Ditte holds her breath and opens the kitchen door.

Although she was ready for the worst, the sight of her naked child on the kitchen floor is startling, but she feels relieved to have found her. Lou sits in front of the widely opened fridge, which is whizzing frantically. It's futilely trying to cool its meagre contents, something that resembles leftover lasagne and a pack of vanilla-flavoured soy yoghurt. Lou is bent over, her vertebrae visible under her light russet skin.

It's the same position her daughter used to adopt when she was younger, when playing or reading. Something she always did on the floor and in hardly more clothes than panties or shorts, especially during summers.

Now, she's surrounded by crumpled-up pieces of brown baking paper and semi-liquid puddles in lush oily-ish colours—a dark hibiscus pink, a deep buzzy yellow, a carroty stark orange, a scintillating lime green, and a clear cobalt with glitter.

Her soaps, it crosses Ditte's mind. It are the soaps Lou has been collecting. Her daughter loves those soaps, why would she waste them like this?

'Lou?' Ditte breathes out the air which she took in in the living room—a sigh expressing both relief for having found her child and fear about the apathy that is holding her captive. The smell must have inebriated Lou.

'Lou?' Ditte is careful not to respire through her nose.

Ditte lightly touches her skin below her daughter's neck and then Lou bursts into tears. Her sobs crash through her sweaty chest. The solace Ditte felt for finding her child is instantly washed away by the wave of Lou's anguish.

'She's gone, Mama,' Lou manages to make clear in hiccupping despair in between two series of sobs. 'Wolfke...she...she broke up.'

Ditte is lost for proper nouns and verbs, let alone adjectives, to counter Lou's breakdown. Lou is clinging to her like a floater. And all Ditte manages to say is her daughter's name.

§

236

Ditte doesn't know how long they've been sitting there, embraced. The fridge casts a dark blue shadow over them. Dawn must be about to offer its cool release outside. Inside, the daily heat is dampening. Water drips down from the open fridge door, forming a fine trickle on the vinyl that evaporates before it can reach her right leg on which Lou is resting her head. Her daughter is finally calm—or rather drained. Ditte is exhausted from the emotions too. The fridge is no longer whirring and its light is out as well.

Ditte is painfully aware that her leg, the leg which Lou has turned into her haven, has gone to sleep. With her available right hand, she massages her thigh. A series of tingles shoots down to her calf, causing a cramp in her foot. Much as she doesn't want to disturb Lou's peace, she can't last much longer. She's too conscious of her discomfort. Her lower back has also started to hurt. Her tailbone is pressing through her skin on the hard floor, a concrete slab with a thin layer of linoleum, probably without any underlay. That'll be a bruise for sure. It can't be comfortable for Lou either.

'Lou?' she whispers.

Lou slowly turns her head towards her. Her daughter's eyes are extremely wide. The dilated pupils nearly completely wiped out her green-brown irises. It's a terrifyingly empty look.

'Let's go home.' Ditte consciously bolsters up the final word 'home' with fresh air of reassurance.

Lou scrambles to her feet in silent agreement. Thankful, Ditte follows Lou's example and stamps her foot on the ground to bring some life back into it.

'We should get you some clothes.'

Limping a little, and holding on to the wall, Ditte hobbles out of the kitchen, checking after every second step that Lou is following.

'Mum?' Lou's voice doesn't sound like her at all. It's fragile and lacking her usual confidence.

Lou is sitting on the bed behind her, while Ditte is going through the clothes on the floor. She's looking in vain for clean items, stuffing whatever is wearable in the zipped open gym bag she found near the dead plant. There was dirt on it. The inside, however, was clean enough. When she hears Lou's voice, another surge of panic bubbles up inside her stomach.

'Mum?'

Trying to ignore her apprehension, Ditte smiles at Lou and encourages her to go on.

Lou waves one hand at her dejectedly. 'No, never mind.'

It's important not to push her. To let Lou tell the story, *her* story, on *her* terms. That's what Jeppe would say, Ditte reminds herself. And nobody knows Lou better than Jeppe. Lou will tell her whenever she's ready.

Ditte holds out a pair of black cotton knickers to Lou that appears to be unused. 'Here. Don't worry, we've got time.'

Lou barely manages to stick her legs into the holes of the underwear. Ditte has to help her to pull them up over her buttocks. Lou's whole body is shuddering. Not visibly, but Ditte can feel it when touching her, like the cold sweat on her skin. It's extremely warm in the apartment, but Lou seems almost frozen to death. She needs to get some clothes on her. Ditte pulls a sweatshirt over Lou's head and finds a pair of shorts.

Now shoes. There's only a pair of white courts in the bedroom closet. Lou wore them once, on her high school graduation day to please her. They bought them together, or more truthfully, Ditte bought them for Lou. Lou couldn't properly walk in them back then. In her current state, she won't be able to put one foot in front of the other. Of the sneakers Lou usually wears, Ditte can locate just one, buried under the bed. She finally finds a couple of scuffed Havaianas with dark blue soles and yellow-green straps in the bathroom. Those will do.

Swinging the sports bag with her left hand over her shoulder, Ditte uses her other hand to support Lou along the way from the bed to the front door and beyond.

§

Ditte looks concerned at the full plate Jeppe brings back into the kitchen. He's gone all out to make the æggekag. Jeppe's vegetarian version of the traditional Danish omelette, for which he uses thinly sliced potatoes, onion, garlic, and chives, is one of Lou's favourites. She didn't taste it.

Since they arrived back home, Lou has been lying on the couch in the living room under a blanket for days. Jeppe has been channelling his love and care into preparing meals he knows Lou likes. Mostly simple comfort food from her childhood. He has done so tirelessly, putting in his best, spending nearly a month's grocery budget on the needed ingredients, but everything comes back practically untouched. Lou didn't take more than two bites from Jeppe's *risalamande* yesterday either, though it had taken him almost two hours to cook the rice dessert.

Apart from the few words in the apartment, Lou hasn't spoken about what has happened. All Ditte has found out since is that Wolfke doesn't respond to Lou's messages or calls. Not that Lou told her this. Ditte has gathered so much from the fact that all Lou has done is stare at her TOM, at a screen filled with her own messages and echoes of unresponsiveness.

Ditte takes the plate from Jeppe and touches the golden omelette with the top of her index finger. Cold, not yet chewy, still edible. She takes a fork out of the kitchen drawer behind her, which turns out to be part of the good cutlery. The silver one with the mermaid handles.

It should be stored away in the black cabinet in the living room. The fork must've been misplaced after they last used it; when they had dinner with Wolfke and Lou. Ditte puts the fork down on the countertop and reaches for a regular one for daily use. She'll put the fancy one back where it belongs later. First, she needs to eat something. She hasn't had lunch herself. If she wants to keep her nerves, she mustn't start to skip meals as well.

Ditte chews and swallows without tasting, sighing in between almost every two bites. This has got to stop.

She needs to know what happened to be able to help Lou. Hastily, Ditte swallows the last soggy chunk of egg and potato. With a loud clang, she resolutely puts her plate down. Picking up the mermaid fork, she strides into the living room.

Lou is lying on the saggy old couch with a sand-blue quilted blanket pulled over her head. Her knees are pulled up, her body is curled into a crescent shape. The curtains are closed. She seems fast asleep, but Ditte knows better. Lou's breathing is too shallow and her position is off. Her daughter always sleeps on her back with her arms stretched out next to her head, like a starfish. She usually grinds her teeth as well. Over the years, Ditte has got so used to the sound of her daughter's tooth enamel grinding down, that it has become soothing. Now it is uncannily silent.

Ditte sits down on the end of the corner sofa. A spring presses against her thigh through the couch's fabric cover. The sofa has seen better days. Once a bright lilac, it has turned into a faded mauve. She should ask Jeppe to repair the spring. He's good at that sort of fixing.

She places her empty hand on Lou's bare feet, which stick out from under the throw. 'Lou?'

Lou grumbles and pulls her feet up, away from her touch. The tiny movement is enough to chase away Ditte's patience. A resounding decisiveness takes over instead. Patience will only get you so far. Sometimes it's necessary to be resolute. She needs to know the full story, that's why she is a scholar at heart. Though her academic work has little to do with taking a stance or telling true stories these days, isn't it the one thing that counts in this world? All that matters in the end is whose story is being heard and believed. And if someone deserves to be seen, it's her daughter.

Ditte abruptly pulls down the quilt, exposing Lou's blank eyes, which are partially hidden behind a cascade of curls. In the diffused light in the room, the usual caramel colour of her hair turns auburn.

Ditte grabs Lou by her wrist and firmly points the mermaid-silverware at her as if it is some sort of weapon or magic wand. 'Lou, you have to tell me. What happened?'

Lou stares down at the fork, surprised. Her lips part a little, like halves of yellow-white cockleshells. Ditte used to collect them with her father during holidays as a child. The little air bubbles rising through the sand at low tide would give them away. Lou clenches her jaws together again.

Somewhat ashamed of her outburst, Ditte lowers the utensil. 'Lou?' she tries one last time.

'It's no use, Mum,' Lou whispers and turns on her side, her back to her mother.

Ditte sighs and gets up to put the utensil back in the cupboard. She randomly opens a drawer. It turns out to be the one with the Polaroids showing her and Jude, and not the one with the cutlery. She angrily tosses it in nonetheless.

It'll get better. Lou will learn how to cope with the

loss. Or rather, she'll accept it. Like they all have. Like she has when first losing her best friend Jude, then her former job and colleagues.

However, unlike Ditte, her daughter can't turn to her favourite artworks, literature and songs to get through it. Albeit they are forbidden, Ditte can revisit them in her mind in times of need. That has proven to be tremendously helpful.

A poem by Bishop, which she got to know so well, as it used to hang opposite the pulpit in the lecture hall, has become her main refuge. The realisation that a person from such a different day and age had felt the same way as she did, that this long-dead poet could reach out to her, always reassured her. If everything else was lost, they couldn't take that away from her. Lou, however, doesn't have a lot to revisit, apart from a few children's tales and nursery rhymes.

Suddenly inspired, Ditte reaches for one of the Polaroids. She might as well give it a decent purpose. Taking a pen from another drawer, she sits down at the dining table to write on the back of the photo. She knows it's technically illegal and normally she wouldn't think of doing it, but desperate times call for desperate measures. The blue ink bleeds a little on the glossy paper, yet Ditte makes sure every word is legible:

> *The art of losing isn't hard to master;*
> *so many things seem filled with the intent*
> *to be lost that their loss is no disaster.*

...

*—Even losing you (the joking voice, a gesture
I love) I shan't have lied. It's evident
the art of losing's not too hard to master
though it may look like (Write it!) like disaster.*

A soft grinding noise fills up the room. Lou is sound asleep now. Ditte puts the pen down. Careful not to wake her daughter, she walks over to the sofa to quietly place the picture on the armrest next to Lou's head, making sure it's the first thing she sees when she wakes up.

§

The walled former farmhouse where Wolfke and her family live is largely overgrown with Virginia creeper and clematis. Both are strikingly straw-coloured. The clematis desperately holds on to some lonely purple, nearly black flowers.

Her daughter might not want to tell her what happened, but maybe Ditte will discover more here. Lou would hate her for doing this if she found out, yet Ditte can't leave her to languish. It might turn out to be a misunderstanding. Maybe Wolfke and Lou aren't lost.

Ditte checks the address on her phone once more. There's no house number on the building. Or at least she can't find it, still this must be the right one—37. The apartment block on its other end starts with 39, 39a, b, c and so on.

Ditte idles impatiently in front of the honey-coloured brick building. There doesn't seem to be a door anywhere. Taking a few steps back to the cobbled street, she scrutinises the farmhouse carefully. She walks around it hoping to find an entrance somewhere in its brick rampart. Nothing. Not even a window.

She peeks through the wilted layers of leaves covering the front and scans the bricks. Then, finally, wood, almost the same deep yellow colour as the bricks. She pushes against it and the gate, it is indeed a gate, gives way. With both hands, she pulls the desiccated Virginia stems aside and stumbles, headfirst, over the bluestone threshold.

The courtyard she finds herself in is an unexpected oasis of greenery. It's sheltered by the coolness of the four high brick walls and the generous shade cast by the overhang of the gabled roof. To have a garden is already a luxury. To have a garden like *this* in the middle of an otherwise dried-out city is an absolute privilege.

The draw well in the middle must provide the vital water for the plants and trees to grow so lushly and in such numbers. There are small decadent fruit trees, peaches and lemons, a fig, a walnut *and* an almond tree, and the flowers are unusually bright. Poppies and purple coneflowers mostly. In the corner, there's a widely leafed banana tree with real bunches of bananas. They are small ones, no bigger than a children's hand. Still, Ditte hasn't seen a banana in years.

A slender woman is standing next to the tree. Her upper body is turned to the gate and she's staring right at

Ditte, a still-dripping metal watering can in her hands. Everything about her is remarkably light. Pale legs in ecru linen shorts, ivory arms in a white loose shirt. There are silvery slippers on her feet.

The rose-golden necklace with a large pendant she's wearing, however, feels out of place on her. At first glance, the pendant appears to be what Ditte knows as the Hamsa Hand or Hand of Fatima. The unfolded hand with two symmetrical thumbs is a religious symbol, often associated with motherhood. Forbidden of course, and indeed, it isn't. The pendant is shaped like a real hand.

It strikes Ditte how the woman is so visibly Wolfke's mother apart from the frown and laugh lines, which embellish her eyes and mouth. There are grey streaks in the hair near her temples too, which he has tied up in a careless bun. The signs of age make her beautiful in an authoritative way.

Eveline is staring at her reprovingly, and Ditte hastens to explain herself. Her long earrings dangle along politely. 'I'm sorry for bothering you...I didn't mean to trespass. I couldn't find the front door or the doorbell.'

Wolfke's mother puts the can down and narrows her eyes.

Ditte takes a step forward and reaches out her hand. 'I'm Ditte. Lou's mum, I was hopi—'

Before Ditte can finish her introduction, Wolfke's mother shuts her up incensed, 'Lou's mum huh? You have a lot of nerve to come here after what your daughter did.'

Ditte didn't expect a warm welcome, but she hoped

they could talk from one concerned parent to the other. Surely, being a mother herself, Eveline would understand that she wants to make sure her child is safe and happy. She hoped they could have a cup of tea together or something else to break ground. The hostile reaction throws her off completely.

'I'm sorry? I don't know...what do you mean? My daughter? Your daughter has...' Ditte restrains herself. She shouldn't start making accusations, that'll get her nowhere. She reformulates her last sentence. 'Lou, I mean, *Lou* has been heartbroken, she doesn't eat, doesn't sleep—'

Eveline utters a short, dry laugh, putting down the watering can. 'Well, that serves her right. A *whole night*, do you hear me, a *whole night* Wolfke spent in jail. All because your precious Lou told on her. To save herself. Luckily, Wolfke got away with a warning. It could've been a lot worse. She was wise enough to tell your daughter to get lost afterwards. And *I* don't want anything to do with *you* either.'

Raising her voice, Eveline has come closer, pointing her index finger at Ditte. She's close enough for Ditte to determine the colour of her polished nail. A pearly berry.

Shrinking and turning back, almost tripping over the threshold on the way out, Ditte tries once more, pleading on behalf of her daughter. 'Please Eveline, may I say Eveline? Can you at least tell Wolfke that Lou misses her, that she loves her...she should talk with her.'

Eveline watches her benignly, her necklace glinting in a streak of sunlight that got around the walls lining the courtyard. 'Wolfke *shouldn't* do anything, and neither should I. Now get out of here!'

§

Ditte and Jeppe are sitting at the kitchen table, the door to the living room securely closed, not risking any chances of Lou overhearing them. Ditte has just told him about her meeting Eveline.

'I don't believe her,' Jeppe speaks softly. 'Lou would never do something like that.'

Ditte nods in agreement. 'No, I don't think so either. If she did, however, she must feel extremely guilty.'

'She didn't, Ditte.' Jeppe sounds slightly agitated.

'You're right. Of course not. I'm shocked they arrested Wolfke. I hope they don't come after Lou too. We don't know what Wolfke told them. If she thought Lou was behind it, who knows what Wolfke would be capable of.'

'And Lou still doesn't want to talk about it?'

'No, I think she's mad at me.'

'Hmm yeah, you should've asked her if she was fine with you going to talk to Wolfke's mother.'

'I'm not worried for nothing, am I?'

She's hoping for his usual catchphrase, that everything will be fine. That's not what he says. 'No. And it isn't just the police I'm concerned about. She's wasting away here, Ditte. And not only Lou. Perhaps Alma and Razi are more like you. But don't be mistaken. They're suffering too. I mean, you don't feel happy with your work anymore either. Maybe, it's not a bad idea to...'

She eyes him inquiringly.

Despite having started his speech passionately, Jeppe hesitates for a moment. 'Well, to be honest, I think we should get away. Your parents' holiday home...a change of scenery will be good for all of us. And in Denmark, Lou's allowed to be herself. No constraints on creativity there. You know your parents would love to have us close. They miss you and the kids. Your father is getting older. He's no longer at his best. Your mother can use our help. I know it would be a strenuous journey, but it might be worthwhile.'

'You want to move there permanently?' Ditte gasps.

They have given up so much to stay in the Netherlands, to lead a life of relative comfort and to have some financial security. It isn't so easy to leave that behind. Ditte knows it's her fault they are in this situation. She should never have taken that job when Eric offered it to her. Instead, she should have packed them all up to flee the country. The thought of uprooting the children, who were still doing well back then, kept her from it. She believed she was doing the right thing.

'Perhaps...why not? But perhaps we should think of it as a long vacation first. Start with a month or so, or two, maybe three?' Jeppe responds. 'Let's go and see how we like it. We don't have to make a final decision yet.'

If they go there, they will most likely not return. It'll be nearly impossible to enter the Netherlands again. Jeppe too must realise this. And yes, the regime is less strict in Denmark, but she knows from her parents how hard it is to make a living there too. She's gathered as much from their sparse letters that get through the border control. They had given up on emailing, as their messages would hardly ever break through. GOFACS considers Denmark a dangerous country by default after all. The envelopes of the letters are also always torn open when they arrive. The customs officers read them first, before sending them on.

Not that life was so easy here, but in Denmark, they'd have to start all over. Lou, Alma and Razi would have to brush up their language skills before they'd be able to find work or continue their studies. And it remains to be seen whether she herself would be able to get a position at a Danish university. Ditte doubts it. She's tainted by the 'academic' work she has done here. She'd be lucky to get a job as a high school teacher.

Ditte gets up to open the kitchen door and peers at her daughter's back to confirm what she already knows. That it's necessary, that it's vital. She can do this, will do this. *The art of losing isn't hard to master.*

She turns to Jeppe and smiles at him precariously. 'Okay then.'

»«

CHAPTER 14

EVELINE

Lou's mother has been gone for quite some time, but Eveline is still worked up. As she paces around the garden, she knocks over the half-full watering can. She curses. At least a litre of water flows onto the brown cracked soil before she can put the metal thing upright again. Aimlessly, the water seeps into the fissures in the dry clay earth without reaching any plants. What a waste.

She doesn't like gardening that much, but it is the elite's national hobby. It's always safe to talk about gardening after all; an innocent way to display concern for the withering environment. Not that those few gardens make a real difference to the irreversible climate change that set in decades ago. They are merely symbolic. But besides it being a prestigious project, gardening has become a necessity. Fresh produce in the grocery stores has become ridiculously expensive, when it's there, which is not always.

With ever-expanding periods of drought affecting the garden, she has to apply all kinds of tricks to ensure the plants can make use of the water she feeds them. Eveline has built little earthen dams around the flower and vegetable beds. In addition, she has dug in empty plastic bottles close to the roots of the fruit trees and the berry bushes—currants, gooseberries, and wild raspberries, her favourites. The bottle openings point upwards and protrude above the ground. She has poked a few holes in the bottoms before burying them, so the water poured into them is released slowly and where it is needed the most.

With the watering can in her hand, Eveline pushes open the two-metre-wide glass sliding door to the kitchen. Still half-blinded by the sun, she puts it down on the chestnut kitchen counter, next to the under-mount sink.

'I don't recognise who you are anymore,' Zac hisses sharply. The unexpectedness of his words startles her. They reverberate on the kitchen's drummed ceiling and the echo intensifies the contempt with which he charged them.

Eveline turns around. She didn't notice him when she walked in, yet Zac is sitting at the kitchen table. She still can barely make him out. Red and blackened after-sun gobs are obstructing her vision. She blinks and rubs her eyes.

'How could you do that to that poor woman?' Zac spells out the reason for his accusation.

She can see enough now not to miss the resentment on his face. His cobalt blue eyes are narrow, his eyebrows objectionably point downwards, and the vertical wrinkles on his forehead are darker than usual. One hand holds a cup of steaming coffee, the other is clenched beside it on the tabletop. Zac must have overheard the shouting match with Lou's mother.

Eveline inhales sharply before launching her offensive. 'She's a mother fighting for her child. Sending her on a wild goose chase wouldn't have helped.'

Zac rubs the bridge of his nose with his thumb and index finger. 'She's a kind woman, Eveline. I know her, sort of. I took some classes with her.'

'So what?' Eveline pushes back. 'As if I could've told her the truth? Imagine that. Telling her *I* set it up? It would've been all for nothing then. What good would that have done?'

'Still, you could've been nicer. You could've simply said you didn't want to talk about it. That it's not your business and that the girls should sort it out on their own. She's smart—what if she catches wind of what truly happened? We wouldn't want to attract any attention. With my history, it's better to lie low.'

She should've known. Zac doesn't care about Lou's mother, about her, or Wolfke. It's always about *him*. He takes a swig of coffee while holding his mug tightly, his knuckles whitened. There's a picture of a half-naked woman on it—a vintage pin-up girl rendered in black and white. It's his favourite mug. Eveline hates it. She has told him so many times. Now, it works on her like a red rag to a bull.

Making a theatrical gesture with her hands as if to

wave Zac away, she ends their conversation. 'Offense is the best defence, Zac. And it's happened already, so this discussion is pointless. Besides, I have work to do. I need to prepare tomorrow's cases.'

§

Wolfke is humming a tune when she arrives home after school. It's been a while since she has been so cheerful. Ever since her "arrest" last month, she has looked a bit dejected. Today, she even kisses Eveline on the cheek. Eveline can't remember the last time she did that. Normally her heart would've leapt, but now she's alarmed. It's a Judas kiss. Her daughter is putting on an act.

Wolfke perches on top of the kitchen table, next to the gold-wired fruit basket, her legs dangling in the air. She takes out one of the figs which Eveline picked this morning and takes a vigorous bite of the pink flesh.

Eveline was monitoring her daughter on a daily basis until last week. Right after Wolfke spent a night in jail, it had been relatively easy to convince her to take her TOM with her everywhere she went—'You never know, Wolfke. You understand why it's necessary, don't you?'

Her daughter had readily complied. Eveline checked her whereabouts every other hour. She also called the head of the school at the start of each day to ask if her daughter had indeed arrived. Wolfke is smart and might perhaps have given her phone to a classmate to trick her.

It all worked well at first, but then Wolfke started to complain that Eveline was treating her like a prisoner on probation. Zac chipped in as well, taking Wolfke's side instead of doing what was needed to protect her daughter. He believed Eveline was overreacting, that she should trust Wolfke.

Eveline knew she shouldn't have given in. She received the dreaded call from the head teacher that her daughter had skipped school again this morning. It was followed by a stressful day of not knowing where she was, as Wolfke had turned her phone off.

Zac told her not to worry, that Wolfke would come home soon and all would be well. Indeed, she got back at the usual time as if it had been a normal school day, acting all innocent, eating figs for goodness sake. But apart from that, nothing is right. It all feels too repetitive.

Eveline is about to call her out when Zac opens the sliding door from the garden to the kitchen. The window rubbers squeak. He had gone to the grocery store and is holding a jute tote bag in each hand. He glances at Eveline, trying to assess the situation—is it safe to enter or is he interrupting a fight?

'What's for dinner, Dad?' Wolfke mumbles in between two mouthfuls of the succulent flesh of a second fig.

Zac steps over the threshold and places the grocery bags on the table. 'I'm thinking of pesto pasta. There's enough basil in the garden. Maybe you can go out and pick some, Wolfke?'

'Later,' Eveline interjects. 'First, you need to tell me where you were today, Wolfke.'

'What do you mean, where I was today? At school of

course.' Wolfke doesn't blink as she lies and takes another bite of fig.

'School called. You weren't there. And you turned off your TOM as well.'

Wolfke wipes the fruit juice from her chin with the back of her hand.

'Where were you?' Eveline insists.

'Why's that your concern?' Wolfke obstinately thrusts out her chin.

'I'm your mother. I care. I've been worried sick.'

'Bit overblown, don't you think? I arrived in time for dinner. Dad isn't worried.'

'Leave me out of it,' Zac answers, as always taking the chance to get out of a difficult situation. He couldn't get out of the kitchen fast enough, back into the garden.

Wolfke jumps off the table and is about to follow him outside when Eveline grabs her arm. 'Where were you?'

Eveline clasps her hand tighter around her daughter's upper arm, until her middle finger and thumb touch. She stares sharply into Wolfke's eyes. A sparkle in them lights up as Wolfke tries to pull loose.

'I was with Lou, ok!' Wolfke shouts when she finally manages to tear away from her. She rubs her reddened arm. 'Happy now?'

'Lou? Why...After what she did to you?'

'She didn't, Mum. I talked with her. She had nothing to do with it.'

'Can she prove that?' Eveline asks, knowing she

can't.

'She doesn't have to. I believe her.'

The bitter taste of fear smacks Eveline in the mouth. She'd been prepared for it all, she had her story ready. She'd planned to lie through her teeth if Wolfke found out about her involvement. But of all the scenarios she had imagined, none included Wolfke believing the words of her sweetheart.

Eveline is painfully aware there isn't anything she can say to make a difference. Nothing can match irrationality, especially when paired with blind love. She has to try however.

'Believe, believe?' Eveline yells in ever-greater despair. 'What good is believing?'

As she expected, Wolfke rolls her eyes.

§

Eveline hasn't heard from Wolfke in weeks, and she has no idea of her whereabouts. Neither does Zac, or her friends from school. Her daughter has vanished without a trace, just, as it turns out, like her girlfriend Lou.

A day after their fight, Wolfke left without a word of warning. Her wardrobe was empty and her guitar was gone. Eveline went over to Lou's family house hoping to find her there, but the brick terraced building was vacant. A moving company was blocking the curb and bringing in the belongings of a new family.

Her greatest fear has become true. Her daughter has cut the cord, the unbreakable bond between them. It hurts more than she could have ever imagined. The pain of losing her is unbearable.

To stay sane, Eveline keeps herself busy in the garden. For the past two days she has been collecting walnuts from the tree in the back. Yesterday, her mind drifted off to Wolfke nonetheless, and she ripped off the skin of the palm of her hand with the pointy pieces of crushed shells. The wound began to bleed. Yet she continued gathering walnuts and spread them out on the carpet in the living room to make sure they dried well.

When they bought the farmstead years ago, Eveline and Zac had assumed the walnut tree was dead. They started renovating the building first. When they finally took on the garden half a year later intending to chop the tree, they were surprised to find it fully leafed.

Maybe it will happen like that between her and Wolfke as well. Perhaps her daughter needs a little time to see and understand how much her mother loves her, and that she has her best interests in mind. But Eveline simply can't wait for that to happen. At the least, she needs to know where Wolfke is and that she's ok.

Kiara has promised to dive into it, to use her contacts and position with the police, pull some strings. Now, finally, there seems to be news. Her friend invited her to meet her in *Café Meuse* on the *Onze Lieve Vrouwenplein* to discuss it.

The park isn't secure anymore. According to Kiara, they put up more surveillance cameras. Her friend's apartment isn't an option for the same reason. It's constantly observed for general safety reasons. Kiara thought the bar would be a better choice. It's a calm place and she knows the owner.

For a moment, Eveline considered suggesting her house to meet, but Zac is moving out today. With Wolfke gone, there's no reason to pretend anymore. He found a flat in the blink of an eye and has managed to secure a regular job as a cleaner. She can't believe they hired him. He must have lied on his resume. Zac should have known better. The truth will come out at some point. It always does. That's no longer her concern though. Still, she didn't want to see him go so she agreed to see Kiara in *Café Meuse*.

Shortly after sunrise, she leaves their house—or is it merely her house now? To get to the bar, she has to take the bus to the city centre. Zac has claimed the car. It's the only thing of value he'll take with him. Eveline doesn't care. She hated that car anyway and she can register for a new vehicle. It's going to be one from the modern range. No more vintage rubbish.

The self-driving, nearly transparent bus arrives exactly on time. There are three other people on it, each of them sitting in a separate far end. Staring out through the acrylic glass, no one says a word to her. Eveline doesn't greet them either. She scans the ticket on her TOM, sits down in the last empty corner and fixes her eyes on the outside surroundings as well.

There's soft music playing in the background. Some classical piece she doesn't know. No lyrics, so within the rules. Her mind drifts off to Wolfke, and she doesn't consciously register the buildings and the sparse trees as they flash by. Eveline is thus surprised when she reaches her destination ten minutes later.

The stop is twenty metres away from the bar. She carefully watches where she places her heels as she walks the short distance, making sure they don't get stuck in the wide grouts between the cobblestones. On the floor of the hall in *Lumière,* their decisive clicks sound like a whip cracking. Here on the cobblestones, it's quite another matter. She shouldn't have worn them, but she hadn't thought much about it this morning and put them on as usual.

Café Meuse is indeed empty when she arrives, as her friend predicted. Kiara won't get there for another half hour. Eveline sits down on one of the cushioned chairs outside and peruses the drink menu. There's a drawing of an old-fashioned lifebuoy and thick braided ropes at the top of the card. The bar has a poorly executed maritime theme. The square tablecloths on the tables are stripped navy and cream-white. There's a round wooden steering wheel placed on the front door. A photo of the meandering river Meuse has been printed on the large window panel.

It's one of the few bars to still have human waiters. Most pubs and restaurants have been fully automated, making a private meeting paradoxically more exposed to third parties, as the chance of recording equipment being present is higher. The waiter, the only staff member—probably the owner known by Kiara—is a bald-shaven man somewhere in his thirties. He's wearing a boxy shirt and tight black jeans.

Eveline examines the menu again before waving him over. They have red wine. It's expensive and most likely not good, but somehow it feels appropriate for today. Martin's favourite drink, she hasn't had it in years.

The waiter seems somewhat annoyed when she places her order and more so when he brings it. She can't blame him. It's early in the morning. He must take her for a secret lush. One of the many spineless citizens in need of booze to live their lives, using the lack of other entertainment as an excuse for doing so, as if fiction and alcohol were the same thing. Who else would order wine at this time of the day? Although wine wouldn't be an addict's first choice unless they were a wealthy one.

It doesn't help she looks a little bit rumpled too. Eveline tried to fix her hair this morning, put on makeup and is wearing her fancy suit—the cherry one with knee length, flared skirt and the jacket with short sleeves. But she couldn't hide the purple bags under her eyes. She is a shadow of the woman she used to be.

She takes a greedy sip of the scarlet liquid. The wine is too astringent. Eveline takes another swig nonetheless. She's agitated. To kill time, and distract herself, she opens her TOM and scrolls through the news items on the GO-FACS home page. The small message is tucked away at the bottom of the news stream. She hadn't given it further consideration, not since she had more important things to worry about. Every word hits her right between the eyes.

GERMAN DISSIDENT POISONED

Yesterday, Mr Roy Schulze, a German writer and broadcaster, was found dead under mysterious circumstances in his house in Cologne.
According to the German authorities, Schulze committed suicide by taking sodium azide. Online anonymous eyewitness reports, however, testify of an incident in which Schulze was stabbed in a restaurant with a fork, most likely poison-tipped. Three weeks ago, Mrs Schwarzer, former head of the Berlin news service Der Tagesspiegel, *was the victim of a similar lethal attack in Berlin.*

Eveline's stomach contracts. Hastily, she checks the background articles. There she finds a picture of the victim, in sober tones, fitting for the dead. It's Roy.

She scans the sentences. No mention of his asylum application in the Netherlands. Not a word on the fact that they, the Dutch, she herself, are responsible for his death. It's classified information, of course. She knows that, but still.

Trembling and in an attempt to pull herself together, she empties her glass in one go. That turns out to be a bad idea on an empty stomach. The wave of acute nausea takes her by surprise. Realising she won't make it to the restroom in time, Eveline yanks her camel leather handbag open and retches audibly. The undigested wine spatters over the contents.

The open bag sits in her lap, under her chin. She breathes heavily, her nostrils flared. The foul smell of her puke makes her gag again and she quickly puts it away under the table and leans back in her chair. Did the waiter see it? She's not sure. He's in the back of the bar, entering something in the cash register on the counter.

She needs to get her act together, if she's ever going to have a chance at finding Wolfke, at getting her back. Eveline checks her clothes for stains—luckily, they're still clean—and takes a lemon-flavoured mint. She always has some on her, usually in the inside pocket of her jacket, as is the case now. Exhaling deeply, she straightens her shoulders.

'Good gracious Eveline, are you okay?' Kiara exclaims a little too loudly when she arrives at her table.

Eveline has to look at her friend twice before recognising her. Her pink-blonde curls have made way for a straightened grey coupe with a lavender shimmer. She hasn't seen that colour on her before. Kiara is wearing a taupe linen suit with three-quarter-length sleeves. The jacket is tightened above her waist with a ribbon. It befits her. Kiara can pull off anything.

Taking a seat, her friend talks to her, concerned, 'You look exhausted.'

'Yes, no, I'm fine.'

Should she tell Kiara about Roy? Perhaps not, not now at least, maybe someday. She needs to focus on what matters most, on what might be within her control: her daughter. She can't do anything for Roy anymore anyway.

He's dead. What good would it do to bring up his asylum procedure? It could get her in trouble, and so possibly diminish her chances of finding Wolfke.

Kiara sniffs and wipes her nose. She must have picked up the scent from the bag under the table. Her friend frowns at the sight of the empty wine glass. 'You should really cut down on alcohol, Eveline.'

'I don't dri...never mind, yes I will. Let's focus on what we're here for, can we?'

'I want something to eat first, and I think you could use a bite as well.' Ignoring her protests, her friend turns around to call the waiter over to their table. 'Two café-au-laits and two croissants with jam please. Fast, and bring the bill as well.'

'I have ongoing meetings all day, I don't have too much time,' Kiara explains after the waiter has left in a hurry to prepare their order.

'You gotta let me pay. You're doing me a huge favour,' Eveline says, hoping that Kiara might say something about Wolfke already, but her friend doesn't.

'Ah, no need to.' Kiara casually waves her hand in front of her chest. 'I'll consider it a work meeting.'

The breakfast arrives within minutes, much faster than the glass of wine that Eveline had ordered. She watches her friend as she takes a bite of the fluffy curved pastry. Kiara simply exudes power.

Eveline doesn't taste much of the croissant, the wine's sourness still predominates. The strawberry marmalade is also lost on her. But Kiara was right, she must've been hungry without knowing it. The food helps to clear up her head. Sipping her coffee, she decides Kiara has been putting it off long enough.

Eveline puts the cup back on its saucer. 'So, what did you find out?'

Kiara casts down her purple-painted eyelids. 'You won't like it...'

Eveline's heart skips a beat, but she has to know. She can do this, for Wolfke she can do anything. 'Whatever it is, I can take it, Kiara.'

'Well, as you know, the last trace of Wolfke in the Netherlands is cold, from two months ago. She bought some groceries—a pack of Chikkocaf, two nut bars—since then, nothing. She hasn't used her phone, no one has seen her, and there's no footage of her on the cameras across town or in other Dutch cities.'

'Yes, yes, that's old news.' Eveline is growing ever more impatient.

'So, I decided to focus on her friend and her family instead. They disappeared around the same time. And given what you've told me about them...Anyway, we found them. They're in Denmark. In Blåvand, to be precise.'

'And W-W-Wolfke?' Eveline stutters hopefully.

Kiara smiles mildly. 'She's with them and she's fine.'

Eveline utters a sigh of relief and starts to laugh and cry at the same time. 'That's such good news! The doom scenarios I had in mind...you have no idea, Kiara. She's in Denmark and she's safe! Blåvand, right? Does it have an airport? Do you have the address? I can't wait to see her.'

Kiara hesitates.

Eveline eyes her questioningly.

'Yes, well...that's what you won't like, Eveline. You see, she doesn't want to talk to you.'

The sheer joy of finding her daughter gives way to disbelief and dejection. Eveline is appalled. 'But I am *her mother*,' she utters despairingly. 'Can you not force her somehow? Make her come back?'

Kiara watches her in dismay. 'We have no jurisdiction there. If she had been a minor, we could've done something, but now...'

Kiara slides a crumpled and carelessly opened envelope across the table. 'She wanted us to give you this.'

Eveline runs her fingers along the jagged tear in the envelope.

'Of course, we had to read it first,' Kiara apologises.

'Of course...' Eveline whispers.

'Okay then. I have to be at a work meeting in ten minutes, so I'm off. Will you be fine?'

Eveline nods listlessly.

§

Her daughter's letter curled in one hand, Eveline staggers across the *Onze Lieve Vrouwe Plein*. She hasn't read it yet. The waiter gave her a scornful look when she was about to. He wanted her out of the way. Stumbling along on the cobblestoned pavement, she seeks support at the facades and the storefronts.

Finally, across the square, she stops at a garbage can

near the pedestrian bridge across the Meuse. She grabs her set of keys out of her ruined bag and wipes the keys more or less clean on the clumps of grass that stick their tawny heads up between the sidewalk tiles. The rest of the bag's contents—five lipsticks in different colours (she still cannot choose), a hairbrush, and a pack of cherry gum—are beyond saving, but can easily be replaced. The bag itself, on the other hand...She's had it for so long. Zac gave it to her as a present when Wolfke was born. Eveline inspects the acrid puke. It's a lost cause. With a heavy heart, she stuffs the bag in the bin.

The stop for the bus back home is on the other side of the bridge, so she starts to climb the stairs. The steps are wide and low, and force her to walk at an unnatural pace. Eveline slowly goes up each step.

At the top, the bridge turns out to be practically empty. It's too early for day visitors and too late for locals to go to their work in the city centre. A black bird with a white blaze, most likely a coot, is hiding in the shadow of the bridge's high arch. It scuttles away at the sound of her heels popping on the ferro-concrete slabs.

Eveline stops to stare at it. Her eyes wander over the city, a fata morgana which is lit up by the red autumn sun. Maastricht is steaming and searing, like the letter in her hand. Here is as good a place and time as any. She leans her forearms on the bridge railing to open the envelope.

Dear mother,
Dear Eveline,

Lou and her mother urged me to write this letter.
They say I'll regret it someday if I don't.
Not sure if that's true,
but anyhow, you're concerned about me,
and I guess, somehow, I care about you.
That's what Lou's mum believes at least,
so I want you to know I'm fine.

I know you'd like to come and find me,
but if you love me as much as Kiara claims,
you'll let me live my life,
let me find out who I am besides your daughter.
Maybe we can see each other,
once I know the answer.
I'll let you know if or when I do.

Don't contact me

Wolfke

Eveline sticks her head over the railing, the sun on her neck, the letter loosely in her right hand. The water level in the riverbed under the bridge is low. It stinks of decay in the city. No wonder, given the long periods of drought it has suffered.

Another coot is bobbing in the small remaining watercourse below her, with two baby coots in her slipstream. A couple of centimetres to the coot's side, a third chick is struggling in a puddle of mud, fighting for its life. With every movement, it sinks away deeper. Instead of helping the little bird, the adult coot watches it wrestle. It only leans over to push it back into the mud whenever it almost manages to free itself.

It's common for animals to mistreat their offspring out of survival instinct when the young are too weak, or when there are too many mouths to feed. Coots are notorious for doing so, Eveline knows that. She can't help thinking if the reverse also occurs. Is it natural for young animals to reject their parents?

Eveline watches the tragic scene, unable to tear herself away. After much floundering, the chick finally drowns. The coot serenely swims around the corpse one last time, as if to assure itself it is truly over. Then it floats away, apparently unaffected.

»«

EPILOGUE

Copenhagen, Denmark

I have heard the mermaids singing, each to each.
I do not think that they will sing to me.
(The Love Song of J. Alfred Prufrock—T.S. Eliot)

MARTIN

The publishing company is housed on the ground floor of a majestic corner building in art nouveau style. Martin is right on time for his appointment, but the publisher keeps him waiting nonetheless. He idles around the anteroom, looking at the decorative *jugendstil* wall friezes of rolling fields, trees and Danish villages. They can't keep his attention. He's too excited.

A chance is coming his way now, finally. *Dizklaim Publishing* is hopefully going to make an offer. It's the only company that has shown any interest in his work, which is a film script, but his agent sold it to them as a novel. Knowing no one relevant in the movie business and with just a few contacts in the waning world of books, the agent is crap. He still works on commission too, a whopping forty per cent, but Martin cannot cough up the large upfront fees other agencies ask for. Today, he feels lucky. One is all it takes, as they say. And who knows, once the book is out, its movie may follow.

Martin sits down on one of the see-through chairs, a slick plastic piece designed for looks, not comfort. He watches the continuous newsreel on the large TV panel, which serves as a dividing wall between the lobby and the reception desk. The broadcast is an amalgam of the latest agreements on the distribution of climate refugees, a report on another protest march against Denmark's relatively relaxed position towards fiction, and of course, the UK elections.

As usual, the current British Prime Minister, who's running for office for the fourth time, is on fire. 'One point one million asylum seekers a year. Within ten years that amounts to the entire population of London. Those so-called poor climate refugees...' The man makes quotation marks with his fingers while spitting out the last three words. 'They're fortune hunters who don't respect our culture, who hold out their hands—'

The words no longer shock Martin. He has heard them too many times before. On TV, but in the streets as well. He hasn't managed to get rid of his Dutch accent, which is reason enough for some people to call him names like 'deadbeat', 'mooch', and sometimes even something as dehumanising as 'climate change parasite'.

Martin leans a little closer to the screen. He wonders if Prior shot this speech as well. His former professor has done all of the Conservatives' campaign videos in the past decade. Martin never thought Prior to be one of them, or that he would make such a drastic turn. Prior's artistic work has also changed. Gone were the independent women, in came the unimaginative stories about men-dominated worlds. The worst flick was a post-apocalyptic drama released two years ago, in which all the women had died from a mysterious disease. It had sickened Martin so much he couldn't see it through to the end. He ought to feel disappointed in his former hero. The fact of the matter is that it suits him well. It will benefit his book.

Dreaming of the fame and the raving literary reviews that will be his, Martin inspects his trainers. He cleaned them this morning, but they got dirty again. On his way over here, it started to rain unexpectedly. One of those rare summer showers. He rubs over the spots with his thumb, trying to clean them. He should've taken the bus, but he can't afford a bus ticket. Luckily, the Østerbrogade is not so far from his home in the Tingbjerg district. Nine kilometres is doable.

The Ghetto of Copenhagen, that's what people who don't live there call Tingbjerg. He rents a sordid room in the quarter—twelve square metres on the top floor of a three-storey apartment block. The once bright yellow plaster on the outer walls is as grizzled as the homeless families in the dust-ridden streets. Some of the men smell sour: Carlsberg and unwashed skin. Still, they're kind and friendly, and the neighbourhood *is* his home.

When Martin gazed into the cracked bathroom mirror this morning, he realised he started to look more like the straying men than he'd thought. He turned forty-three last week. His hair still looks good. It's thinner and a bit grey and not as glossy as it used to be, but nothing some hair oil can't fix. His face, however, is a shorn mess—a landscape of small, desolated islets of hair and tiny blood-red bumps. The flesh and skin under his chin have become flaccid. His nose is crooked from the time he got beaten up in Maastricht years ago. The tip of it is turning purple. He drinks too much.

Martin had expected more for himself when he left

the Netherlands in a hurry, shortly after that incident. When he was a kid, he and his dad spent all their summers on the seaside in East or West Jutland. They would catch hermit crabs and roast them over a bonfire. It had been the first place to pop up in his mind when he decided to make a run for it. Besides, some of the best filmmakers in the history of cinema came from Denmark—Dreyer, Von Trier, Vinterberg, Bier...

At the time, Martin didn't realise that Denmark would be impacted by the situation in Germany as well. He would be one of the first of many to cross the border in the years ahead. Luckily, the government hasn't reacted to the collapse of their neighbouring country in the same way as the Netherlands. Instead of limiting access to the internet and restricting fiction officially, the Danish administration has opted for education—such as free workshops in media literacy in every local library—and an army of analysts that tracks down and publishes the sources of fake news. With climate change driving people out of their homes in the past years as well, there are too many exiles in the European areas that aren't drowning or burning. That's probably the same here as in the upland of the Netherlands.

Like most refugees with a residence permit, Martin lives on a small allowance, in exchange for which he has to work in a local nursing home a couple of days a week. The prerequisite to receive his paltry handout. For a long time, all he had to do was keep the residents company, talk to them, hold their hands and drink coffee, offer them *real* human interaction. A few elderly clients had drifted off so far they hardly noticed he was there. Therefore, he sometimes used the time to write instead. That stupid head nurse had to report him of course. Since then, he has had to wash the reusable adult diapers instead. He hates the sight and smell of them. If all goes well this afternoon, he'll never have to touch them again.

Martin gives his shoes another rub with his thumb, but the mud stains won't come off. He uses some saliva and the hem of his T-shirt instead, which works better. He's fully bent over and engaged in the cleaning when the publisher calls him into her office.

§

The publisher is young, perhaps half his age. Twenty, twenty-one maybe? She's wearing a pinafore made out of tweed-like fabric and impeccable green brogues. According to the large name tag on her spotless glass desk, her name is Lien—*Lien Nguyen, MA (she/her)*.

She points Martin to a fluffy, pink lounge chair. He takes a seat. She, however, remains standing. Leaning against the front of her desk, her arms crossed, she towers over him.

'OK Martin. I'll get straight to the point as I have ten minutes for you. We are interested, and we want to publish—'

'I am pleased tha—'

She raises her hand to silence him. 'But, but, but! But of course not as it is now. The first thing that needs to go,' the publisher starts to expound her ideas for his book, 'are those references to music, films and literature...Those are so old. We'll have to make it more contemporary. Still, that's easy-peasy. What I want to get down to is how much of this is true. Did it all happen like this? We need to know precisely which bits are genuine, and which not...Well?'

'Oh, uh, you want me to explain that now? It's not straightforward.' Martin uneasily moves back and forth in the low furry chair. 'I mean, it's based on reality, but honestly, I also ran away with it.'

The publisher impatiently waves the back of her hand at him. 'Maybe I should've been clearer when asking the question. You know Prior is the real juice in your story. So, spill.'

'Well, that's all legit.'

'Which means you can prove you made the video?'

Martin didn't expect that question. Why would it matter if he could provide evidence? They're talking about a *novel* here. 'No, of course not. It's been twenty years. I don't have that laptop anymore.'

That should satisfy her sufficiently, but she clearly thinks differently.

'And the account used to post it, could you get access to it?'

He shakes his head. 'That website is long dead.'

'We couldn't ask this friend of yours? The one who uploaded it?' She picks up her phone from her desk and touches the screen with her index finger. 'Ah, here it is, this Zac?'

Martin is a bit taken aback. 'I wouldn't know how to get a hold of him. He wouldn't be willing to help out anyway. I mean, he's *exactly* as I described him.'

'That's a shame,' she muses. 'I would've loved to see that xenophobe Prior go down in flames. That leaked video gave him his street credits. If we could expose that it was all a lie and that he is just an opportunist...too bad. We need to think of a different approach then. We can't label it as fully fictional. That doesn't sell with a human author. Our chatbots produce far better fake stories. No, it needs to contain credible biographical ingredients too. Hmm, we can't claim you made the video without any evidence. But you knew him, didn't you? We can prove that. He must've been an awful man.'

'Well—'

'Of course he was, and you should let your Martin character understand this at some point. Make him turn around and come closer to Eveline. That would also make for a better love story.'

'Eh, it isn't a love story.'

'No? Perhaps not. But it would paint a far more honest picture of Prior. More in line with how we know him now.'

'But that's preposterous.'

'It would be more believable to our readers. And don't worry, I'll ask one of our collective writing groups to rewrite it to avoid one-sidedness. Nobody writes and publishes alone these days. That's far too risky. Especially when you are not writing from your point of view, or the perspective of a character like yourself. You aren't female, Martin, let alone a woman with Danish-Somalian roots. You can't speak on her behalf.'

'Do you think it's that unrepresentative? I tried to empathise, to include—'

Irked, she cuts him off, 'Ugh. Suggesting that Eveline betrays her daughter? That she's responsible for the death of a German refugee? Eveline, who's sexually liberated *and* your former lover? You didn't even bother to give her a last name. None of the women in your book have one. The true villain here is this Martin. He gets away with it all, doesn't he?'

Confounded, Martin runs his hand through his hair. He didn't expect her to put him to the test like that. It sometimes feels as if he's no longer allowed to say anything or that there's somehow no room for his ideas. And he actually wants to give marginalised groups a chance to get their stories heard. Moreover, he enjoys stories by female and non-white writers and directors. Like that seventies feminist film from the last century in which a woman leaves her husband for another woman...*A Woman like Eve*. That's the one. He likes that film.

'I didn't intend it that way—' he stutters apologetically.

She closes her eyelids and massages them with her fingertips. 'Ah, come on. His voice is the most dominant. You open the book with him. And that almost all-knowing external narrator...'

She shakes her head in disbelief. 'Don't worry, we're

good gatekeepers. We won't publish anything that will put you in danger, or us. Here at *Dizklaim,* we take care of our authors. I have a group of excellent writers in mind for you, sensitive to the whole range of identity issues. They do great things with our algorithms. Important stories are collective, Martin, they always have been. I'll let them review and revise this. If all goes well, we will publish it on our online forum within two months.'

'Okayyyyy...' He sounds diffident.

'Not all at once, of course. We'll chop it up. No one reads longer than five minutes at a time. We'll have to add some extra cliffhangers to keep readers coming. Not your strongest point...And we'll make sure to create a good-looking main author identity. We'll go for a male, white one, as close as possible to the truth. There's some interest again in stories by men like you, to understand where they're coming from. But, no offence, we can't use your face, you aren't sexy enough to attract our readers. You're a bit old already and well, your hair...'

§

Martin is out in the street again. He should be happy. He'll make some money, but he feels hard done by. Instead of going home directly, Martin decides to take a detour to the harbour, to the bronze sculpture of *The Little Mermaid*. It's the only spot in this city that feels genuinely familiar.

When he came here, the mermaid offered him consolation, a point of reference in a city which felt completely alien. He had been in Copenhagen with his father before. But he was only eight years old at the time, and it had been a single-day trip. He didn't recognise anything when he arrived here, apart from the mermaid. She helped him to feel rooted.

He's nearly there. Although the pavement is gleaming with rain, it's busy in the small street leading up to the statue. Crowds feel welcome if you have something to celebrate, but Martin isn't sure if he does. He doesn't want to slow down and slaloms agilely through the people-made-maze. After a few metres, he gets stuck. The people in front and behind him have stopped to listen to two street artists standing on the concrete block that marks the start of the pedestrian area.

He must admit the woman playing the guitar knows what she's doing. And the other young woman, who's singing, has a remarkably pleasant voice. Martin bends backwards to watch them. The audience is holding him captive, but if he could have moved, he would have been rooted to the spot all the same. The singer: it's Eveline! Yet not a day older than when he last saw her.

The song's lyrics are a bit sentimental for his taste, but he's hooked by her looks and voice, and he listens nonetheless, drinking in every word:

> *They wreck the truth.*
> *They take from you.*
> *Too greedy,*
> *In the art of losing.*

Let's be the scum.
Don't let them run,
Slide easy,
With this art of losing.

You are the scream,
That makes me gleam,
So deeply.
You're my art of losing.

She looks so much like her. He could've sworn it was her, but the young woman isn't Eveline. Her voice is grittier and there's a dimple in her chin. The colour of her eyes is brown—or is it green? Anyway, it isn't blue like Eveline's. It's a different girl.

It's been so long since they parted. Martin has thought of her many times, of course he has. She's in his script for goodness sake. But he believed he had dealt with his past. Writing the story had been his way to make peace with it, to make things right, or at least make them feel all right. So why can't he breathe?

He desperately wants to move now, to come up for air, but the gaggle won't let him. The air is thick with sweat and the various perfumes from the people around him. Sebum, vanilla, and oranges, overripe oranges…the coffee on their breath. After the third song, he's nearly suffocating and feels as if about to pass out.

Finally, there's some movement in front of him. With some pushing and wringing, he manages to set himself free. Leaning against the side of the kiosk where they sell ice cream and soda at ridiculous high prices, he puts his hands on his knees and his head between them. He gasps. It feels as if he has escaped something other than the crowd.

More or less recuperated, he follows the way to the waterfront. Coming closer to the statue, Martin is surprised to see police officers and journalists with cameramen next to the expected bunch of tourists. Just like the quay, they have raised the mermaid once again since he was here last time. Another boulder has been added to the pile of stones on which the figurine sits. The water level rises in unpredictable ways these days.

But that's not why the police and the media are there. Somebody has sprayed the new stone on which the small mermaid sits. Two words in black paint, one below the other:

RACIST
FISH

It's not the first time the figurine has been damaged. The poor girl was beheaded a couple of times. Usually, the purpose of those protests made sense to Martin. It was about whale hunting or the position of women in Danish society. Sexist fish, he might have understood that. A woman who gives up everything for a man...But racist, why racist?

'It was about time somebody did something about that statue,' a young man next to him mutters.

He must be barely twenty. Martin tries to gauge whether the man is serious. There was no trace of irony in his words. His pensive and at the same time provocative frown reminds Martin of how he was himself when he was younger.

It makes that Martin wants to understand. 'Why, what do you mean? It's a beautiful work of art.'

'Perhaps, but she betrayed her kind. She did everything to pass for something else. Including giving up her voice and in the end, her life.'

'But she's fiction. And she isn't black. She's a mermaid.'

'Is she?' the guy asks in a Socratic manner while staring at the statue.

Martin follows his gaze. But no matter how hard he tries, he only sees a mermaid captured on the brink of turning into a human, having both legs and a fishtail.

The man sighs at the sight of Martin's troubled expression. In a soothing, somewhat condescending manner, he sets out to explain, 'Yes, she's fiction. You're right about that. And that's the problem exactly. Fiction is utterly unstable. It changes meaning, depending on who's reading or watching. That little mermaid might not be real, but she surely is bloody fake.' The guy points with his chin in the direction of the statue. 'She may seem solid as rock, but make no mistake, she is as turbulent as the sea around her. So, yes she can be black. She can be anything. It's exactly this which makes her dangerous. Like all fiction, she is an ever-changing lie. Fleeting. Elusive. Untameable.'

'Ah.' The nondescript sound with which Martin responds practically sounds like a Eureka. Its cheerfulness contrasts sharply with the gloomy picture the young man just sketched, sparkling nearly as brightly as the sun reflecting on the waves crashing into the mermaid's boulder pedestal.

Decidedly giving up on him, the young man walks away, without realising Martin finally got it: a writer or artist may have intended one thing, but it's up to readers, time and context what it'll end up being. Over and over again. It can change direction as easily as the wind blowing in the harbour. But unlike the man, Martin doesn't think that this is a problem. Yes, fiction might be dangerous, but it's stunningly sublime too. It's a unique opportunity to catch a glimpse of lives beyond one's own. There's a beauty within that.

Above all, Martin finally understands what happened to him and Eveline. Their fights about Prior's film amongst others—they simply spoke different truths. Equally and simultaneously valid, yet opposing truths. He wishes he'd known this back then. He would have listened to her, rather than trying to convince her he was right. *That* was his fault.

The police have finished their investigation. Like most members of the press, they are packing up their things to leave. The wind tugs at Martin and pulls him closer to the waterfront, to the mermaid in all her multiplicity. He examines the green-patinated face. Her eyes are focused on the sea, the home she once left behind.

She doesn't care if he is there or not. He's just one out of the many millions who have visited her, whose voices she passes on to those who take the time to listen. To those who dare to be silent.

She is black, but she is also white and everything in between, and still, non-existent. She's innocent, racist, sexist, fake, true. She's female and male and beyond. She's him. She's Eveline.

»«

DISCUSSION GUIDE

1. When Martin discovers that his favourite professor and film director Jude Prior is in trouble because of the fake video he made, he wavers about taking responsibility. Do you understand Martin's response? What would you have done if you were in his position?

2. When the EU collapses as a result of fake news, Ditte decides to stay in the Netherlands, even when the country's regulations get increasingly stringent. Can you empathise with this? What would you have done?

3. Not knowing that the video of Martin's professor is a fake, Eveline believes the cancellation of him and his work is justified. What do you think about this? If the video was real, should one indeed no longer watch Prior's films?

4. In the epilogue, the publisher tells Martin he should not write about experiences which are not his own, even when fictional. Does it matter for how you read a fictional story if the writer's identity is similar to the identity of the main character(s)? Should personal experiences and the identity of a writer be a yardstick against which we judge the value of a novel?

5. Eveline accuses Martin of male privilege. Do you agree with her that Martin is privileged? Why is

he/isn't he?

6. The relationship between Martin and Eveline is fraught with miscommunication. Talk about the moments when they do not communicate well.

7. In the first chapter, Martin speaks about truth in fiction. Misquoting Oscar Wilde, he argues that fiction offers us possibilities to experience truths about love, loss, death and life. According to Martin, these are different kinds of truths than the ones offered by science. Can you relate to this? Have you experienced and learned truths through reading fiction? Which ones?

8. In the second part of the book, all characters struggle with a life devoid of fiction. Could you imagine living in a world like this? What would you miss the most? Is fiction indeed essential to a full and meaningful life?

9. Fiction plays an important role in the relationship between Lou and Wolfke. In particular, Lou experiences a strong connection between love, desire and imagination. How are these experiences connected? Can you relate to this?

10. Part two of the novel largely revolves around the dynamics between Eveline and her daughter Wolfke, as well as Ditte and her daughter Lou. Both mothers want what is best for their daughters and try to keep them safe above all. Still, they make drastically different choices in doing so. How do these two mother-daughter relationships dif-

fer from each other? How do the mothers relate to their daughters? And how do Lou and Wolfke relate to their mothers in turn? Do you understand Eveline's and Ditte's attempts to help their daughters? What would you do in their position?

11. *Fake Fish* is told from the perspectives of four highly different characters. How did the shifts in perspectives influence your reading experience? Did you relate more to one specific character? Did this change as you read the novel?

12. The epilogue invites you to look back on the novel and to question what is real or fiction. How does the epilogue change your perception of the 'reality' of the story told in *Fake Fish*? How does the epilogue and the novel make you reflect on the relationship between fiction and reality?

13. *The Little Mermaid* is a recurring image in the book, and it plays a crucial role in the ending. Talk about the different parts in which the mermaid figures and what she stands for.

14. One of the book's mottos is Oscar Wilde's claim that 'a truth in art is that whose contradictory is also true.' What do you think this means and how does this idea reflect on the story of *Fake Fish?*

LISTEN, WATCH, READ & VISIT FAKE FISH

Fake Fish is shot through with filmic, musical, literary, artistic and geographical references, either explicitly or implicitly, which are listed below.

Music

- *Cold Little Heart*—Michael Kiwanuka, 2016 (Chapter 1)

- *Alt hvad hun ville var at danse*—Tina Dico, 2014 (Chapter 3)

- *Chiquita Banana*—Monica Lewis, 1944 (Chapter 4)

- *Rebellion*—Arcade Fire, 2004 (Chapter 8)

- *Free Falling*—Tom Petty & The Heartbreakers, 1989 (Chapter 9)

- *Apache*—The Shadows, 1963 (Chapter 10)

- *So Easy*—Noud Theunissen & Josje Weusten, Synth Society (Chapter 10)

Novels, Poetry and Plays

- *Das Parfum*—Patrick Süskind, 1985 (Chapter 1)
- *La Bête Humaine*—Émile Zola, 1890 (Chapter 1)

- *The Great Gatsby*—Francis Scott Fitzgerald, 1925 (Chapter 1)

- *Disgrace*—John Maxwell Coetzee, 1999 (Chapter 1)

- *Tirza*—Arnon Grunberg, 2006 (Chapter 1)

- *The Picture of Dorian Gray*—Oscar Wilde, 1890 (Chapter 2)

- *The Hill We Climb*—Amanda Gorman, 2021 (Chapter 3)

- *We Wear the Mask*—Paul Laurence Dunbar, 1895 (Chapter 3)

- *Immigrant*—Rupi Kaur, 2017 (Chapter 3)

- *One Art*—Elizabeth Bishop, 1976 (Chapter 3)

- *Spreek*—Wiel Kusters, 1979 (Chapter 3)

- *Romeo and Juliet*—William Shakespeare, 1597 (Chapter 4)

- *Den Lille Havfrue (The Little Mermaid)*—Hans Christian Andersen, 1837 (Chapter 7 and Chapter 9)

- *De Vilde Svaner*—Hans Christian Andersen, 1838 (Chapter 9)

- *Alias Grace*—Margaret Atwood, 1997 (Chapter 10)

- *Identity Crisis*—Ben Elton, 2019 (Chapter 10)

- *Leaving. A Poem from the Time of the Virus*—Cees Nooteboom, 2020 (Chapter 10)

- *We gaan op berenjacht*—Michael Rosen, 1989 (Chapter 11)

- *Raad eens hoeveel ik van je hou*—Sam McBratney, 1994 (Chapter 11)

- *The Love Song of J. Alfred Prufrock*—T.S. Eliot, 1915 (Epilogue)

Films and Series

- *Inglourious Bastards*—Quentin Tarantino, 2009 (Chapter 1 and Chapter 6)

- *Pulp Fiction*—Quentin Tarantino, 1994 (Chapter 1 and Chapter 9)

- *Death Proof*—Quentin Tarantino, 2007 (Chapter 1)

- *Band of Brothers*—Stephen Ambrose/Tom Hanks, 2001 (Chapter 1)

- *Dr. No*—Terence Young, 2016 (Chapter 1)

- *Her*—Spike Jonze, 2013 (Chapter 2, Chapter 8 and Chapter 9)

- *Breaking Bad*—Vince Gilligan, 2008 (Chapter 4)

- *Better Call Saul*—Vince Gilligan & Peter Gould, 2015 (Chapter 4)

- *Narcos*—José Padilha, 2015 (Chapter 4)

- *El Chapo*—Ernesto Contreras & José Manuel Cravioto, 2017 *(Chapter 4)*

Cocaine Coast—Carlos Sedes & Jorge Torregrossa, 2018 (Chapter 4)

- *Once Upon a Time in Hollywood*—Quentin Tarantino, 2019 (Chapter 4 and Chapter 9)

- *The Matrix*—Lana & Lilly Wachowski, 1999 (Chapter 4)

- *Lock, Stock, and Two Smoking Barrels*—Guy Ritchie, 1998 (Chapter 4)

- *The Usual Suspects*—Bryan Singer, 1995 (Chapter 4)

- The Hulk—Ang Lee, 2003 (Chapter 6)

- *Ocean's Eleven*—Steven Soderbergh, 2001 (Chapter 6)

- Skyfall—Sam Mendes, 2012 (Chapter 6)

- *Goldfinger*—Guy Hamilton, 1964 (Chapter 6)

- *Flikken Maastricht*—2007-present (Chapter 6)

- *(R)Evolution*—Toneelgroep Maastricht, 2021 (Chapter 6)

- *Grizzly Man*—Werner Herzog, 2005 (Chapter 6)

- *Fight Club*—David Fincher, 1999 (Chapter 6)

- *1984*—Michael Radford, 1984 (Chapter 9)

- *Django Unchained*—Quentin Tarantino, 2012 (Chapter 9)

- *Sideways*—Alexander Pain, 2004 (Chapter 9)

- *Triangle of Sadness*—Ruben Östlund, 2022 (Chapter 11)

- *Light of My Life*—Cassey Affleck, 2019 (Epilogue)
- *A Woman like Eve*—Nouchka van Brakel, 1979 (Epilogue)

Artworks
- *Le Déjeuner sur l'Herbe*—Édouard Manet, 1863 (Chapter 2)
- *Untitled (Dutch cow in green from above)*—Jasper Geers, 2013 (Chapter 3 and Chapter 10)
- *De Maagd*—Michaél Borremans, 2014 (Chapter 4)
- *Halfautomatische Troostmachine*—Michel Huisman, 2001 (Chapter 6)
- *The Little Mermaid*—Edward Eriksen, 1913 (Chapter 7 and Epilogue)
- *Amphitrite's Capture by Poseidon*—Hof van Tilly, 1714 (Chapter 10)

Essays and Academic Books
- *The Truth of Masks*—Oscar Wilde, 1886 (Part I and Chapter 1)
- *Narration in Fiction Film*—David Bordwell, 2015 (Chapter 1)
- *The Big Screen*—David L. Robbins, 2012 (Chapter 1)
- *Story: Style, Structure, Substance, and the Principles*

of Screenwriting—Robert McKee, 2010 (Chapter 1)

- *Project Europe: A History*—Kiran Klaus Patel, 2020 (Chapter 2)

- *Banana's, Beaches and Bases: Making Feminist Sense of International Politics*—Cynthia Enloe, 2014 (Chapter 4)

- *Banana Industry in Central America in the Oxford Research Encyclopaedia of Latin American History*—Kevin Coleman, 2020 (Chapter 4)

- *Finding the Truth in the Courtroom*—Henry Otgaar and Mark L. Howe, 2017 (Chapter 5)

- *Maastricht Treaty*—EU Member States, 1992 (Chapter 5)

- *Situated Knowledges: The Science Question in Feminism and the Privilege of Partial Perspective*—Donna Haraway, 1988 (Chapter 6)

- *Faces of Evil: Enemy Image Construction in the American Action Film*—Lennart Soberon, 2020 (Chapter 6)

- *Surveiller et Punir: Naissance de la prison*—Michel Foucault, 1975 (Chapter 6)

- *Useless Concentration: Life and Work in Elizabeth Bishop's Letters and Poems*—Langdon Hammer, 1997 (Part II)

- *A Short History of Migration*—M. Livi-Baci, 2012 (Chapter 10)

- *Agonistic Memory and the Legacy of 20th Century Wars in Europe*—Stefan Berger & Wulf Kansteiner, 2021 (Chapter 10)
- *Imagined Communities*—Benedict Anderson, 1983 (Chapter 10)

Places
- FASoS Lecture Hall and University Building, Maastricht (Chapter 1, Chapter 2 and Chapter 6)
- Mr Smith Speakeasy Bar, Maastricht (Chapter 2)
- Lumière Film Theatre, Maastricht (Chapter 2 and Chapter 8)
- Fort Eben-Emael, Eben-Emael (Chapter 3)
- Moulin Loverix, pancake restaurant, Eben-Emael (Chapter 3)
- Maastricht-Aachen Airport, Beek (Chapter 4)
- Maastricht University Inner City Library, Maastricht (Chapter 5)
- Sint Pieter District, Maastricht (Chapter 5)
- Plein 1992, Maastricht (Chapter 5)
- Café Zuid, Maastricht (Chapter 5 and Chapter 6)
- The City Park, Maastricht (Chapter 6)
- Sphinx, Maastricht (Chapter 6)

- Police Station, Maastricht (Chapter 6)

- The Little Mermaid, Copenhagen (Chapter 7 and Epilogue)

- Bandito Espresso Bar, Maastricht (Chapter 9 and Chapter 12)

- The Belle-Vue Site, Brussels (Chapter 10)

- Blåvand Beach, Denmark (Chapter 10)

- Onze Lieve Vrouwenplein, Maastricht (Chapter 14)

- Hoge Brug, Maastricht (Chapter 14)

- Vibensgård on the corner of Østerbrogade and Strandboulevarden, Copenhagen (Epilogue)

- Tingbjerg, Copenhagen (Epilogue)

Miscellaneous

- *Ten Questions for Werner Herzog*—The IU Cinema, 2014 (Chapter 1)

- *Projections*—Jean-Luc Godard, 1992 (Chapter 1)

- *Audiences like to see the bad guys get their comeuppance*—quote ascribed to Charles Bronson (Chapter 4)

- *SCART Plug Fan Club*—@ScartPlugFans on Twitter (Chapter 4)

- *The ultimate boy's dream you can afford*—Slogan

Burton Car (Chapter 8)

- *Red Felt Protest-Square*—WOinActie (Chapter 10)
- *Copenhagen's Little Mermaid branded 'racist fish' in graffiti attack*—John Henley, The Guardian (Epilogue)

ACKNOWLEDGEMENTS

Although stories are often voiced by an individual author, they are collective in both origin and reception. This novel is no exception and I have many people to thank. I will inevitably forget to mention some, as we are often unaware of who makes a mark on our life and work. If you have been overlooked, I apologise. Please know you are a vital part of this narrative.

The earliest germ of this book should probably be traced back to my mother, with whom I share a passion for literature. She has supported me tirelessly from the moment I started to write short stories and poems as a child. Thank you so much, mama.

My obsession with literature was nurtured into adulthood by my high school teachers at Bernardinuscollege Heerlen and my professors at Maastricht University. Thank you for introducing me to the works of Renate Dorrestein, Vonne van der Meer, Cees Nooteboom, Margaret Atwood, Rachel Cusk, J.M. Coetzee, Oscar Wilde, Elizabeth Bishop, Ian McEwan, Kazuo Ishiguro, and many others. All writing starts with reading after all.

I cannot begin to express how indebted I am to my students in creative writing and literature at the Faculty of Arts and Social Sciences and University College Maastricht for bringing newer authors, such as Kiley Reid, Bernardine Evaristo and Sally Rooney to my attention. I love our respectful and inspiring discussions. Martin and Eveline could learn a lot from you. Keep reading and above all, writing!

Thank you to my friends, family and colleagues for hearing me out about my book, and for asking difficult questions. Some of you were directly involved in this project. My best friend Olga was my first real reader. Her excited response to my "vomit draft" and her original ideas to develop it further were crucial for continuing this project. Olga, I have never met a more empathic and non-judgemental person than you. I am so glad I get to call you my friend.

I also want to thank John and Keith for the time they took to edit my work, and for calling me out on my "Dunglish". Diënne and Jeroen from *Bandito* ensured that the coffee in this novel is made by the book. Let's hope the fictional one tastes as good as your real stuff.

I am thankful to my friend David, the artistic director of *Lumière*, for suggesting film books and for having created such a great film theatre, which has the most interesting programme. Let's hope it will never turn into an asylum centre.

Tim, your impressive, thought-provoking art installations enthused me to weave the impact of climate change into my story. Thank you also for letting me use your bathtub anecdote in altered form. Jasper, your wonderful paintings have been a source of inspiration for this book too.

Aagje, your support for my project has been

heart-warming. Thank you for being such a great department head. Jan, your expert feedback and enthusiasm have proved invaluable. Thank you for convincing me to put my work out there, and most of all, for your friendship.

My good friend Maarten deserves to be mentioned too. We immediately connected through our shared love for writing, Cees Nooteboom, islands, and a preference for walking on a specific side on the curb. Thank you for your insightful feedback on my drafts and for trusting me with your work too. *Alles raakt alles.*

The fellow writers and tutors at Faber Academy London were superb. The course *Finish Your Draft* gave my novel the extra push it needed. Thank you so much for your guidance, Tom and Mandy.

I am immensely grateful my book found a home at *Sparsile Books*. I could not have found a better one for it. Dear Lesley and Margaret, I love how you go against the current commercially-driven trend in publishing, instead creating room for high-quality literary fiction that is engaging and eclectic. Thank you for giving me a chance to be part of this journey. Lesley, you instantly understood the story I was trying to tell. The advice from you and the reading panel as well as the feedback and editing done by Stephen were priceless.

Noud, my intelligent, handsome, musical partner-in-crime, my lifelong love, without you there would not have been a novel at all. You tirelessly read every new version of each chapter and challenged me to be better by asking the most difficult questions about them, which

I would dismiss as irrelevant or avoid answering first, to then often realise I indeed needed to tackle them. Moreover, you helped to create the time and space for me to write, and dealt patiently with my fickleness, keeping the faith when I lost mine (which was often). I could not have done this and so many other things without you. Always and always 'saaie mis'. Your *lady writer*.

Veerle and Stine, my beautiful daughters. You are currently too young to read this book. When you are old enough, it will probably make you "cringe". I still dedicate this novel to you. You are the most impressive, wise young women. Your braveness and creativity kept me going. I am so proud I get to be your mother.

Last but not least, each reader is part of the creation process of this narrative. By reading it, you will tease out (unintended) meanings, connecting the story to your lives and inner worlds. Thank you for turning my fiction into truths.

Printed in Great Britain
by Amazon